A. Night
In Hollywood Forever

ANDREW J. FENADY

Five Star • Waterville, Maine

First Edition
First Printing: August 2006

Published in 2006 in conjunction with Tekno Books and Ed Gorman.

Set in 11 pt. Plantin by Christina S. Huff.

Printed in the United States on permanent paper.

Library of Congress Cataloging-in-Publication Data

Fenady, Andrew J.
    A. Night in Hollywood forever : a novel / by Andrew J. Fenady.
—1st ed.
        p. cm.
        ISBN 1-59414-379-X (hc : alk. paper)
        1. Novelists — Fiction.   2. Detective and mystery stories—
Authorship—Fiction.   3. Kidnapping—Fiction.   4. Los Angeles
(Calif.)—Fiction.   I. Title.
    PS3556.E477A63 2006
    813'.54—dc22   2006007955

For Angela Lansbury
no one was ever more
appropriately named

For Mary Frances
forever

Prelude

I haven't been looking at the calendar lately—matter of truth—in all my life I seldom looked at a calendar.

I don't keep track of holidays, anniversaries, or birthdays, especially my own birthdays. Every birthday is closer to death-day, so, to hell with it.

But it's been quite a few months since I officially went out of the private eye business on Larchmont Boulevard in Hollywood and into the mystery writing business at the Writers and Artists Building in Beverly Hills.

During those quite a few months I've earned zero dollars writing and pocketed over thirty grand from former clients who just won't believe I'm no longer a card carrying PI—sometimes I don't believe it, either.

But my stomach abhors a vacuum, and thirty Gs goes a long way toward fueling the belly and paying the rent. And it breaks the monotony of looking at an empty page rolled into the vintage Royal.

Every few days I'd unroll one empty page and carefully insert a fresh empty sheet.

And during those quite a few months I'd dumped dozens of wastebaskets filled with unrolled sheets. It might be an exercise in futility, but at least it's exercise. That, and going to the Hollywood YMCA, had kept me in shape and allowed me to take a break from those damned Lucky Strikes.

The title of the mystery novel I'd been working on is *The*

Big Changeover and that's as far as I'd got—the title.

One day, for no particular reason—except that I couldn't think of an opening for the great mystery novel I was going to write—I started thinking about how the capers in the great mystery novels and movies began.

In *The Maltese Falcon*, a lady who called herself Miss Wonderly walked into Sam Spade's office with some cock and bull story that led to murder and the search for the fateful black bird.

In *The Thin Man*, Nick Charles at a speakeasy ran into a beautiful young woman named Dorothy whose father Clyde Bryant had disappeared.

In *Farewell, My Lovely*—also known as *Murder, My Sweet*, Moose Malloy appeared in Philip Marlowe's office one night in search of his old flame, a dame named Velma Valento who had vanished while the Moose was a guest of the California Department of Corrections.

And of course, in *Double Indemnity*, Walter Neff, played by Fred MacMurray, sat bleeding at a desk with a dictation machine confessing to Barton Keyes, played by Edward G. Robinson, how he had conspired with Barbara Stanwyck to murder her husband—making it look like an accident—to collect the double indemnity insurance policy.

I'm not quite sure how this so-called caper really started—or exactly when—but it really doesn't matter how or when anything starts.

What matters is how it ends.

Still, how or when something starts has to have something to do with how or when it ends.

Maybe this whole thing began in 1863 when a baby named William Randolph Hearst was born.

Or when, twenty-four years later, he persuaded his father to let him run one of the Hearst newspapers.

A. Night In Hollywood Forever

Or in 1894 when the Russian Tsar, Alexander III, decided to commission a priceless Easter egg—fashioned of gold and jewels by a craftsman named Peter Carl Fabergé—to be presented to the Tsar's wife that year and a new one every following year. The tradition was continued by Alexander's son, Nicholas II, until the Bolshevik revolution that ended in the deaths of the royal Russian family—fifty eggs later.

Or in 1917, when W. R. Hearst, a fifty-four-year-old married man, met a beautiful twenty-year-old Ziegfeld Girl named Marion Davies.

Or a few years later, when W.R. formed Cosmopolitan Pictures to star his sweetheart in a series of pictures to compete with America's Sweetheart, Mary Pickford.

Or during the Great Depression, when W.R. decided Marion Davies would play the ill-fated Alexandra, the last Russian empress. That's when he purchased a real Fabergé Imperial Egg to be used as a prop in a picture that was never made.

Maybe it started in 1951, when W.R. died, or in 1961, when Marion died, and the secret of the Fabergé went with them to their graves.

Shakespeare wrote, "The evil that men do lives after them—the good is oft interred with their bones."

But, good or evil, where was the Fabergé interred?

In *Touch of Evil*, Marlene Dietrich said, "What does it matter what you say about someone after he's dead?"

But sometimes it does matter, because sometimes it can help solve a mystery in that person's life.

Almost a half century after her death, the Fabergé that W.R. bought for Marion Davies was valued at over ten million dollars.

When did it all begin?

I don't know.

But all of that was the prelude—the overture.

When my part in the story starts, the ten-million-dollar dingus was up for grabs.

Except nobody knew where it was.

But that day I wasn't thinking about the ten-million-dollar dingus. That day, when the phone rang, I didn't even know it existed.

Howsomever, I knew Mike Meadows who was on the phone and made me an offer.

Five thousand bucks for just a few hours of my time, with no risk, escorting a sex goddess to a Hollywood soirée.

When I say no risk I mean no physical risk—like getting beat-up, shot at, or shoved into a buzz saw. But the temptation *was* physical—because the sex goddess was Frances Vale, who in some years gone by had gone to bed with hundreds of lucky lotharios—including me—and who had been in fantasy beds or other places with millions of young and old men—and, I guess women—all over the planet.

Not that I wouldn't enjoy another night's lodging with Frances Vale—the Fairest of the Rare—Rarest of the Fair— but ever since I started keeping company with Goldie Rose, who has an office right across from mine and writes hard-boiled mystery novels in eleven days, and who has a heavenly face and a helluva body, I have been abstemious—well, make that monogamous.

Goldie Rose's family name had been Triandafelos, which in Greek means rose—like my family name had been Nyktas, which in Greek means night.

Goldie's got silver-blue eyes on a countenance that doesn't need makeup, short, honey blonde hair, a clean, clear California complexion, long, lovely legs and—well, never mind.

For months I've wanted to marry Goldie. My mother wants me to marry Goldie. If my father were alive, he'd want me to marry Goldie. My best friend, Lieutenant Myron Garter of the Beverly Hills Police Department, wants me to marry Goldie. I can't think of anybody who doesn't want me to marry Goldie—except maybe Goldie.

She had said yes. Even agreed on the place, Saint Sophia's Greek Cathedral on Pico and Normandie. Trouble was—and is—she never exactly agreed on the date. It would either be spring, summer, autumn, or winter, but she didn't narrow it down to the year.

"Alex, things are fine just as they are," she'd say, "let's give it a little more time . . ." then she'd put her arms around me and one thing would lead to another . . . but not to Saint Sophia's.

More often than not, it would lead to Goldie's bed and— *"a trip to the moon on gossamer wings"* —so I'd shut up and enjoy the ride—not just to the moon—so high I could buzz the stars.

I've had more than my share of women, and been had by more than my share, but there's never been a woman in my life like Goldie Rose. My serenity is through, but it's worth it . . . and then some.

When I got the call that afternoon from Mike Meadows at Tri-Arc Studios offering me five grand to escort Frances Vale and a million dollars' worth of ice to the soirée, I had no notion that it would trigger a fusillade of violence, mystery, and murder that would make my past misadventures from battlefields to LAPD to Hollywood private eye—and the bullets I'd dodged and some I didn't dodge—look like an old MGM musical.

How the hell did I know that if I hadn't called up and left a message breaking my date with Goldie that night, she probably wouldn't have gone missing the next day—or, that I'd walk hand in hand with the ghosts of William Randolph

Hearst and Marion Davies—or, that I'd spend so much time at the city's most famous cemetery called Hollywood Forever before I was dead—or, that I'd confront a cast of deadly characters that make those in *The Maltese Falcon* look like a bunch of born-again Baptists—or, that it would all lead to a treasure trove that survived the Russian revolution—a Fabergé Imperial Egg aptly called The Tear of Russia.

There was no way of knowing.

There was no way of guessing.

In the movie, *Forrest Gump*, Tom Hanks said that, "life is like a box of chocolates."

Not my life.

It would be more like *Five Graves to Cairo*—maybe including mine.

Chapter I

Months ago, when I first sat down to write about the events and characters involved in my decision to switch so-called careers from private investigator to potential mystery writer—events that started that night in Palm Desert when Mrs. Cynthia Alderdyce had hired me to escort her and a couple million dollars' worth of ice to and from Walter Annenberg's New Year's Eve party—events that led to a holdup by a couple of bogus cops and to a chase—gunfight—crash and another leg wound—mine—events and characters which prompted me to, at long last, heed my mother's advice to "get out of this cockeyed private eye business before I have to bury you"—I wrote the whole thing down as it happened to me and to the other people involved in that screwy story—a story that I could never publish due to a promise I had made to a spicy old tomato—Mrs. Alderdyce.

This story is even screwier.

As for being published—well, let's put it this way—yeah, it did get printed, but . . .

In the movie *The Man Who Shot Liberty Valance*, a character says "when fact becomes legend, print the legend."

In this case, what got printed was neither exactly fact, nor legend.

The dictionary defines "legend" as an unverified, romanticized story.

Well, I've verified as much as possible and romanticized as

little as possible—but I'm part human, so I might have missed a little on both counts.

What counts is the story got printed—most of it did—and nobody got hurt—except for those who got in the way, those who didn't get out of the way, those who deserved it, and some who didn't—oh, and those who died.

Mike Meadows, the high cogalorum at Tri-Arc Pictures, was never one to waste words coming to the point. When his secretary, Clara—for almost twenty years she had been his secretary, not assistant, well paid and proud of the title—put Meadows on the line he didn't bother with preliminaries, went right to the main event.

"Night, your girlfriend's done it again."

"Who's my girlfriend, I forget."

"You know damn well—Frances Vale, who's going to win an Academy Award for *When Winter Comes.*"

"Glad to hear that. Is the fix in? How'd you do it?"

"Nobody can fix that. Not anymore. But she's a cinch for best supporting actress—at least she was until she called me a few minutes ago . . ."

"Is she going to pull a George C. Scott and refuse the nomination?"

"That's what it amounts to. She refuses to go to the premiere tonight."

"That sounds like Franny . . ."

"Unless . . ."

"Unless what?"

"You take her."

"Is this a gag?"

I knew it wasn't. Mike Meadows doesn't gag around. But I had to say something and that's all I could think of.

"Listen, Alex, I've built this up as the biggest opening

since the Grand Canyon. The proceeds go to the Judeo-Christian Charities. Everybody's going to be there. I've arranged for her to wear a million-dollar necklace, The Star of Good Hope. But she called me up a few minutes ago and says she's a no-show unless you take her."

"She off the wagon?"

"Nope. Says she won't go with any of those phony four-flushers in the picture. Says if it weren't for you she wouldn't have done the part, and unless you take her I can take the million-dollar necklace, the picture and the Academy Award and shove it all where it's impossible."

"Maybe she's bluffing . . ."

"You know better than that."

I did.

"Alex, five grand for about five hours of your time . . ."

"Are you serious?"

Another stupid remark. Mike Meadows is always serious. So is five thousand dollars.

"Have you got a tux?"

"Yeah. Me and the moths."

"You've just got time to clean up and put it on. The limo'll pick you up at 5:30 and take you to her place. I'll call and tell her it's all set. Five Gs and beside that, Night, you've got my marker you can call in any time you want to."

"Mike . . ."

"Alex, yes or no?"

He already knew the answer and so did I.

Goldie had left her office around noon. She had just finished another hard-boiled novel. Usually it takes her eleven days. This one only took ten and a half. It was called *Holy Whore* by Gray Lugar—one of her *nom de plumes*. She's got about a dozen.

Goldie had poked her beautiful face in the door and said

15

she needed to relax for a few hours before we had dinner that night at The Petite Greek over on Larchmont.

I had told her I'd pick her up about seven and pecked away on the typewriter just like I was actually writing some Chandler-like dialogue for *The Big Changeover*.

So, after Mike Meadows hung up I called Goldie at home—only she wasn't at home so I left a message on the machine.

"Dear Gray Lugar, have to break our dinner date tonight. Something urgent's come up. Money. I'll explain tomorrow. *Kali Nikta* and sweet dreams."

A couple hours later I had showered and shaved for the second time that day, and slipped on the old double-breasted tux I'd bought on sale at Carroll and Co. a few years ago.

There were two items on the dresser. I rarely carried them both at the same time. One was my .38 Police Special. The other was a gold pocket watch. A hunting case Elgin. Inside was an inscription.

Alexander Nyktas

It was my grandfather's watch and name. He had given it to my father and my father had given it to me.

Just as I looked out the window and saw the limo pull up the phone rang. I figured it was probably Goldie or . . .

"Oh, hello, Mom."

"How are you, Alex?"

"Just going out, Mom."

"With Goldie?"

"No, Mom."

"With Myron?"

"No, Mom."

"You want to tell me who with?"

"No, Mom."

"Can't you say anything except 'no, Mom'?"

"No, Mom, not right now."

"Alex, if you've got a new girlfriend, I don't want to meet her."

"Even if she's Greek?"

"Is she?"

"There's no new girlfriend."

"That's good. Are you in trouble again, Alex?"

"No, Mom. I'll explain tomorrow."

"I love you, Alex."

"I love you, Mom."

"Have you finished your book yet?"

"Not yet, Mom."

"Finish it."

"Yes, Mom."

"And don't forget to dedicate it to me. Good night, Alex."

"Good night, Mom."

A few minutes later I was in the backseat of the limo Mike Meadows had sent over.

In the front seat sat the driver who had introduced himself as Irv Wiznewski and never spoke another word that I can remember. He did hum a little.

Irv looked more like a cop than a limo driver, and actually he was a sort of cop. A security guard for the jeweler who had loaned Mike Meadows and Frances Vale The Star of Good Hope to wear at the premiere of *When Winter Comes* that night.

But on the way to Malibu where Frances Vale lived I wasn't thinking about cops or jewels. I was thinking back on the conversation between me and the Fairest of the Rare, Rarest of the Fair that day at the coffee shop on Larchmont Boulevard, where I had just given up my office and the private eye business.

★ ★ ★ ★ ★

"Alex how come you don't have your office anymore?"

"Because I don't need it. I quit the detective business. I switched to another line."

"What line?"

"Don't laugh, Franny, but I'm going to be a writer."

"Laugh? Hell, Alex, I know you." The way that she said it sounded strange—and intimate. *"You can be any damn thing you put your mind to."*

"Thanks, Franny . . ."

"Alex, walk across the street with me. Have a cup of coffee. Please. For old times?"

"Okay."

We walked across the street to the B and L Patisserie, sat at one of the outside tables and ordered coffee. Even in the sunlight, in spite of the dope and booze and God only knows what else, her face was unlined except for a few crinkles around the eyes and that beautiful mouth. Even her throat was smooth and tight. Maybe she had had some work done. If she did, it worked.

"What are you looking at, Alex, old times?"

"You look great, Franny."

"I been straight for years. No shit, no pot, no booze. Straight as Robin Hood's arrow."

"Good for you, Franny."

"It wasn't easy. There were times when I thought the walls would come tumbling down—and so would my head. It wasn't easy but I did it. I do look good don't I, Alex?"

"You look good, Fairest of the Rare, Rarest of the Fair."

"Tell that to that son of a bitch."

"What son of a bitch?"

"Mike."

"Mike Meadows?"

She nodded and sipped her coffee.

"*Franny, there're a lot of son of a bitches in this town. Mike Meadows is not one of them. And you know that better than anybody.*"

"*Not anymore I don't. You know what he talked me into? Had me sign the goddamn papers and everything.*"

"*What?*"

"*A part in his goddamn lousy picture. Part? Shit, more like a bit, about three scenes playing a goddamn hundred-year-old mother to some snot-ass television actress I wouldn't let stand in for me if she was the only other woman left in the world.*"

"*Who's the television actress?*"

"*What's the difference?*"

"*Who is it?*"

"*Jackie Mathews . . .*"

"*Franny, Jackie Mathews has made three big pictures, hasn't done television for years. She's a star.*"

"*Never was a star. Isn't a star now. Never going to be a star. A lousy TV actress and he wants me to play her hundred-year-old goddamn drunken mother. I don't need that shit!*"

She said it loud. Too loud. People sitting near us and walking on Larchmont turned and looked, and not because she was beautiful.

"*So what do you want from me, Franny?*"

"*If I'm going to do it, I want you to come up to Carmel with me. Like you used to. I know Mike'll pay your fee like he used to. If he won't, I will.*"

"*Franny, Mike used to hire me to keep you off the booze and the pills and the dope and the . . .*"

"*Say it, Alex, go ahead and say it. Off the studs. Because I couldn't get enough of a lot of things in those days, right?*"

"*You already said it, kid.*"

"*I'm no kid and I know it! But I still won't play this part and the son of a bitch won't let me out. Alex, I'm afraid if I go up there*

19

something bad'll happen. So just come with me. A couple of weeks, 'til I settle down."

"Why won't Mike let you out? That doesn't sound like him."

"He says it's for me. That I'll win an Academy Award. Who gives a shit! It'd be for 'supporting actress' anyhow, I'm no goddamn supporting actress."

"You weren't much of a goddamn actress at all when Mike signed you thirty years ago."

"It wasn't thirty!"

"All right, twenty-nine."

"Alex, please, I feel like I'm drowning. Come with me, keep me afloat, Alex, please."

"Franny, as the Irish say, 'I'm sorry for your trouble, but you haven't got real trouble. Other people do. So, I'll tell you what you and I are going to do. You're going to go to Carmel and play the hell out of that part and start a whole new career. And me, I'm going to get into my car, drive away from Larchmont Boulevard and start a whole new career."

I got up from the chair and tossed more than enough money onto the table.

"Alex," she hollered. "You're just like him. A son of a bitch!"

But that wasn't the end of it.

She did go up to Carmel and start shooting. But a few days later I got a call from Mike Meadows saying that Frances Vale had walked off the set. She was on a binge, holed up at her Malibu house and unless she was on the company jet that afternoon, he'd have to replace her with Ann Gavery and start shooting her scenes all over. He didn't want to do that—not just the money—but he had had this part tailored for her. Every scene. Every word. Every move.

He said she was scared to death of being an actress instead of everybody's fantasy lover.

Would I give it a try?

When I got there she and some jock were both naked in the Jacuzzi, each with a drink in one hand and a joint in the other. She introduced him as a Black Belt.

I said it looked like he left it at home, then reached in, pulled him out by the hair and broke his nose with the heel of my left hand. A little harder would have driven the bone of his nose into his brain and killed him.

He was beat and he knew it.

Inside, I shoved her into the shower and let her soak for about five minutes. I got pretty soaked myself.

Then I turned off the shower, grabbed a towel and pushed her into the bedroom. She stood there dripping. Naked as April morn. All right, September morn. But she still looked like what she used to be, the Sex Goddess of the olden, golden days.

And in my mind's flashback, as the limo turned onto 101 and rolled toward Malibu, I could still see the scene.

There was something lustrous about her body that made it seem like she was moving even when she stood still. She still had it, and she knew it. I tossed the towel at her. She held it with one hand but let it touch the floor.

"Dry off," I said.

"Do I look like that TV actress's mother to you?"

"Fairest of the Rare, Rarest of the Fair, you look great. And you can be a great actress."

"Mike sent you, didn't he?"

"Nobody sends me anywhere. I came because I wanted to come. I read that script," I lied. "He stuck his neck in a buzz saw for you when nobody else wanted you for the part. He's given you

21

the chance to act, instead of shaking your tits and your ass and licking your tongue like . . ."

"Like what?"

"You know what. Mike Meadows might be the last decent human being in this indecent town. He sure as hell is the last one who believes you can play this part. And you piss on him. And why? Because he believes in you more than you do. That's why. Because you're afraid to act. So you take the easy way and act like a slut. Goddammit, Franny, the walls haven't come tumbling down—and neither have you, go up to Carmel and act! Really act! Show those son of a bitches what you can do with this part. Because they're the son of a bitches, not Mike Meadows."

"It's too late. I walked off."

"You can walk right back on again. No, not walk, fly. He's got a jet waiting for you. That's how much he believes in you. If you're not on that plane they're signing Ann Gavery for the part."

"Ann Gavery! Why that fat old bitch, she couldn't act . . ."

"They wanted her in the first place, everybody wanted her except Mike."

I didn't know if any of that was true, but I knew she hated Gavery's guts. "That's who they want and that's who they're going to get unless you're on that plane. Get on it! Fly, Franny. Fly! Soar right into that part and reap a second glory. This is your last chance, Franny. Your last and only chance. Don't screw it up!"

She took a couple of steps closer to me and let the towel drag on the carpet. She wasn't wearing any makeup. She wasn't wearing anything. God she was still beautiful.

"You're all wet," she smiled that smile that had driven a million men crazy. Ten million. "I'll go up," she said. She loosened my tie and started to unbutton my shirt. "But first we've got to get you dry."

A. Night In Hollywood Forever

★ ★ ★ ★ ★

What happened next is nobody's business. But Frances Vale made the plane, and she made the picture.

The limo, driven by Irv Wiznewski, pulled up in front of her house in Malibu.

Chapter II

Irv Wiznewski waited in the driveway while Hannah Blue, Franny's housekeeper, opened the door and let me inside.

Also inside were two fellows who made Wiznewski look like the small kid in the neighborhood.

We exchanged names and handshakes. Their names were Brock and Claude. I felt the effect of each handshake for about ten minutes.

They, too, were security guards who would follow in another car close behind to escort us to and from the Kodak Theatre where the premiere and party were to take place.

They weren't going to go inside the theatre because nobody would be dumb enough to try and swipe the Star in front of thousands of people—so they were explaining to me—until she walked down the stairway from the second floor of the beach house.

Frances Vale wore a clinging pale blue satin evening dress with a décolleté that clung so there was no doubt that there was nothing underneath except nature's extraordinary endowments to one beautiful woman. At her throat she wore The Star of Good Hope.

But, at that moment neither Brock nor Claude was looking at The Star of Good Hope.

Their aim was a little lower.

So was mine.

"Real ones shimmer," she said, "diamonds, I mean."

A. Night In Hollywood Forever

In that satin gown Frances Vale shimmered all over.

The three of us, Brock, Claude and I, stood staring—just like kids in a candy store. The difference was that I had already tasted some of that candy.

She shimmered closer to me. I resisted the urge to step back—or forward.

"Glad you could make it, Alex." She glanced at Brock and Claude who were making it back to earth. "We'll ditch the duennas later." She touched the diamond at her throat, "After we get rid of this. Alex, aren't you going to say how nice I look?"

"You look nice."

From the outside, at first glance, the Kodak complex looks like it was plastered together from leftover D. W. Griffith and C. B. DeMille sets—Babylonian and Egyptian.

But as the battery of searchlights swept across the structures and penetrated the night sky, there seemed to be a sort of magic transmigration back to the glory days and nights of Hollywood.

This was the corner of Hollywood and Highland, where once sprawled the famous Hollywood Hotel, playground of Valentino, Pickford, Fairbanks, Chaplin, the Gish sisters, Swanson, Theda Bara, Mary Miles Mitner, Mabel Norman, Jack Gilbert, the Barrymores—where later, Louella Parsons broadcast her radio program while Dick Powell sang songs like "Hooray for Hollywood" which Johnny Mercer wrote for the Warner Bros. movie called, what else?—*Hollywood Hotel*.

Our limo, along with all the other limos, made a left from Highland onto Hollywood Boulevard where hundreds of noisy "fans" sat in bleachers and stood on the sidewalk as the vehicles disgorged celebrities—including Frances Vale and the anonymous jerk next to her. I didn't know what happened to Brock and Claude, but guessed that they couldn't get any closer for the time being.

The Kodak is almost across the street from the Roosevelt Hotel, where the first Academy Awards were presented in the Blossom Room in 1928. Since then the ceremonies have taken place at a dozen places all over town and since 2002 the Kodak has hosted the event. Tonight it was hosting the premiere of Tri-Arc's W*hen Winter Comes*, starring Jackie Mathews, who was walking on the red carpet just ahead of us but was not getting nearly the attention, applause and squeals as was the "supporting actress" whom I walked beside—actually a half pace behind.

Since the premiere benefited the Judeo-Christian Charities, many of the attendees wore yarmulkes and collars. I noticed that a lot of those fellows were giving Franny the up and down as we went along.

There were the usual interviews by the usual interviewers including the grand ol' man of the "Just for Variety" column, Army Archerd.

Army was still talking to Jackie Mathews when we walked up. Mathews started to walk away, but Archerd took hold of her arm and there the two ladies stood for everybody to see—and compare.

It was no contest, and Jackie knew it. She managed a "Hi, Frances, you look swell, but then you have for a long time," and off she swept.

Frances greeted Army warmly, mentioned the name of the picture, Mike Meadows, the million-dollar Star of Good Hope she was wearing and the jeweler from whom it was borrowed, and even introduced me as a "dear friend."

Then up the escalator we went toward the theatre where Mike Meadows damn near smiled as Franny kissed him on the left cheek.

A. Night In Hollywood Forever

The Kodak Theatre is magnificent.

The picture was—as they say—a smash, and in every scene the two of them were in, Frances Vale made Jackie Mathews look like wallpaper.

On the way out of the theatre there were twice as many sycophants swarming around Frances Vale as there were around Miss Mathews and the phrase "Academy Award" was bouncing all over the joint.

As we passed Jackie, Frances said it just loud enough, "Better luck next time, kid." And we moved toward the escalator to take us down to the main floor.

Mike Meadows was surrounded by a herd of congratulators, and this time he did smile and wave at Franny.

On the way down on the escalator I whispered to next year's Academy Award winner, "Franny, you were great in the picture . . ."

"Thanks, Alex, we're going to spend the night together . . ."

"No, we're not . . ."

"Yes, we are . . ."

"No, we're not, and did you have to say that to Jackie Mathews?"

"Piss on her."

That's when the priest at the bottom of the escalator smiled, spoke and reached out.

"Excuse me, Miss Vale . . ."

It all happened so fast, in retrospect it seems like slow motion.

He had gray hair, sort of long for a priest, wore steel-rimmed glasses over a wrinkled face with a benevolent smile.

His hand that reached out held a small medal attached to a silver chain.

27

". . . Miss Vale, this is a Saint Genesius medal blessed by . . ."

The chain and medal slipped from his hand.

". . . Oh, I'm sorry . . ."

He started to bend toward the sidewalk but abruptly stopped, grasping his back in pain.

Franny looked at me, then at the fallen medal. Instinctively, I stooped like a naïve Boy Scout executing his good deed for the day and didn't see exactly how it happened—but it happened.

Franny was also looking down as the holy man in one swift stroke cut off the necklace at her throat with some sort of small clippers, grasped the Star and chain, turned and melted into the assemblage of priests, rabbis and other first nighters before anybody, including moron me, realized what had happened. It was so brazen that nobody could have believed it—because nobody would be dumb enough to try and swipe a million-dollar diamond in front of thousands of people—talk about chutzpah.

I stood there with Saint Genesius in one hand and an Eagle Scout–look on my stupid face while Franny pointed into the crowd.

"The son of a bitch stole it!" she said almost to herself, then hollered so hundreds of us heard, *"the son of a bitch stole it!!!"*

I tore into the swarming sea of tuxedos, evening gowns, priests, rabbis and assembled humanity, shoving aside innocent bystanders while trying to spot the gray-haired son of a bitch running away.

But he was too smart to run—at least for the time being.

I made my way toward the edge of the crowd and spotted the steel-rimmed glasses on the sidewalk, then saw in the dim distance the figure of a man dressed in black walking away while tearing the hair off his head and revealing a bald pate. He then pulled off the stiff collar and dickey that had designated him a man of the cloth.

"Hey, you!" I hollered.

He threw away the wig and dickey, then moved fast toward the only direction that wasn't populated by passersby—the metal skeleton of a five-story structure under construction.

I thought I had the son of a bitch cornered and I could hear the shrill sounds of police whistles, even sirens, and bullhorns instructing "Everybody stand still! This is the police! Everybody stand still! Freeze! Don't move! Don't anybody move!"

I did have the son of a bitch cornered. There was no way he could go but up—unless he shot me.

Luckily he didn't have a gun. Jewel thieves generally don't.

So up he went.

But he took the express.

There was a cable suspended near a power box. He wrapped the cable around his arm and hit the switch. Both he and the cable ascended considerably faster than it would take to climb the metal ladders of the structure.

I stood and watched as he made it up toward what would be the fifth story—then I snapped the power switch to "off."

I could go after the cops or go after him.

To hell with the cops. I wanted to get him myself and besides he might disappear while I was gone.

So up a ladder I went.

Toward him and the Star—and the stars in the blue-black sky that twinkled with indifference at the both of us.

By the time I got to the third story the Lucky Strikes were taking aching effect on my lungs and the old wound in my left leg was telling me to quit.

Not me!

Up I climbed—but a little slower.

From time to time the searchlights below swept across the naked outline of the building and the tuxedoed outline of me—and the man in black above framed in the moon glow.

And down below I saw a dozen or so figures scampering toward us—some in uniform and some not. A couple of those figures, not in uniform, started to climb a ladder.

But this was my dance and I wasn't going to let anybody cut in.

I got to the fifth story and stepped onto the scaffolding about ten feet away from my prey.

"End of the line, padre. Hand it over."

He looked below and saw the two men climbing up.

So did I.

I recognized them. Brock and Claude. Each with a gun in his hand as they climbed.

There wasn't enough room on the scaffolding for all of us.

"Stay back, fellas. I got him."

They ignored my instructions and kept coming.

I was just a couple of feet away from him.

"Hand it over, pal, and nobody'll get hurt."

There was a seemingly resigned look in his moist eyes. He smiled and lifted the Star and chain out of his pocket.

I was close enough now to see the makeup melting off his face from the sweat. And I could see that he wasn't old. About my age. In the prime of life.

"Sure," he said.

He held the Star out in his left hand and when I reached for it he swung with his right. I ducked and grabbed the Star—and maybe I shoved him—don't want to remember— but over he went, twisting and turning while he screamed until the scream was silenced by cement.

As Brock and Claude came close I held out The Star of Good Hope and let it shimmer in the moonlight.

Chapter III

Mike Meadows called off the party.

But he didn't mind a bit.

The jeweler got back the Star and Mike got a couple million dollars' worth of publicity for the picture.

There were flashbulbs and television cameras all over the place and all over me.

Under the circumstances, I was a model of modesty.

I did have a session with the cops, but it was short and painless. The cop in charge was Lieutenant Frank Rodriquez, LAPD, Hollywood Division. The other officers were Detectives Don Higley and Philip Mansour. Brock and Claude were right there to back up my story. The cops said there was nothing on what was left of the body to identify the corpse, but they'd ID him through prints after the SID boys scraped him off the cement.

"Night," Meadows said, "you'll get a big bonus for this."

"And a new tux?"

"I'll buy you a dozen new tuxes."

"Alex," Franny smiled. "Aren't you going to take me home?"

"I've had enough excitement for one night. Better luck next time, kid." I turned and walked away.

And it turned out all right for everybody—except for the guy splattered on the cement.

The Saint Genesius medal was still in my pocket.

And in my watch pocket there was still the Elgin.
I lifted it out and put it to my ear.
It was still ticking.
And so was I.

Chapter IV

As the saying goes—I slept fast that night.

By the time I got home it was past two a.m. By habit I turned the television set on to Turner Classic Movies. I used to alternate between TCM and AMC to watch old features, but these days AMC plays five minutes of movies and five minutes of commercials. *Foreign Correspondent* with Joel McCrea was just starting on TCM. I had seen it too many times, so I switched to the Westerns Channel. *Colorado Territory* with Joel McCrea was just ending. It was the Western version of *High Sierra*, directed by Raul Walsh, the same man who had directed *Sierra* where Bogart played "Mad Dog" Roy Earle. I liked McCrea, but he was miscast as the desperado called Wes McQueen in the piece. Wes McQueen was no Roy Earle. Walsh had wanted Robert Mitchum, but Mitchum was unavailable. Too bad. I turned off the television set and turned on to a fresh bottle of Gordon's Gin.

By the time I finished a couple double doses of Gordon's Gin laced with Schwepp's Tonic, it was past three.

By the time I blurred the image of a man twisting and turning and screaming and splattering, it was past four.

By the time the phone rang, it was just past seven.

I figured it was probably Goldie, or . . .

"Hello, Mom."

"My son, the hero. My son, the idiot."

"Mom . . ."

33

"You're famous . . ."

"Mom . . ."

"And lucky to be alive."

"Mom . . ."

"Don't ask me how I know. It's all over the newspaper and the TV."

My mother's always been an early riser and unfortunately that day was no exception.

"Alex, I thought you were out of the danger business."

"I am."

"As of when? This morning? What time this morning? Why didn't you tell me you had a date with that so-called sex goddess?"

"It wasn't a date."

"What was it?"

"Business."

"Monkey business. Are you all right?"

"A little groggy, Mom."

"You should get some sleep."

"I'll try."

"Did Goldie know you had a date with the sex goddess?"

"I phoned her . . ."

"You ought to marry that girl—Goldie, I mean—not the sex goddess."

"I intend to, Mom."

"Good. Was the movie any good?"

"It was good, Mom."

"Not too dirty?"

"Rated PG, Mom."

"Maybe I'll go see it. I'm proud of you, Alex, but stay out of the danger business and finish the book."

"I will, Mom."

"I'm going to keep the newspaper story for my scrapbook

that I'm starting today. I'll call you later, son."

"So long, Mom."

I lay back down and tried to sleep but it was hopeless, that day's adrenaline was already pumping. I shaved, showered, had coffee and toast with marmalade and some yogurt, and then phoned Goldie. I figured I ought to give her my version of what happened, but she still didn't answer, so I left a message saying I'd see her at the office.

Driving with the top down to the Writers and Artists Building in my near-new Sebring convertible, for which I had traded in the LeBaron which was full of bullet holes and dents, compliments of an unfriendly Uzi—the friendly dealer on LaBrea, Maurice Claff, gave me two thousand bucks, including the bullets still imbedded in the fuselage—I thought about my good fortune in securing an office in that grand old landmark thanks to a good word from Mrs. Kramer to her friend Henry Fenenbock, Jr. who owned the landmark.

Unfortunately, Mrs. Tina Kramer had died since, but her daughter Marsha and Marsha's husband Jim Keller still ran Kramer's Tobacco Store on Santa Monica Boulevard, where I still got my Lucky Strikes while Marsha took up where her mother had left off warning me to quit smoking cigarettes and switch to a pipe.

Not much else had changed around the old neighborhood except at the Beverly Hills Police Department just down the street. My old pal and former LAPD partner, Myron Garter, now Lieutenant Myron Garter with the BHPD, was still there, but Police Chief Marvin D. Iannone had retired from what had been a pretty steady job. There had only been seven chiefs since Beverly Hills was incorporated in 1914.

And it just so happened that the new chief, Dave Snowden, was a pal of mine, so, actually things got better for me. Not that I was still in the detective business but it's always handy to have a pal or two on the police department. The more prominent the pal, the better—and you couldn't get any more prominent than Chief of Police.

There was another change for the better in the neighborhood. In the old, olden days, catty-corner from the Writers and Artists Building there used to be Carroll and Co., just about the best men's clothing store in town. A few years ago Carroll and Co. moved to 425 N. Canon Drive. The grand old building was torn down and a newer, more garish structure was built to house, of all things, a Tommy Hilfiger emporium. Hilfiger and Co. lasted just a couple of years and now Brooks Brothers had renovated and moved in, redeeming some of the former class of the corner location.

The three-story Writers and Artists Building had officed some of the most famous scribblers and celebrities in Hollywood history, including Doug Fairbanks, Mary Pickford, Billy Wilder, Ray Bradbury, Michael Blankfort, Daniel Petrie, Jack Nicholson, Chuck Barris, Oscar Saul, Al Ruddy, James Komack, Bill Bixby, and on and on.

The current crop of writer tenants—all published or credited screen and television writers—except A. Night—included, of course, my bride-to-be Goldie Rose, plus:

E. Elliott Elliot, who looked and spoke like an immaculately tailored Clifton Webb and long ago won two Academy Awards and hadn't had anything produced in two decades but had made a fortune in Beverly Hills real estate.

Wes Weston, a Texan about seven feet tall who dressed and talked like Randolph Scott and who years ago "created" a Western TV series called *Cattle Drive*—which he ripped off of John Wayne's *Red River*—and ran for nine years making him a millionaire and who was now waiting for Westerns to come back. Meanwhile you can see *Cattle Drive* on the Hallmark

Channel on Saturdays and Wes Weston on weekdays at the Writers and Artists Building.

Morgan Noble was another tenant. She's a woman—although sometimes it's hard to tell—with bobbed hair and bosom. She dressed in men's clothes and politically was a direct descendant of Ayn Rand. Morgan wrote the same kind of novels as Rand only dirtier, so they sold reasonably well.

She and E. Elliott Elliot carried on a long running hate-hate relationship.

He called her Madam Ovary and said she had two right wings.

She announced that the *E* in his name stood for Effete.

Then there were the Bernstein brothers, Bruce and Bernie, who not only wrote together, but finished each other's sentences.

"Hello there . . ." Brother Bruce.

". . . and how are you?" Brother Bernie.

"We're going out . . ." Brother Bruce.

". . . to have lunch." Brother Bernie.

"Care to join us . . ." Brother Bruce.

". . . for a bite?" Brother Bernie.

"No, thanks. Not today." Alex Night.

Or any other day. It made me dizzy just to be with them—like watching a Ping-Pong game up close.

Things went on just about like that at the Writers and Artists Building every day.

But not that day.

I could see that things were different by the Beverly Hills police cars parked out front—and the officers standing by.

Chapter V

I parked my near-new, half-car in the underground lot behind the building, mashed all the right buttons so the top and windows all came up, and walked 'round front to see about the uniformed visitation.

I recognized two of the officers standing at the entrance—and vice versa. Buddy Carr and Jim Sawaya.

"Hey, fellas, what's going on?"

"Big reception," said Carr, "for last night's hero—Alex Night. Brass band'll be here any minute."

"Quit clowning."

"The mayor's gonna give you a medal," Sawaya smiled. "What did Frances Vale give you last night, Night?"

"Hey, you got that million-dollar diamond on you?" Carr beamed. "I'd like to take a look at it."

"I'd like to take a look at Frances Vale," Sawaya winked. "Close up."

They went on for about thirty seconds.

"Saw you on TV, who does your makeup?"

"Who does your publicity?"

"Is it true they're gonna make a movie about you?"

"Is it true what they say about Frances Vale?"

"Gangway!" I said and brushed by them into the entrance.

I walked past the directory and the plaque on the wall that had been attached there for I don't know how many years.

A. Night In Hollywood Forever

Henry Fenenbock, a friend
To all writers and artists
From his tenants

I paused to light a Lucky, then started up the stairs.

Each of the upper two stories consists of a wide but moody center hallway flanked by warren-like, twelve-by-fourteen-foot offices. No central air-conditioning. No hot water. No elevators.

Spartan and inexpensive. But exclusive. It's not easy to become a tenant. The waiting list runs into months and years.

Henry Fenenbock, Jr. maintains an office—number 205—in the center of the second floor. My office is on the third floor where all the noise was coming from and where all the people were standing.

But not in front of my office. In front of Goldie Rose's office across the hall.

I recognized most of those people—the tenants, E. Elliott Elliot and his ebony walking stick, Morgan Noble, Wes Weston, and the Bernstein brothers.

Henry Fenenbock, Jr. was there along with his girl Friday, Judy Kirk—a Valkyrie blonde.

I also recognized Lieutenant Myron Garter of the Robbery-Homicide detail of The Beverly Hills Police Department—and the topper to my surprise, the chief himself, Dave Snowden.

As I came closer I kept looking for Goldie Rose, but she wasn't in the hallway. I figured she was in her office.

I figured wrong.

I don't know which of them was the first to spot me, probably Myron Garter, or which of them was the first to start it, probably Myron Garter, but they all commenced to clap and even cheer.

I went along with the gag and bowed obligingly and puffed away on the Lucky as the chorus picked up from where Carr and Sawaya left off downstairs.

"Home is the hunter, home from the hill." E. Elliott Elliot.

"Lay on McNight!!" Morgan Noble.

"Hear they're gonna make you an honorary Texas Ranger." Wes Weston.

"Night and day you are the one . . ." Brother Bruce.

". . . beneath the moon and under the sun." Brother Bernie.

"Coming up to give us a hand, Alex?" Lieutenant Garter grinned.

By then the applause had died down and I stepped toward Goldie's open door to look inside.

"She's not here, pal," Garter said, "but somebody else was, last night or early this morning."

"What're you talking about, Myron?"

"Breaking and entering."

"Where's Goldie? Is she all right?"

"Well, we think so, but we don't exactly know. Doesn't answer her phone, thought maybe you . . ."

"Maybe I what?"

"Might know. Did you . . . see her last night . . . I mean after the excitement?"

"Hell no. I went home and went to bed. Did anybody go over to her place?"

"Yeah, we sent a team. Nobody answered."

"Did they break the door down?"

"You know they can't do that."

"I can."

"Take it easy, Alex . . ."

"Don't give me the easy . . ."

"They got a fast warrant and went in. Empty. Only mes-

sage on the answering machine was yours. Car's gone.
Doesn't she go away for a few days sometime?"

"Yeah, I guess so. Anything missing? From the office, I
mean . . ."

"Hard to tell. She doesn't have much here . . . word processor, some books and . . ."

"Yeah, I know . . . oh, hello, Dave." I tried to smile at
Snowden. "Since when does the Chief of Police show up at a
burglary?"

"Since I was on my way to breakfast and saw the squad
cars. Old habit from Costa Mesa." He did smile.

Snowden used to be the police chief there—where the
crime rate was considerably higher than in Beverly Hills . . .
robbery, rape, homicide—there hadn't been a homicide in
Beverly Hills in over two years.

Henry Fenenbock, Jr. took a step forward. He's a pleasant,
affable fellow with an easy smile, but he wasn't smiling now.

"In the entire history of this building there's never been a
break-in."

"Another first for Writers and Artists," Elliot noted.

"I was the first one here this morning," Morgan Noble
said. "And . . ."

"Doing your usual snooping about, no doubt." Elliot
smirked.

"And . . ." Morgan ignored Elliot's remark, ". . . found the
door open, obviously forced open, and the office empty, so I
notified the police . . . without touching anything, of course."

I looked at Garter.

"Yes, Alex, we'll go over it for prints."

"I want to file a missing person . . ."

"You know you can't do that for forty-eight hours,
boychick."

I did know it, so I didn't answer him.

"All right, fellas, carry on," Snowden said. "I'm going to get that breakfast. It'll be okay, Alex," he nodded as he went by.

"Look, everybody," Garter glanced around, "why don't you all go to work and let us get to it."

Writers never want to go to work, never. They all find any excuse not to sit down and look at an empty sheet of paper or a blank monitor—the room's too hot or too cold—they have to go to the toilet—pencils need sharpening—the typewriter needs a new ribbon—the keyboard needs cleaning—the pictures on the wall need straightening—the wastebasket needs to be emptied—or it's lunchtime.

These writers were no different, but reluctantly, they began to drift off toward their respective *oubliettes* while the cops went about their business.

"First time." Fenenbock shook his head as he and Judy Kirk walked away. "First time in all these years anything like this has happened."

"There goes the neighborhood," Weston observed.

Fenenbock was not amused.

Neither was I.

I didn't like it.

Not because of the break-in, but because Goldie, my beautiful, wonderful Goldie wasn't in her office across from mine and wasn't home.

I pulled out my keys and started for my office so Myron and the print boys could go to work when E. Elliott Elliot came alongside and damn near put the hand without the walking stick around my shoulder—a most unlikely gesture by the E. Elliott Elliot the world knew and disdained.

"My friend," he said just above a whisper, "besides being a wise, old party, I have an extraordinary instinct which in this case tells me that our Miss Rose is well and safe and will be with us soon, very soon."

"I appreciate that, Elliott. You're a damn nice fellow."

"Don't let it get around, I've spent a lifetime dispelling the notion."

As I opened the door I could hear the phone ringing. I hoped it would be Goldie. It wasn't. It wasn't my mother, either. It was Detective Don Higley from the LAPD—one of the cops who had talked to me last night.

"Night, I thought you'd want to know about that guy who did the Brodie. We ID'd him."

"Yeah, sure." I snuffed what was left of the Lucky into an ashtray.

"Name was James Glazer. Unbalanced. In and out of mental hospitals for years. Often posed as priest. Rap sheet of petty thefts. First and last time he tried for the big time. No living relatives we know of. That's the story."

"Thanks."

I hung up and punched the button on the phone to listen to the messages.

There were plenty, but none from Goldie. Most of them were from what is now called the "media," leaving numbers that I never intended to call back.

I mashed the "off" button when I saw the two of them walk into the room without the formality of knocking.

One was average size, the other above average, considerably above average.

"Morning, Night," said Average. "My name's Joe Saturn. This is Pete Donner. We're from *Reality Magazine* and we're here to hand you five grand for the exclusive story about that guy you dumped last night and the affair between you and Frances Vale."

He pulled a little recording machine out of his pocket and clicked it on.

"We want the story in your own words, you know, 'The

Private Eye and The Public Sex Goddess,' and Pete here will just take a few pictures of you while you tell it like it is between you and Vale and how you nailed the phony priest and saved The Star of Good Hope and the sex goddess . . ."

Saturn talked faster than anybody I ever heard, and Donner was already taking pictures with one of those micro cameras.

I took about all I could, and that took about thirty seconds.

I came around the desk, slapping the camera out of Donner's hawser hand and grabbed the recorder away from Saturn.

They both stood, stunned, but not for long. Donner came at me like a bull, but I was no china shop. I kicked him in his vitals then slammed the edge of my hand hard into his Adam's apple. He sputtered and coughed in agony while I slapped Saturn silly, once, twice, then I lost count.

That's when Lieutenant Myron Garter and a couple of his men came into the room to see what the ruckus was about.

"Alex! For Chrissake!!"

I guess they were a little surprised at what they saw.

Donner was on his knees trying to vomit and Saturn's face was blue as a hydrangea.

After what happened last night and that morning, I guess I had to take it out on something or somebody, and those two slime balls just fit my pistol.

"Alex," Garter repeated. "What the hell's going on? Who are these guys?"

"They're intruders," I said as calmly as I could muster. "From *Reality Magazine*. Need I say more?"

"Not unless you want to press charges," Garter said with a straight face.

"Let it pass this time," I replied, just as straight.

"Get out," Garter barked at them and pointed to the open door.

"What . . . what about our . . . equipment?" The hydrangea sputtered and

pointed to the recorder and micro camera on the floor.

I stepped over and ground a heel into each piece of equipment.

"Take 'em with you." Garter shrugged.

They didn't. But did manage to stagger out.

Garter's head motioned a "dismissed" signal to the two cops. They obeyed the signal.

Myron closed the door, produced an El Producto, and lit the cigar while I went around the desk to the swivel chair, sat and lit a Lucky.

We looked at each other through smoke clouds for a few seconds. Over the years we had been close enough to hell together to smell the fumes. We were just about even in the saving each others' lives statistic—and swapping favors department. We started out as pals in the LAPD Academy and ended up as partners until I went into the private eye game and he went west into the Beverly Hills Police Department.

But the friendship beat went on—through tough and tender times. Myron Garter had had many tender years with his wife Rhoda—until she lost the baby they were finally expecting and sometime after that Myron caught her and a Coldwell Banker real estate salesman *flagrante delicto* in the Garters' own bed. The occupants were both lucky to escape with their naked skins. You never know what goes on in the house next door. Myron didn't know what was going on in his own house.

The Garters got a divorce and over the next few years they both got fat from overeating until a few months ago, when Rhoda overdosed on pills and came skin-close to dying.

When she came to at Cedars-Sinai, Myron was there and they've been back together ever since. Even went to a Fat Farm together.

They lost weight and found—I don't know what to call it—but it seems to be working better than being fat.

"You know you're going to die a horrible death, don't you?" he finally said.

"What?"

"Look what happened to Bogart."

"Bacall?"

"Cigarettes."

"He lived to a ripe old age."

"Fifty-seven."

"That's a ripe old age."

"Not when you're fifty-six."

"I'm nowhere near fifty-six."

"You probably never will be if you keep that up." He pointed the El Producto toward my Lucky.

"What's that in your mitt? A cinnamon stick?"

"Cigars don't kill. Cigarettes do. A horrible death. That's the last time I'm going to say it."

"Promise?"

"No."

"Anything else on your mind?"

He nodded toward Goldie's office.

"She'll turn up, Alex. It's too early to start worrying."

"Better than being too late."

"We'll do everything we can."

"So will I."

"Sure you will, but do us both a favor, will you, pal?"

I didn't answer.

"Just don't go around slugging people left and right."

"How about right and left?" I gave him a smile.

He gave me one back. Then he got up, went to the door and opened it.

"After last night you're not thinking of going back into the private eye routine are you?"

"Hell no."

"Good. Tell your mom I say hello."

"I will. Same to Rhoda."

"Right."

He took a step into the doorway.

"Alex . . ."

"What?"

"We're looking for Goldie's car."

I just nodded.

He went out and closed the door, leaving the room to the cigar and cigarette smoke—and me.

Through all that smoke I couldn't help thinking about it. The first time she walked into this room.

The door was open and she stood by the nameplate.

"Mr. Night?"

I just might have acquired a new favorite blonde. She was beautiful, with lips that looked like they had just licked something sweet—and fresh as a spring garden. I weighed her in at 126 pounds. Blue eyes that didn't have, or need, makeup. Short honey-blonde hair. Slender, but strong, hands. A clean, clear California complexion. Long, lovely legs. She wore a dark blue skirt and jersey blouse that matched her eyes.

"Ye . . . yes," I stammered.

"I'm G. Rose across the hall. May I use your phone? Local call."

"Miz Rose, you may use anything I have."

"Thanks. Just the phone. I don't have one in my office. Too distracting."

I stood there mumchance while she walked to the phone and punched in a number. She walked even better than she stood still. And that jersey blouse pendulated just right. She smiled at me as she listened to a recorded message, then spoke into the phone. "Sorry, Duke, can't make lunch today. Right in the middle of a murder." She hung up and tapped the phone twice.

"Who done it?" I said cleverly.

"That's what I've got to figure out this afternoon."

"Good luck."

"Luck hasn't got a damn thing to do with it. By three o'clock I'll narrow the murder down to four suspects on page 223. By noon tomorrow on page 308, those six immortal letters T-H-E-E-N-D."

"That's it?"

"That's it."

"How long you been working on it?"

"Same as all the others. Eleven days."

To borrow a phrase from Dashiell Hammett, she made it sound as easy as eating gravy.

"You write a novel . . . an entire novel . . . in just eleven days?"

"Exactly. Twenty-eight pages a day. Totals 308 pages per novel."

"Simple as slicing salami," I said, thinking I was improving a little on Dash.

"Not quite," she admitted.

"And they all get published?"

"That's the idea."

"Have I ever read one of your books?"

"Maybe."

I riffled through the tables of my memory. There were a lot of female mystery writers lately, Julie Smith, Sara Paretsky, Sue Grafton, Linda Barnes, Patricia Cornwell . . . "G. Rose," I said aloud and repeated, "G. Rose . . ."

"No. No . . ."

A. Night In Hollywood Forever

She walked out of the door and for a moment I thought that that was the end of the conversation, but she beckoned from the hallway.

"Step across into the Twilight Zone," she invited.

With no hesitation and great anticipation I followed her through the hallway and into the opposite office. The room was the same size as mine, but appeared larger because of the furnishings, or lack of furnishings. Spartan. Strictly utilitarian. A computer-type table, a word processor, two straight-back chairs. Not even a coatrack, just a screw-in hook behind the door. No phone. On the floor two tall stacks of books, hardcovers and paperbacks by several different authors.

She let me just stand there a moment for the full effect. It was effective. Then she pointed to the books. "That's me. John Grim, Bart Cord, Gray Lugar, Russ Spiker, et cetera, et cetera, et cetera."

You could have knocked me over with a jersey blouse. "I have read you. You're tough."

"At these prices, tough comes easy. Especially when the payoff includes television and an occasional low-budget movie. What do you write, Mr. Night?"

The truth was that about the only thing I had ever written was bills to my clients, plus some stuff for a short story course I took at UCLA, so I thought I'd play it cute. "I'm still a virgin."

She let it pass.

"You can call me Alex."

"Okay. Is Night your real name?"

"Nyktas. In Greek it means . . ."

"Night."

"Right. How'd you know?"

"My real name is Triandafelos. In Greek it means . . ."

"Rose. Yes, Santa Claus there is a Virginia."

"How's that?"

"Never mind."

"Well," she smiled. "We do have something in common."

"Not too much." I gave her the up and down.

"I'm happy to say."

"Yes." She looked at me, then at the door. "Well . . ."

"I know, page 223. Uh, any time you want to use the phone . . . or anything else . . ."

"I know."

"I mean a dictionary . . . thesaurus . . ."

"Thanks, I have one of each at home."

"You write at home, too?"

"Not mysteries."

"What?"

"My doctoral thesis."

"Oh, on what?"

"It's called, 'The Crime of Punishment.'"

"You're deeper than you are tall. How long have you been working on that?"

"Two years."

I would have liked to linger a while longer. What I would have really liked was to seduce her, or have her seduce me. But as Scarlett O'Hara remarked in the last reel, "Tomorrow is another day." And this was not the last reel. I felt it in my bones. I walked to the door, doing my best imitation of John Wayne making an exit, paused by the nameplate, turned and gave the woman I loved my million-dollar smile. "If you do need anything, just whistle. I'll be right across the hall. By the way, what's the G stand for?"

"Goldie." She pointed to the processor. "But right now, I'm 'Trig Barker.'"

"Yeah, well, Happy Ending, Trig."

That's where and how it began for the two of us just a few months ago.

And while I sat there that day in that same office I

couldn't help but wonder where she was—and when she'd come back.

And whether it would be a happy ending for the two of us.

E. Elliott Elliot, the self-proclaimed sapient, had done his best to be encouraging and so had my best friend, Myron Garter.

I'm not a man who by nature builds dungeons in the air.

But this time it was different. There was a dark shadow across my mind's eye—like in those damn *noir* movies where things seem bleak even in daylight—where there is disquiet even in the silence of a room—where on a warm summer night something unspeakable lurks behind a rustling bush.

Where someday fate or some mysterious force can put the finger on you or me for no reason at all.

Was it fate or some mysterious force that the damn premiere happened to be last night? Or that Frances Vale happened to decide she wouldn't go without me? Or that I decided to break my date with Goldie in order to put five grand in my pocket?

She had only been missing a few hours. She might show up any minute smiling, and give a perfectly reasonable explanation of where she had been and why.

We'd both have a good laugh—and all her friends in the building and the cops would, too.

But what if she didn't show up?

And who broke into her office?

Coincidence?

Not likely.

And besides—there was a feeling that I couldn't shake—the feeling that if Goldie was well and safe, like Elliott said, then I wouldn't feel the way I did.

Chapter VI

I sat there in that office for how long I don't know, and for how many cigarettes, I lost count.

For a while I took the phone off the hook so I wouldn't get any more idiotic calls from the "media," or some former client wanting to hire me again, or some company wanting me to endorse some brand of underwear.

But after a while I put the phone back on the hook in case Goldie was trying to reach me. Just as I did there was a soft knock on the door.

"Come in."

E. Elliott Elliot stepped in, walking stick in one hand and carrying a couple trade papers in the other hand. He put them on my desk.

"My copies of *Variety* and *The Reporter*. You made the front pages of both. Thought I'd bring them by before that androgynous thief pilfers them."

"I heard that," Morgan Noble's voice came from the hallway as she stepped into the open doorway.

"Of course you did. As usual you're sticking your nose where it doesn't belong."

"God only knows where your nose has been."

"I thought you and your ilk didn't believe in God."

"God with a small *g*."

"Of course, everything about you is small, particularly your talent."

"Speaking of small, what's that between . . ."

"Look, would you two mind taking this act on the road?"

Morgan Noble disappeared down the hallway.

Elliott bowed slightly and pointed his walking stick toward *Variety* on the desk.

"Army did quite a piece on you, too, almost half his column."

"Yeah, thanks, Elliott."

"You're welcome—and be of good cheer, my friend." Elliott walked toward the door and before he closed it behind him I could hear him say—to himself, I guess, "there was a time when he'd devote an entire column to me."

E. Elliott Elliot's name hadn't been in Army Archerd's column or anywhere in the trade papers for a long, long time.

His time had come and gone. He once admitted to me that "For forty-odd years I made a fortune writing and re-writing the same story with only the names changed to preserve my illustrious reputation and extravagant lifestyle. And all those years I got away with it because I'd been blessed with an ingrained ability to construct an uncluttered sentence and with an uncanny ear for sophisticated dialogue. Unfortunately, uncluttered sentences and sophisticated dialogue are no longer in vogue. However, if good taste and eloquence ever return to this benighted profession, you can be assured of my prominent resurgence. Meanwhile I continue to reap a fortune in a more mundane manner, real estate, primarily Beverly Hills real estate. Not what you'd call a slum lord."

As I picked up the trade papers I couldn't help thinking that E. Elliott Elliot would probably be willing to give up a chunk of that real estate just to see his name on the screen again—or even in Army Archerd's column.

The trade papers, *Variety* in particular, have long had reputations for clever—some say callow—headlines and banners—ever since *Variety*'s stock market announcement: WALL STREET LAYS AN EGG; then rural b.o. assessment: STIX NIX CRIX PIX.

That tradition still survives and thrives at *Variety*. When MGM was sold to Sony: LEO'S BIG FADE OUT; CBS's "memogate": THE EYE WON'T BLINK; Schwarzenegger's election: GOP FLEXS MUSCLE; Eisner's successor at Disney: IGER FINALLY THE BIG CHEESE; and so on and on.

That morning's *Variety* front page: THREE STARS AT PREMIERE: FRANCES VALE, STAR OF GOOD HOPE, A. NIGHT.

The picture got an excellent review and so did Frances Vale, but most of the story was about what happened afterward. Never mind the details. Suffice it to say that this will be prominently pasted in my mother's scrapbook. Army Archerd followed his "Good Morning" lead with "Good Night Rides to the Rescue to Catch a Thief.'

The Hollywood Reporter's Robert Osborne waxed just as effusive.

When the phone rang I hoped it would be Goldie, but expected it to be my mother.

Wrong.

"Mr. Night. This is Clara in Mr. Meadows' office. I have Mr. Meadows on the phone for you."

"Good morning, Alex. Have you seen the trades?"

"No," I lied.

"Great reviews and a million dollars' worth of publicity. Same with the newspapers and television. Never been anything like it. Everybody here's ecstatic."

"James Glazer isn't."

"Who's James Glazer?"

"The thief."

"Oh, him."

"Yeah, him."

"Well, into each life some rain must fall."

"It fell all right."

"We'll see he gets a decent burial, but listen, Alex, first off I've got to tell you Tri-Arc's going to do another picture with Frances and this time she's going to star, name above the title."

"That's nice."

"Nice, hell, it's . . ."

"Great!?"

"Yeah, great. I've had this script for two years, but the board wouldn't touch her—until now—now they're nuts about her . . ."

"Well, I'm happy for the two of you, Mike."

"Yeah, well this'll make you happier. For the three of us. Has my messenger got there yet?"

Right on cue there was a knock on the office door.

"Come in."

The messenger came in.

"Mr. Night?"

"Right."

"Would you sign for this please?"

He handed me an envelope and a clipboard. I took the envelope and signed the receipt on the clipboard.

"Thank you," the messenger said, took the clipboard and left.

"Alex? Alex . . . are you there?"

"I'm here and so was the messenger."

"Open the envelope."

I did.

"Is this a gag?"

"No gag, Alex—and I've got to tell you that The Star of Good Hope was sold this morning."

"For a million?"

"No."

"Oh."

"One million two hundred and fifty thousand."

"The jeweler did all right, huh?"

"So did I."

I could hear him chuckling—and never in my life did I know Mike Meadows to chuckle.

"You mean the publicity . . ."

"Hell, no. I mean that I owned the Star. The jeweler was just the broker. Been trying to get rid of it for years. Nobody would bite. This morning somebody swallowed it and paid the premium, thanks to you and what happened last night."

"I don't believe this . . ."

"You can believe it all right and you can believe that check . . ."

"You said five thousand . . ."

"That was before last night. Go to the bank and deposit it."

"I will before you come to your senses."

"It was more than worth it—to me and Frances and Tri-Arc. Thanks, Alex."

"Thank you, Mike."

I hung up and looked at the check again—made out to Alex Night.

Never before did I have a check in my hand made out to Alex Night for twenty-five thousand dollars.

At that moment I would have been the happiest man in the world if Goldie Rose had walked into the office.

But she didn't.

Chapter VII

The rest of the day was sort of a blur. I do remember Myron Garter coming in and saying the print boys were through and BHPD would follow up.

When I passed by Henry Fenenbock's office, he and Judy Kirk were on the phone with the insurance company. I stopped by Kramer's Tobacco and bought a carton of Luckies, much to Marsha's chagrin.

One thing does stand out. At the underground garage there were dozens of empty spaces and a Lincoln Navigator driven by a little woman with a big man on the passenger seat pulled up right next to the Sebring. When she opened the door it greeted the side of the Sebring with a sharp report. The result was evident.

"Lady!" I couldn't help wincing.

Out came the big man from the passenger side of the Navigator.

"What's your problem, bud?!"

He looked tough, but not tough enough. Under ordinary circumstances I would have . . .

But I didn't.

"No problem, bud."

"What did you call Debbie?"

"I called her 'lady.' I apologize."

"You do?"

"I do."

"Okay, then."

He took her by the hand and swaggered away in triumph.

I let him swagger.

The check in my pocket for twenty-five grand had a compensating effect.

I drove to Larchmont Village, where I still did business at the California National Bank, saw Ivan Carbajal, the manager. One grand went into the checking account, two hundred into my pocket and the rest into savings—I hadn't done that much business with CNB ever before. I don't know who was more surprised, Ivan or me—but I do know who was more content—like a fat spider in a web full of flies.

On the street I met City Councilman, 4th District, Tom LaBonge, a natural-born politician who will someday be mayor of Los Angeles. He greeted me as if I was on my way to vote. We shook hands and I drove home to get some sleep.

But first I drove by Goldie's apartment.

I hoped her car would be parked where it usually was.

It wasn't.

When I got home there was a message on the machine from Frances Vale asking me to call her.

I didn't.

I had a couple of Gordon's Gin and tonics and called my mother before she called me. I didn't have much to say but she did. I listened to her through a couple more gins and a Lucky Strike before she said good night.

I didn't have the heart to tell her about the break-in at Goldie's office or that Goldie was missing.

I hoped that tomorrow I wouldn't have to.

Chapter VIII

That night I dreamed the devil was shaking a fist at me.

The next morning I called Goldie's home number—and got the message machine.

I didn't leave a message.

I made breakfast and, for the second day in a row, skipped working out and swimming at the Y.

I was in no mood for the raspberries, rhubarbs and bullshit from the boys in the locker room—particularly those boys in the business or want-to-be in the business—actors, producers, directors and writers who would delight in dirty cracks about Frances Vale, or a million-dollar diamond, or a defunct detective now a want-to-be mystery writer. All that could wait until another day—or two.

By mid-morning I made the climb up to the third floor of the Writers and Artists Building. Most of the writers and artists were already writing and arting, but the one I love wasn't. There was still a yellow police tape across her door proclaiming CRIME SCENE—DO NOT REMOVE.

And across from her door, in front of my door, there was something else.

Actually someone else.

A man sitting on one of those canes that unfolds into what must be a very uncomfortable seat—and he was not exactly sitting—leaning and he had a regular-type cane in his other hand.

He looked like he was in his late seventies or early eighties, and also looked like Charley Grapewin, who played the alcoholic lawyer in *Johnny Apollo*—only not as healthy as Grapewin looked in the picture that starred Tyrone Power, Dorothy Lamour, Edward Arnold and Lloyd Nolan.

I would have bet that this old man could not have climbed up to the third floor, but he must have—unless someone carried him.

He waited until I was about ten feet away. His voice came out a lot stronger than he looked—almost sounded like a challenge.

"You Night?"

"Me Night," I smiled. "You Tarzan?"

"Not funny, Night. You want to stand out here and talk or let me come inside?" He nodded toward the door.

"Neither."

"It's gonna be one or the other, brother. I didn't come all the way up here to get eighty-sixed."

The truth was I sure as hell wasn't going to get any writing done that morning—not with that police tape across the hall and wondering about Goldie's whereabouts—and the old man did go to all the trouble of climbing the stairway to heaven and he sure could use some rest before making the descent—so I figured I'd do my good deed for the day and humor him.

Besides, there was something about that man that commanded—if not respect—attention.

Somewhat disused maybe, but still assertive.

Without further remark or hesitation I unlocked and opened the door, stepped inside and bade him follow.

He did, and stood for a moment appraising the room.

There wasn't much to appraise. A rolltop desk, a wooden swivel chair, a straight-back chair, a Naugahyde couch, a nonelectric Royal typewriter, a telephone with a long cord—plus a dictionary, a thesaurus, a hot plate, a dented aluminum coffeepot, a couple of restaurant coffee cups and spoons, a ream of unlined white paper, two pipes on the desk, a half pound of Kramer's Mixture tobacco, a box of kitchen matches, and assorted ashtrays.

"Don't put up much of a front, do you?" he said.

"The decorator I hired'll be here any minute, meanwhile you want to walk to the window and enjoy the view?"

"No." With effort he sat in the straight-back chair and held on to both canes. "I usually don't need these sticks, but today I felt a little wobbly."

"Would you like me to fix you a cup of coffee?"

"I'd like you to fix me a Scotch and milk."

I just shook my head.

"That's what I thought," he said.

"Look, Mister . . . whoever you happen to be . . ."

"Ever hear of Charles Oliver Dash?"

" 'C.O.D.'? Yeah."

"That's who I happen to be . . . and that was my byline. 'C.O.D.' "

"Sure. You used to be . . ."

". . . like Cagney in *The Roaring Twenties*—'a big shot.' "

"I was going to say a 'newspaper man.' "

"That's right, a big shot newspaper man—during the roaring fifties, sixties and seventies . . . big bylines, big money, big booze, big blondes, big Pulitzer Prize . . . until the big fall . . . so much for *curriculum vitae*."

" 'The big fall'?"

"I wrote an interview with John Wayne for my syndicated column. He was an old pal and I'd interviewed him dozens of times before. Usual questions and I knew I'd get the usual answers—besides he was sick and I didn't want to bother him and also I got sidetracked by a bottle of Scotch and a beautiful blonde. The interview got printed in hundreds of papers. There was only one hitch . . . It turned out that at the time the interview supposedly took place Duke was already dead. Died hours before."

"Yeah, I do remember something about that."

"So do I. So does everybody in the newspaper game. That was the end of that—'that' being my career."

"One mistake?"

"That's all it takes when you've made a lot of enemies as well as friends. My friends couldn't help me and my enemies . . . well, let's say there were more daggers in my hide than in Caesar's."

"You sure you don't want some coffee?"

"I want some help . . . from you."

"Me?!"

"The man who saved The Star of Good Hope."

"Don't believe everything you read in the papers."

"I don't, but I did some checking on you."

"Did you check the fact that I'm retired from the private eye business?"

"People have been known to un-retire."

"Not this people."

"I'll pay you for your time if you'll just listen for five minutes."

"I don't want any pay and it won't do any good but go ahead."

"At home I've got a whole folder full of details, but I'll just give you the bare bones. Ever hear of 'The Tear of Russia'?"

"No."

"Ever hear of the Imperial Fabergé Eggs?"

"Yes."

"At one time it was known that fifty of them existed. Recently nine were sold out of the Malcolm Forbes estate to Viktor Veksellberg, a Russian oil and aluminum tycoon. Do you know the price?"

"No."

"Mister Night, name a fantastic figure."

"I'm no good at guessing games."

"This is no game. How much is The Star of Good Hope worth?"

"It just sold for one million two hundred and fifty thousand dollars."

"That's *not* a fantastic figure."

"It's *not?* What is?"

"The nine bejeweled Fabergé eggs were sold for more than one hundred million dollars . . . I repeat, one . . ."

"I heard, one hundred million dollars. What's that got to do with the price of tomatoes?"

"Each egg is worth more than ten million. Eight of those eggs are still missing."

"So?"

"So I'm on the trail of one of those Fabergés . . . 'The Tear of Russia.' "

"Well, I hope you find it and become a rich man."

"I don't care about riches."

"What do you care about?"

"The story—my redemption . . ."

"Another Pulitzer Prize?"

"Maybe that, too."

"What's all this got to do with me?"

"Mister Night, look at me. I'm an old man. A sick man. Diabetes. Going blind. High blood pressure. A bum ticker and a lot more. It's not easy for me to walk and get around. But I can still write . . ."

"I repeat, what's all this got to . . ."

"I need strength . . . legs, somebody with smarts and muscle . . . with courage like you exhibited the other night . . . a man who . . ."

"Hold on, Mister Dash. If you're going to suggest what I think you are, you're wasting your time, I . . ."

He pulled a slip of paper out of his pocket.

"This is a check for ten thousand dollars. There's more where that came from. I cashed in my insurance policy. This is a retainer for your services. If we can find the Egg, I don't know who the money will belong to. But this and another ten thousand belongs to you. The story belongs to me."

"I'm sorry, Mister Dash . . ."

"I'll play the sympathy card. You're my last and only hope . . ."

"You'll have to find another boy."

"I've tried."

"Try some more."

"I can't."

"The answer is no."

There was a knock on the door and I was happy to hear it. I felt sorry for the old man, but . . .

"Come in," I said.

The door opened and Elliott stepped in.

"Alex, I was wondering if you'd like to have lunch . . . oh, excuse me. I didn't know you were . . ."

"No, come in, Elliott, this gentleman was just leaving."

Dash managed to stand and turn toward the doorway.

"Charlie!" Elliott gasped, "My God! Charlie, old friend, how are you?"

"Hello, Elliott," Dash nodded and almost smiled.

"Charlie, what're you doing here?"

"On a fool's errand."

"I do presume you were going to stop by and see me . . . after all this time. Well, were you?"

"I . . . I'm not sure . . ."

"I certainly am. Alex, I trust you realize you've been entertaining one of the few living legends . . . besides myself. Now I am glad I interrupted."

"It's all right, Elliott," I said, "we were finished."

"Good. You can both tell me all about it over lunch."

"Sorry, Elliott, I've got a date."

"That is a pity. Charlie, you and I will reminisce over luncheon about the golden days."

"No, Elliott, I . . ."

"The matter is settled! I insist. My man, Carstairs, will drive us to Musso's. Alex, you don't know what you're missing."

No, I didn't.

Chapter IX

Yeah. That was me. Like the vamp of Savannah . . . "hard-hearted Hannah . . . pourin' water on a drownin' man."

And Charles Oliver Dash looked like he was drowning. But I didn't think I could bail him out even if I felt like trying.

And just then I didn't feel like trying.

I only felt like two things. Finding out what happened to Goldie. Finishing *The Big Changeover*.

And I had a feeling I wasn't going to do either that day.

So I lit a Lucky.

And answered the phone.

"Hello, Mom."

"Alex, you sound disappointed."

"No, Mom, I'm just hungry."

"Too many cigarettes."

"Mom, cigarettes cut down your appetite."

"They do? I thought it was just the opposite. Why don't you come over here. I've got some Avgolemonou soup."

"I can't, Mom."

"Why not? You got a lunch date with Goldie?"

"No, Mom."

"Why not?"

"She's not here."

"Where is she?"

"I'm not sure right now."

That's as close as I was going to come for the time being.

"Well, go get something to eat then finish the book."

"I will."

"Why don't you go to lunch with Myron?"

"He goes home when he can, now that he and Rhoda are married again."

"You and Goldie ought to get married."

"We will, Mom."

"Promises. I love you, Alex."

"I love you, too, Mom. Good-bye."

As soon as I hung up I picked up the phone again because it rang again.

"Hello, Alex."

"Hello, Franny."

"Why didn't you answer my call? I called you at home *yesterday*."

"I didn't go home yesterday," I lied.

"Oh? Did you sleep over at your girlfriend's?"

"You'll pardon me if I hang up now, Franny."

"I'm sorry, Alex. I shouldn't have said that. Matter of fact I shouldn't have said and done a lot of things in my time."

"That goes for most of us."

"I only called to thank you."

"You're welcome. For what?"

"You know what, making me do *When Winter Comes*."

"Mike did that."

"We both know different. Alex, I feel twenty years younger."

"Be careful, you had some bad habits twenty years ago."

"You were one of 'em."

"I wasn't a habit—just handy once in a while."

"You know I signed to do another picture with Mike."

"Yeah, name above the title."

"I'm flying to New York today to do publicity for *When Winter Comes*. Katie Couric, Larry King, even O'Reilly. Mind if I mention your name?"

"Just mention the picture's name and Mike's."

"No shit, Alex, if I can ever do anything at all for you—anything, just say the word."

"The word is 'stay straight.' "

"Straight as Robin Hood's arrow."

"Happy landings, Franny."

Downstairs in the entryway I saw Morgan Noble giving a quick read to Elliott's *Variety* and *Reporter* that had been delivered in the mail.

The Bernstein brothers came down the stairs right behind me.

"Take your time, Morgan . . ." Brother Bruce.

". . . Elliott's out to lunch . . ." Brother Bernie.

"Probably won't be back . . ." Brother Bruce

". . . for a couple of hours." Brother Bernie.

"Go to hell. Both of you." Morgan.

"Don't forget the Klan meeting tonight . . ." Brother Bruce.

". . . bring matches." Brother Bernie.

They had used that one before, but I guess they figured it was worth repeating.

"Both of you go to hell."

I guess Morgan figured that was worth repeating, too . . . with a slight variation.

My stomach was getting pretty sore at me, so I stopped in at Johnny Rocket's.

While I sat at the counter with a hamburger and Coca Cola in front of me, I couldn't help thinking of E.E.E. and C.O.D. over at Musso and Frank's on Hollywood Boulevard.

Musso's is the oldest restaurant in Hollywood—since 1918—and the best.

In the old days it was the watering hole for some of the best writers in town and the world. Ben Hecht, Charles MacArthur, Hemingway, Scott Fitzgerald, William Faulkner, John Lee Mahin, Budd Schulberg, and of course, Dashiell Hammett and Raymond Chandler.

I could just imagine E. Elliott Elliot and Charles Oliver Dash sitting there in that booth by the bar, number twenty-seven, sipping their drinks among the phantoms of the Screen Writers Guild—enjoying prime rib while I took another bite from Johnny Rocket's hamburger.

I told myself when Goldie came back, she and I would sit in that same booth, sip those martinis against which all other martinis must be judged, enjoy our dinner—and then enjoy each other.

When Goldie came back.

The rest of the day was uneventful . . . for me.

Not for some other people I knew.

Chapter X

When you're a private eye you get so you can damn near smell something amiss. Since retiring, my sense of smell—like the ol' gray mare—ain't what she used to be.

The next morning as I walked along Santa Monica Boulevard toward the Writers and Artists Building everything smelled just like it always did in Beverly Hills about that time of day—coffee brewing from the open doors of the coffee shops, kitchen delights emanating from the entrances of the restaurants, fumes from the internal combustion engine traffic crisscrossing the intersection and the ever so slight whiff of pollution commonly characterized as smog.

It was a day that smelled just like any other day.

But my private eye eyesight did notice something that could be considered—if not amiss—unusual.

E. Elliott Elliot's brown Bentley was parked directly in front of the Writers and Artists Building. Unusual, because Carstairs, Elliot's man, invariably double-parked in front of the building while Elliot embarked or disembarked, then Carstairs would drive away until the designated time when Elliot would reverse the procedure.

Never before had I seen the Bentley stationed curbside.

I must admit that, while I did notice the anomaly, I didn't pause and reflect on it. I kept right on walking into the entryway where I *did* pause and glance at my name on the directory along with the names of other artists and writers.

But then I did that every day. It was somehow reassuring before I continued the upward trek to my office.

This day the upward trek was interrupted before I got there.

E. Elliott Elliot, elegant as ever, stood in front of his office as if waiting for someone. It turned out he was.

Me.

"Alex. We saw you coming from the window."

I had hoped the "we" was Goldie and he.

It wasn't.

"Would you mind coming into my office so we can talk? It's a bit more comfortable than your diggings."

I couldn't gainsay that.

For years Elliot had occupied two adjoining rooms, which he had converted at great expense and refurbished in the fashion of a Victorian Club. Like Elliot himself, it reflected another era, proud and courtly, debonair and moribund.

Elliot, of course, didn't wait for my answer. He stepped inside and assumed that I'd follow.

I did—and closed the door behind me.

The "we" that Elliot had referred to turned out to be his driver, Carstairs.

Carstairs was seated in a wingback chair and wore his usual black suit. He also wore a black eye and assorted welts and bruises in varying hues. I also noticed that the knuckles of his formidable fists were swollen. He started to rise but I motioned for him to sit back down.

At first I thought he might've had an accident in the Bentley, but I hadn't discerned any bruises or dents on the machine parked out front.

"Jeesus!" I inquired brilliantly. "What the hell happened to you?"

"Do you want to tell him, Carstairs?" Elliot responded. "Or shall I?"

"You tell him, Mr. Elliot," Carstairs managed through a ruptured lip.

"Very well. Please sit down, Alex."

I complied.

"As you know Charlie and I had lunch yesterday at Musso's. Excellent, as always, and as always, Charlie consumed too much of his usual cocktail, too much Scotch and not enough milk. In the car, he passed out—thank God without throwing up. I instructed Carstairs to drop me off, then see to it that he delivered Charlie safely to his abode and put him to bed or couch.

"Charlie came to enough to walk inside, with assistance from Carstairs. Once inside they came upon an intruder who was in the process of photographing the contents of a certain folder on Charlie's desk. The intruder, a behemoth, did not welcome the interruption. As Carstairs approached a polemic ensued.

"Carstairs gave a good account of himself, but both he and Charlie ended up on the floor. The intruder made a grab for the folder, but good old Carstairs leapt back into the fray. The intruder dropped the folder and its contents and managed to flee the scene with Carstairs unable to pursue due to . . . well, you can see the results of the encounter." Elliot pointed to the driver.

"Yeah, I can see. How's Dash?"

"Somewhat the worse for wear, but sober. I've seen to it that he has an attendant until he further recovers."

"How much of the 'contents' did the intruder manage to photograph?"

"That's academic, because in his hurry to escape he left the camera behind. It's one of those small devices employed by spies in bad movies."

"I assume the folder is the one that Dash mentioned when he was in my office."

"A reasonable assumption," Elliot nodded.

I took a step closer to Carstairs.

"This behemoth, as Elliot called him—can you describe him in a little more detail? Light complexion? Dark? About what age? How was he dressed? Could you recognize him if you saw him again? Did he say anything—have an accent of any kind?"

Carstairs closed his eyes, thought for a moment, conjuring up the image, opened his eyes and answered.

"About six-three, two hundred ten or twenty pounds, light complexion, maybe forty-five years of age, dressed in dark clothes . . ."

"So far you might as well be describing yourself," I said.

"I guess you're right," Carstairs agreed. "He was a little bigger and no he didn't say anything so I don't know about any accent, but he was good with his fists, I've done some fighting in the ring, and he used karate, too, a couple of kicks in the . . . right places."

Carstairs hands inadvertently moved to those "right places."

"Could you pick him out of a lineup?" I asked.

"Well, I'm not sure. It happened so fast and I ended up pretty dizzy."

"Where's the camera from that bad spy movie?"

Elliot picked the camera up from his ornate desk.

I winced.

"I know what you're thinking, dear fellow . . . prints. They would be Carstairs'."

"I . . . I'm sorry." Carstairs lowered his head. "I guess I was still dizzy, just picked it up without thinking."

"I wouldn't worry about it," I said as consolingly as I could. "That damn thing's too small to have any discernable prints on it anyhow."

That seemed to make Carstairs feel better.

"I'll have the film developed," Elliot said, "if that'll help."

"That'll help."

Even as I said it I thought to myself, "Wait a minute Night, why the hell are you getting involved? This is none of your beeswax! Butt out."

My thought must have shown because Elliot gave me that Waldo Lydecker look from *Laura*.

"Alex . . ."

"Elliot. If you're going to say what I think you're going to say . . . don't say it."

"I am going to say it. Alex just talk to Charlie for a few minutes—no, just listen for a few minutes as I did over lunch at Musso's. I promise you'll be intrigued . . ."

"I don't want to be intrigued. Why the hell don't *you* do his legwork for this Pulitzer Prize–story of his?"

"First of all, it calls for detective work, and I am no detective. Secondly, as you can tell from looking at Carstairs, it well may involve some danger, and I *am* an inveterate coward . . . and those are only two of many other good reasons."

"Elliot, what's your stake in all this?"

"*Amicus curiae.*"

"Friend of the court?"

"Friend of Charles Oliver Dash. Don't say it, I don't often let it show, but I do have some friendships, and in this case there's more to it . . . there's obligation. I'm obliged . . ."

"Well, I'm not."

"That's true—not to me or him, but let me tell you a story I've never told anyone . . . Carstairs . . ."

"Yes, sir."

"Pretend you're not hearing this."

"Yes, sir."

"Alex, that first time I introduced myself to you in front of the directory downstairs you said, 'Oh, yes, you won an Oscar once.' 'Twice,' I corrected you—and there they are."

He pointed to the two golden statuettes on his mantel.

"The truth is I only won one and a half. The studio assigned me to write a picture called *Deadline*, a newspaper story. I wrote it despite the fact that I knew nothing about newspapers. Charles Oliver Dash did, so I let him read it overnight.

"It stank and he said so.

"And that night, to the accompaniment of a bottle of Scotch, he rewrote every part of it that had anything to do with a newspaper, which was over half the script.

"In those days if we studio writers wrote a half a page a day, a few hundred words a week, we were doing well. Newspapermen like Dash could write a couple thousand words a day—six or seven stories a week.

"The result of his contribution is that second Oscar." Again Elliot pointed to the mantel.

"Why didn't you give him screen credit?"

"He wouldn't hear of it. Said he couldn't even remember writing it. Maybe I should have persisted, but I didn't. Thus, the friendship and the obligation."

"What's all that got to do with me?"

"Nothing. Absolutely nothing. Not a jot."

"Then why tell me the story?"

"I thought, perhaps if I did, you might be willing to listen to a story he wants to tell you."

"Elliot, listen to this—and you can listen, too, Carstairs—one: I'm out of the detective business; two: I'm in the process of writing a mystery novel; three: I've got something else on my mind—a lady I happen to love is missing . . ."

"Alex, I can counter every one of those arguments, but I won't bother, well, maybe I will briefly—once a copper always a copper—the novel, like heaven, can wait—as for the missing Miss Rose, this will help take your mind off that until her safe return, which I will personally guarantee."

"You will?"

"Yes, I and my rosary. Now will you indulge a couple of old-timers and listen to Charlie's tale? And, besides, it may give you some pointers for that nascent novel of yours . . ."

I was licked and I knew it—and so did E. Elliott Elliot. I could tell by that telltale smirk on his talcumed face.

Chapter XI

When Charles Oliver Dash first came into my office he had looked it over and said, "Don't put up much of a front do you?"

I could have said the same about the place where he lived—but didn't.

It was a tiny bungalow in the Hollywood Hills just off the freeway. Built long before I was, it consisted of about nine hundred square feet divided into three humble rooms and a toilet. We sat in what passed for the parlor—den. The room needed paint. The carpeting was threadbare. The furniture hoary and the walls were lined with long wooden planks between cement blocks piled with books, magazines, newspapers and periodicals. He did have a cigarette-stained desk with a typewriter older than mine, an Underwood.

Elliot had called and told him I was driving over. The attendant answered the door and Dash asked him to sit outside on the stoop while we talked.

The old man was pretty banged up, but not nearly as bad as Carstairs. He asked if I wanted a drink.

"No."

He poured some milk and Scotch into a tumbler. Some of the Red Label spilled onto the floor.

"Don't worry about that carpet," he said, "if it could walk, it'd stagger."

It never entered my mind to worry about the carpet. I sat down and lit a Lucky.

"That's the folder, over there," he pointed toward the desk. "You can take it with you, but I want to tell you a little bit about this first. That okay?"

"Okay."

"I already told you about those nine eggs that were just sold from the Malcom Forbes estate for over a hundred million dollars—more than ten million for each Fabergé. There's an article about it in *Time* magazine, the whole history, but there are some things that aren't in that story or anyplace else. Things that I heard about when I first came to this town from people who were much older than I was then—or now. How much do you know about William Randolph Hearst and Marion Davies?"

"What everybody does, man and mistress. He was a great newspaper man and she was not a great actress."

"She was better than most people thought, 'specially at comedy. Everybody got the wrong impression of her from the hatchet job Orson Welles did in that picture he made, *Citizen Kane*."

"Yeah, I do remember that."

"And that's the way most people remember Marion Davies. Too bad. Hearst met her when he was fifty-four and she was twenty—a beauty in the Ziegfeld chorus. He had four sons and was separated from his wife Millicent Veronica Wilson, an ex-showgirl and compliant Catholic. W.R. went nuts over Davies. He even started a motion picture company, Cosmopolitan Pictures, to make her a star. It cost him millions but he did it."

"Hooray for Hollywood and Hearst."

"But he wanted her to be known as a great dramatic actress. He had a deal with MGM and wanted Louis B. Mayer and Thalberg to have her play the Bard's Juliet, Elizabeth Barrett Browning and Marie Antoinette.

"Norma Shearer got all three parts. She happened to be married to Irving Thalberg."

"Well," I said, "that's keeping it in the family."

"Hearst wanted to keep it in his family even though he wasn't married to Marion. So he decided to produce a picture about Alexandra who was married to Tzar Nicholas—not exactly a comedy. In the end the Tzar's entire family was lined up against a cellar wall and shot. And for that picture they needed a duplicate of a Fabergé egg—only W.R. wouldn't hear of a duplicate. He bought a real one. The Tear of Russia. The property master did manufacture a duplicate, a stand-in, but for the close shots they'd use the real one. The picture was called *The Last Empress*."

"I don't remember it."

"That's because it was never finished. Hearst hired Eric Von Stroheim to direct, a colossal egotist, who shot millions of feet of film and gave Marion Davies a nervous breakdown. She implored Hearst to abandon the picture, and he finally did."

"So?"

"So nobody knows what happened to The Tear of Russia which today is worth . . ."

"Ten million dollars."

"Or more."

"Didn't I read somewhere that when Hearst got into financial trouble during the depression . . ."

"I know what you're going to say, he damn near went bankrupt and Davies sold a lot of her jewels and bailed him out—greater love hath no mistress than to lay down her jewels—but those jewels were all inventoried, and the Fabergé was not among them."

"You sure?"

"I'm sure. Davies wouldn't part with it."

"Wasn't it included in their estates—their wills?"

"Hearst died in 1951—Davies in 1961, no mention of it in either will. But in that folder," Dash took a gulp of his drink and nodded toward the desk, "I've chased down a lot of clues and possibilities . . ."

"So, as Bogart said in *Casablanca*, 'it's a story without a finish.' "

"Every story has to have a finish—if you know where to look."

"Do you?"

"I know where to start."

"Where?"

"Where Marion Davies is buried."

Chapter XII

How the hell do I get hooked into these things? That, among other thoughts, is what I thought to myself while I drove across Hollywood and Vine toward my condo over on Wilshire and Fremont.

Why am I doing this? I glanced down at the yellow folder on the passenger seat. It was more than an inch thick. Charles Oliver Dash had crisscrossed it with heavy rubber bands and handed it to me.

I had asked him if he had another copy.

"No."

"Why not?"

"Then there would be two for somebody to steal instead of one."

I didn't think that was a very good reason, so I intended to make at least one more copy over at Kinko's tomorrow.

I deliberated on stopping at a restaurant and placating the call of my ingestive system, but decided I'd go home and warm up some leftover spaghetti sauce and go over at least part of the contents of Dash's folio.

But first I'd drive by Goldie's place and see if her car came home.

It hadn't, so I proceeded toward the spaghetti sauce.

I wanted to clear my mind of all the clutter, and music usually turns the trick. I inserted a Cole Porter cassette into the dashboard and listened to a rendition of "Anything Goes" then "Easy to Love." By the time I got to the condo and parked in the garage that came with the accommodation, "Every Time We Say Goodbye" had just come on. I let the motor run and kept listening until the song ended . . . "but how strange the change from major to minor, every time we say goodbye."

I pressed the button so the top came up, then got out of the Sebring with the folder, closed the garage door and turned around into a gun pointed right between my eyes.

Chapter XIII

Even though he was wearing a ski mask there was something familiar about the behemoth holding the gun. In a millisecond I recalled Carstairs description of the intruder.

I couldn't tell much about his complexion because of the ski mask and the fact that he wore tight-fitting gloves, but the rest of the description fit.

This time he did speak.

"Hand it over."

No accent.

It's strange, "the change from major to minor," when unexpectedly somebody's pointing a gun at you—especially at close range—the whirlwind of past such occurrences races through the mirror of your memory. It happens in a tenth of a split second. What and where it happened before and how you survived. You skim over the combat situations because there you knew that guns were always pointed at you and nothing was unexpected.

I riffled through the other times, times when my hand was already in my coat pocket and already holding a gun. The pocket suffered a bullet hole and so did the man with a gun—in one case it was a woman. But in this case there was no gun in my pocket and both hands were in plain sight, one hand holding the object of the gunman's quest; the other a set of keys. There was the time I spit an oyster into the face of the scofflaw, but this scofflaw was wearing a ski mask and I wasn't sure I could target either eye with accuracy.

I used a cane once with swift, devastating effect. This time no cane, no devastating effect. Aha! The good, old kick in the vitals! But while the gun hand was extended close by, his body and vitals were a tad too far for certainty. I was running out of options and, though only a second had elapsed, the behemoth with a gun was running out of patience.

"I said hand it over!" he repeated.

I could see his finger tighten on the trigger.

Would he risk a gunshot in these surroundings?

Maybe he would.

But I wouldn't.

'Twas then that the gods looked down favorably upon me.

No, not the gods. One of the tenants.

Mrs. Favarsham, a septuagenarian busybody who rarely missed any comings or goings around the building, hadn't missed this one.

She poked her head out of her second-story window and shouted for all the neighbors to hear.

"Hey! What the hell's going on down there!"

That was my cue and I took it.

I slammed at the gun with the folder and the gun fired. The slug landed I know not where, but not in me. The gun dropped and so did the folder and the set of keys.

He was a worthy opponent. Too damn worthy.

The encounter was well worth watching. By now, due to the gunshot, some of the other residents were at their windows watching.

There were salient blows, foot and fist, fast and fervent. In a barroom fight, whoever hits first usually wins, but in a contest like this, whoever hits last wins. The last hit was landed by me. A good, old-fashioned right cross that nearly tore the ski mask off his face and his face off his neck, which is what I meant to do.

He went down like a shot buffalo, but the son of a bitch didn't stay down. He rolled over, picked up the gun and ran off like a rabbit going to shit. By then he had pulled off the ski mask so he could see better, but I couldn't see his face—or what was left of it.

At that point I was too groggy to see anything except that the folder was still there.

"Should I call 9-1-1?" Mrs. Favarsham bellowed.

"No, thanks," I wobbled and waved at her.

She and the other residents clapped and cheered.

The hometown boy had won.

The hometown boy picked up the folder and keys and managed to take a bow.

I thought of another lyric Cole Porter had written.

". . . like the beat, beat, beat of a jungle drum" . . . that's the way my head felt.

Chapter XIV

I hadn't lost the folder, but I sure as hell lost my appetite. A couple of severe blows to the stomach will do it every time, particularly when compounded by what felt like a couple of chinked ribs.

I decided on alcohol. Not the rubbing kind. The drinking kind.

The Gordon's Gin kind to be specific. A long time ago I had read somewhere that that was the brand Ernest Hemingway drank. Maybe I thought some of his talent for writing would rub off on me. So far I couldn't tell—because, so far, I hadn't written anything.

That's not quite true. I did write the title of the next great mystery novel. *The Big Changeover*, but beyond the title page there was still nothing but blank pages. I wasn't discouraged. There were plenty of other writers who were slow starters, but offhand I couldn't think of any that slow.

After the third gin some of the pain had begun to ease off, so I sat on my comfortable leather chair, put both feet on the matching leather ottoman and took the rubber bands off the folder.

Dash's physical appearance was sloppy, but his research was anything but—all divided into appropriate sections— W. R. Hearst—Marion Davies—Fabergé—Nicholas and Alexandra—The Revolution—Hollywood—Silents—Talkies— San Simeon—the Beach House—Beverly Hills—Investments—Celebrations, and almost a dozen other sections.

I sure as hell wasn't going to read it all that night, but since Dash had suggested I start the search where she was buried I thought I'd take a hinge at the life that led up to that final resting place in 1961.

Marion Davies was born Marion Cecilia Douras in Brooklyn on January 3, 1897, of Greek and Irish bloodlines. Her father, Herbert Douras, mother Rose Reilly, three older sisters, Rose, Reine and Ethel, brother Charles drowned at the age of fifteen in 1906.

All the sisters went into show business. Reine changed the surname to Davies, the rest followed suit.

In spite of her slight stammer, Marion was the most talented, the most beautiful and the luckiest, because she's the one W. R Hearst spotted in the Ziegfeld Follies and that was the start of something big and lasting. It lasted " 'til death did them part."

All the details were in Dash's folder, the movies she made including *Cecilia of the Pink Roses*, *Peg o' My Heart*, *When Knighthood was in Flower*, *Going Hollywood*, *Polly of the Circus*, *Operator 13*, *Page Miss Glory*, right up to her last one in 1937, *Ever Since Eve*. Forty-six films, including sixteen talkies that co-starred Hollywood's top leading men—among them: Bing Crosby, Dick Powell, Leslie Howard, Gary Cooper, Robert Montgomery, Ray Milland, and Clark Gable—almost all of whom were widely acknowledged philanderers, womanizers and seducers, but none of whom dared risk the wrath of W.R. by the slightest misconduct with Maid Marion.

The dwellings Hearst built or bought for the two of them to cohabit, San Simeon, Wyntoon, St. Donat's, "the Dressing Room," the Beach House, the houses in Beverly Hills and all the rest.

"The Dressing Room," or "The Bungalow" as it was

called, was a fourteen-room mansion, not including baths, and was well staffed with servants and attendants—cost $75,000. And this, of course, was the tiniest of Hearst-Davies structures.

There had never been anything like it at MGM or on any other lot—decorated in ornate Spanish castle opulence, located on Davies Square, it served as the social center of Louis B. Mayer—and W. R. Hearst's domain.

It was said that Marion spent more time in The Bungalow than on the stages at MGM. For almost a decade and dozens of pictures the party lasted at MGM, and W.R. picked up the check.

Nothing was too good for Marion—except the parts of Juliet Capulet, Elizabeth Barrett Browning and Marie Antoinette, so Hearst picked up his marbles and Marion and left—he also picked up The Bungalow. It was dismantled into sections and moved to Warner Brothers Studio in Burbank, and later to Benedict Canyon and sold as a private residence.

In the interim W.R. decided he would make *The Last Empress* to make Marion Davies a great dramatic star and collect an Oscar. With W.R.'s influence, money and power of the press she couldn't miss.

While the epic script was being written and rewritten by Frances Marion, Eleanor Glin, Herman Mankiewicz, Charles Lederer, Scott Fitzgerald, and a battalion of other writers, the Hearst-Davies movable feasts continued from Beverly Hills to the Beach House—a multimillion-dollar estate built on a hundred acres with the Pacific Ocean as a backdrop—to San Simeon that would make Kubla Kahn's stately pleasure-dome look like a carriage house, to several other stopovers in the United States, Mexico, Scotland and Europe.

The most famous and frequented was San Simeon, celebrity center of the rich, famous and infamous—movie stars, the likes of Charlie Chaplin, Cary Grant, Dick Powell, Gloria Swanson, Jack Gilbert, John Barrymore, Doug Fairbanks, *pere et fils*, Mary Pickford, Jean Harlow, William Powell, Clark Gable, Carole Lombard, Randolph Scott, Gary and Rocky Cooper, the Gish sisters and more stars than in the night sky—and international celebrities from Winston Churchill, Florenz Ziegfeld, George Bernard Shaw, Somerset Maugham, Charles Lindbergh, Doris Duke, the Duke and Duchess of Windsor, to crowned heads and pretenders to sundry thrones—and, of course, ladies and gentlemen of the press, Arthur Brisbane, John Frances Heylan, Walter Howey, Vincent X. Flaherty, Louella Parsons, Hedda Hopper, Adela Rogers St. John, and scores of others who kept Marion Davies' name in print from coast to coast in dozens of newspapers, magazines and periodicals under the control of "the Chief," William Randolph Hearst.

Also in frequent attendance were Marion's sisters, Rose, Reine and Ethel. It was dizzying just to read about it—and I was getting even dizzier due to Ski Mask's blows and the gin that I had absorbed, but something very interesting arrested my attention just as the phone rang.

"Hello, son."

"Hello, Mom."

"What are you doing, Alex?"

"Research, Mom."

"For the book you're writing?"

"What else?" I thought that was an artful dodge without getting into particulars this time of night.

"How are your eyes?"

"My eyes?"

"Yes, your eyes. With all that reading and writing you're doing, maybe you need glasses."

"No, Mom. My eyes are fine."

"So are mine, you've got good bloodlines, thank God. I only use mine for reading, the glasses, I mean, and the other pair for driving. Did you go to the gym today?"

"No, not today, Mom."

"You should go every day. Keep in shape. You don't want to get soft. Was I right, or what?"

"About what, Mom?"

"About being a writer instead of a detective, about not getting beat up and shot at anymore. Was I right?"

"You were right . . ."

"But don't get out of shape. Keep exercising."

"I exercised today, Mom."

"At home?"

"Yeah, at home." I rubbed my ribs and took a swallow of gin.

"What're you doing? Sounds like you're gargling?"

"Just a nightcap, Mom."

"Don't drink too much. How's Myron?"

"Fine."

"And Rhoda?"

"Fine."

"Still together?"

"Still together."

"Good. And Goldie?"

"Fine, Mom."

"Good. Well, it's getting late. Think I'll go to bed."

"Good idea. Me, too."

"Good. You've done enough writing for one day."

"Good night, Mom."

"Good night, Alex."

After I hung up I went back to Dash's folder and the part that had arrested my attention. Earlier it had arrested the attention of Dash—there was one visitor to San Simeon and to the other residences of Hearst-Davies who was in attendance much more often and for longer periods than any other—a "relative."

Not Marion's sister, Rose—Marion's niece, Patricia Van Cleve Lake, Rose's daughter by her first husband, George Van Cleve.

Or was she?

Patricia practically grew up with Hearst and Davies. She spent much of her childhood at San Simeon and everywhere Marion and W.R. went—from San Simeon, Wyntoon, the houses in Beverly Hills, the Beach House or The Bungalow—they took with them Patricia Van Cleve and Marion's beloved pet dachshund, Gandhi. Financially, and in every other way, Patricia's every need and want were taken care of by her "aunt."

There were rumors, rumors that no one dared mention, within hearing distance of Hearst-Davies. Those rumors were fueled by Patricia's physical appearance.

She was tall, blond, with blue eyes, a long, narrow face and nose that looked like it was borrowed from a long-ago photograph of W. R. Hearst.

In June of 1937, Patricia Van Cleve was married at San Simeon to the actor Arthur Lake, who for years in movies had played elevator operators, Western Union messengers, soda jerks and other jerks, mostly bit parts.

The year after he married Patricia, Lake landed the plum role of Dagwood Bumstead, in the movie version of the comic strip, "Blondie," co-starring Penny Singleton. The string of moneymaking movies—twenty-eight of them—went on for twelve years and was also a highly successful radio series.

By coincidence, the "Blondie" comic strip had since its inception run in the Hearst papers. Arthur Lake, who was excellent in the part, commented more than once that in getting the role, "I had a couple of people rooting for me named Marion Davies and William Randolph Hearst."

In 1993, Patricia Van Cleve Lake, hours before dying, revealed the truth she had known and kept secret for all those years, the truth about her real mother and father. On her death certificate Patricia Van Cleve Lake's parents are listed as Marion Davies and William Randolph Hearst.

For the few who still doubted the claim, there was still more evidence.

When I had said to Charles Oliver Dash that this was a story without a finish, he said that every story has a finish if you know where to look.

He suggested that I start to look where Marion Davies is buried.

There is a mausoleum where several members of the Douras-Davies family are interred. Rose Reilly Douras, Barnard J. Douras, Arthur Lake and Patricia Van Cleve Lake—and Marion Davies.

I remembered that on Shakespeare's tombstone there's an inscription that says something like "cursed be he who disturbs my bones."

Could the ten-million-dollar Fabergé be interred with Marion Davies' bones?

Could I find out without disturbing her bones?

The mausoleum was located at a cemetery called Hollywood Forever.

Chapter XV

It's a curious thing—sometimes you go to bed dead tired and want to go to sleep—but even though it's past midnight, the day doesn't end.

Actually I was not asleep and not awake. It was that mental no-man's-land where you can't quite control your brain. Since I was in that in-between territory, I tried to guide my thoughts toward Goldie and the times we made love— never in this bed—she was there all right, in my thoughts, but so were William Randolph Hearst and Marion Davies and I couldn't help but think about the two of them making love all those years in all those places.

He a hatchet-faced, lumbering giant, and she a petite, vivacious, orchidaceous, curvaceous beauty.

About all they had in common physically was blue eyes— and Patricia Van Cleve.

But all those years they were together physically—all those months and weeks and days and nights.

She was with him as he ran his empire and her life. She saw him in action and took care of him, and my thoughts floated to that first time Goldie saw me in action—sort of—and took care of me. Maybe I thought of it because of the effect of my encounter with Ski Mask—or maybe just because I couldn't control my thoughts, but I recalled another encounter.

It was shortly after my retirement as a private investigator. I had recently rented the office at the Writers and Artists

Building and was still using a cane from a leg wound in another heroic episode involving the criminal element.

I had just made a lunch date with Lieutenant Myron Garter, and wished I was going to have lunch, or better yet, dinner, with the tenant across the hall, Miss Goldie Rose, when out of the recent past there appeared in the doorway a moose of a man who was determined to settle an unsettled score. A few days before, he had been hired by someone I had displeased to give me a going-over. Instead, he ended up on the receiving end—his head did—of the cane I'd been using. His name was Bull Connors. He closed the door, lifted a sap out of his rear pocket and whacked it into his plentiful palm.

"I'm gonna give you a paint job," he announced. "You made me look foolish to my friends. You cracked my head."

"I'll apologize. I'll tell your friends I snuck up on you, hit you from behind. Besides, Bull, it was self-defense."

"No more talk," he said, and I knew he meant it.

The events of the next few minutes were jumbled. The fight itself, blows and counter blows, a bit hazy. I've known fighters in the ring to have the same experience, win or lose. They can't remember the physical encounter itself, but they can tell you what the trainer in the corner said and what the lady in the third row was wearing and swearing. Suffice it to say sounds of warfare penetrated through the walls and into the hallway and warrens of the venerable structure. Glass breaking—objects being thrown—bodies banging against walls, mostly my body—grunts—groans—collisions—kicks, and all manner of Herculean combat, all ignoring the rules and regulations of the Marquis of Queensbury.

Somehow, I did manage to gain possession of my Malacca and fend off some of the blows of Bull's sap. But it was like trying to ward off a raging bull with a feather boa.

Outside, writers had come forth from their warrens, no doubt welcoming the interruption as writers always do.

I could hear somebody hollering "Call the cops!"

"Right," I hollered back. "Call the cops!"

That's when our entwined bodies, Bull's and mine, burst through the door with cannonball velocity. The spectators wisely retreated as the carnage continued.

The spectators included E. Elliott Elliot, Morgan Noble, Wes Weston, the Bernstein brothers—Bruce and Bernie—and Goldie Rose. Morgan Noble gave evidence of near euphoria, in fact this probably was as close to climaxing as she had come in years.

Wes. "I'll take the big guy and give six to one."

Elliott. "Typical Texas mentality."

Wes. "Any takers?"

Goldie. "For God's sake, somebody do something before he gets killed." By "he," I assumed she meant me.

Morgan. "I've seen better fights in movies."

Elliott. "At porno houses, no doubts."

Goldie. "For God's sake, somebody do something!"

All the while Bull was wildly swinging his sap and I was countering with the cane until the cane snapped from impact on Bull's forearm. But Bull did drop the sap. I glanced at the stub of my cane, tossed it away and charged the stunned Bull with a volley of lefts and rights.

Goldie turned to someone who was now standing next to her. "Call the police," she said.

"I am the police," Myron Garter replied.

"Then do something!" Goldie suggested.

Both Bull and I were on the floor. Bull had the advantage. He was on top. I don't know which part of me hurt the most, my head which had taken several punches from Bull's iron-cantaloupe fists, my shoulders and arms which had absorbed the sap shots, my ribs which I'm sure must have cracked again, or my shin which felt like

I had been shot there again. I was about to give up and allow my-self the welcome relief of being beaten to death when Myron swung into action.

He didn't exactly swing.

Myron Garter moved—not fast, not slow—he picked up the fallen sap, hauled back with all his strength and slugged Bull Connors across the skull. This resulted in two sounds, the sharp crack of bone rupturing inside Bull's head and the dull thud of Bull's body slumping onto the floor of the hallway. I cannot re-member two more welcomed sounds.

"How's that?" Garter said, looking at Goldie.

"That's good," she responded.

By now two uniformed Beverly Hills policemen had climbed the stairs and joined the party. Immediately they recognized Lieu-tenant Myron Garter.

"Lieutenant," said one of the officers. "How'd you get here so fast? We just got the call."

"That's why I'm a lieutenant." Garter pointed to Bull Connors who, amazingly, was already stirring. Almost any-body else would have been out for a week, or dead. "Book this one."

"Yes, sir," snapped one of the constables.

They cuffed Connors, hands behind his back, half lifted, half dragged him to his feet. He swayed like a bleary Buddha, but kept his balance.

"What's the charge?" asked the other constable.

"Destruction of property, mayhem, assault with a deadly weapon." Garter slapped the sap into the officer's palm.

The two policemen convoyed Mr. Connors toward the stairs as the spectators cleared a pathway.

"Alex . . ." Goldie touched my broken cheek.

"Goldie, please don't ask me if I'm all right."

"I won't, but . . . are you?"

"No. Lieutenant Myron Garter, Beverly Hills Police, this is Goldie Rose, writer-type."

"Hi," smiled Myron.

"Lieutenant," Elliott extended his hand. *"I am E. Elliott Elliot, also a writer-type, and as a citizen of Beverly Hills, I commend you on your expedient action."*

"Thank you," said Myron as they shook, then he looked at me.

"I don't suppose you feel like lunch?"

"Pass," I said.

"Call me when your head clears."

"Sure thing."

Myron Garter walked away, to have lunch I suppose.

"Get him into my rooms," Elliott ordered. *"I have a first-aid kit."* Elliott broke out his first-aid kit, which I'm sure had never been used until then, and as I reposed on an oversized leather chair, Goldie, with the hands of an angel, made ministrations on my assorted bruises. Never before had I felt such a soothing, healing benediction. I'll always remember the welcomed touch of Goldie's hands and the droning sounds of Elliott's unwelcomed epigrams. I wasn't paying much attention—to him.

But from then on Goldie and I paid more attention to each other. Much more.

Maybe it wasn't the love of the century like Hearst and Davies—or Gable and Lombard—or Tracy and Hepburn—or Bogart and Bacall—but it was something we both wanted and needed.

I wanted and needed her now—and just before I fell asleep, I wondered if she still wanted and needed me.

Chapter XVI

The next morning I didn't take my mother's advice again.

I skipped the morning workout at the YMCA. One: I had enough of a workout the day before with Ski Mask. Two: I was bruised and battered all over from the encounter and didn't feel like displaying and discussing the effects with all or any of the members.

I parked the Sebring, and folder in hand—I'd go to Kinko's after the drumbeat in my head had become a little less percussive and a little more sotto—walked past the first-floor shops at the Writers and Artists Building. The corner was occupied by Boulmiche, an upscale ladies' clothing boutique, then Standard Cutlery, Café Massimo, and the Shoe Clinque. They had all been Fenenbock tenants for years, some for generations.

I paused at the directory, then ascended the stairs cursing Ski Mask with every step.

Not good news. The yellow police tape was still in place across Goldie's door.

Inside my office I called Garter's direct line. He picked up on the third ring.

"I know what you're going to say, pal. I already did it."

"Did what? Find her?" I knew he hadn't or else he or she would have called if she were able.

"Not yet, but I did the next best thing." He tried to keep it light. "Filed a Missing Persons Report, filled in all the details.

There's already a flyer out on the track system all over the county, state and country."

"Thanks, Myron."

"Sure thing."

"How's Rhoda?"

"We got a contest going and she's losing."

"Too bad."

"No, it's good—for her. The contest is who can lose the most weight. She's got me beat by three pounds."

"Then I won't ask you out to lunch."

"I'm going home at lunchtime—but not for lunch," he chuckled. "See you, boychick."

"Thanks again," and I hung up.

Myron Garter had always had a facial and vocal resemblance to William Conrad, the actor in *The Killers* and *Body and Soul*, but in the couple of years during his divorce, he also took on a physical resemblance by putting on about fifty pounds and looking more like Conrad did as Frank Cannon, then the fat man in *Jake and The Fat Man*.

The police psychologist told him that he was trying to compensate for the loss he had suffered—his wife.

During that interval it was rare not to see Garter without the remains of a Snickers bar in his mouth. Often a Snickers bar and an El Producto cigar at the same time. The top button and buttonhole of his shirt could never quite converge. He was in imminent danger of being outed from BHPD. But since the reconciliation Lieutenant Garter has lost three or four stones while reclaiming the conjugal benefits of his marital bliss.

I had been seeing a lot less of him, but enjoying his company a lot more.

I undid the rubber bands, opened Dash's folder and turned to where I had left off in C.O.D.'s section about Marion Davies.

That's as far as I got when there was a knock on the door.
"Come in."

The door opened and Carstairs came in.

"Mister Night, Mister Elliot wants to know if you can see him in his office?"

I nodded, picked up the folder and followed Carstairs—the two of us still bruised from our respective contests with Ski Mask.

Carstairs opened the door to Elliot's suite, then went on his way down the hall and, I presume, to the Bentley.

I was surprised to see that E.E.E. had another visitor, C.O.D., who was sitting in a wingback chair while Elliot stood at the side of his desk.

"For someone who can't get around, you sure do get around," I said to the visitor and sat in one of the two straight-back chairs.

"I asked Carstairs to pick up Charlie this morning. Thought a strategy session would be productive, then we'd enjoy lunch at Massimo's and . . . good Lord!" Elliot squinted at me. "What happened to you?"

"Somebody tried to get this," I held up the folder. "I assume it was the same somebody who was at Mister Dash's house. Did you get the film developed?"

"It's on my desk," Elliot pointed with his ubiquitous walking stick. "Seems he didn't get much . . ."

"If at first you don't succeed . . . well, that's two strikes. But never mind that, there's something I want to know, Mister Dash. How did word get out?"

"About what, Mister Night?"

"About the fact that you were on the trail of the missing Fabergé."

"I guess I should have told you about that."

"Tell me now."

"*Mea Culpa*. Me and my big mouth. Make that big, drunken mouth."

"Chew it a little finer."

"At a recent luncheon at the Los Angeles Press Center—I'm a lifetime member—I was one of the founders and there was a time, one of its most celebrated, if not esteemed members. These days I'm just an obsolete, drunken, old fool they ignore or tolerate for what they hope is not much longer. At any rate, at this last luncheon for a certain honored guest—I had a leetle too much to drink and started spouting off about a big story I was working on . . ."

"A story about the missing Fabergé?"

"During WWII," he nodded, "there was a saying 'loose lips sink ships;' I'm afraid my lips were too damn loose that day. After a while I realized the error of my way and clammed-up . . ."

"Did you mention the folder?"

"I . . . must have . . . can't quite remember . . ."

"Well, evidently, somebody did remember." I placed the folder on top of Elliot's desk.

"You think it was another newspaperman?" Elliot inquired, looking from Dash to me.

"If so, they play awfully rough these days."

"I don't think any newspaperman there would believe me . . . these days," Dash wiped at his mouth.

"Somebody did," I said. "But let's skip that, too. You mentioned that I ought to start where Marion Davies is buried."

"Just a suggestion."

"Not a bad one. There's only one trouble. How do I get into the mausoleum to start looking?"

"That's not much trouble," Elliot smiled. "I think I can arrange that."

"You? How?"

"Many celebrities are resting there."

"So?"

"So, I intend to repose among them, not soon, however."

"What's that got to do . . ."

"The owner of Hollywood Forever is a good friend of mine, Tyler Cassity—so is his right-hand man, Andy Martinez. Both splendid young fellows."

"Not much surprises me these days, Elliot, but this sure as hell does."

"Not at all. When Tyler purchased the cemetery a few years back, I procured a choice plot overlooking the lake there at a cost of one hundred thousand dollars. It is currently valued at over two hundred thousand . . ."

"You invest in all sort of real estate, don't you, Elliot?"

"It's not for sale—that's an eternal investment—but I do believe I can arrange a visit to Miss Davies' tomb. It, too, is near the lake. Some of our finest former citizens are neighbors there, C. B. DeMille, Tyrone Power, Janet Gaynor, Harry Cohn . . ."

"Elliot."

"Yes?"

"Those people are dead at the present time, aren't they?"

"Yes, of course."

"Well, that eliminates them as suspects in the matter of the Press Center lunch where Mister Dash . . ."

". . . spilled the beans," Mister Dash concluded.

"Right," I nodded toward him, "unless you can recall other times or places where you also spilled the . . ."

". . . proverbial legumes. No, I can't think of any such occasions."

"Good. That narrows it down considerably."

"Oh, wait. There is one other fellow in whom I confided, but he wouldn't pull a double cross on me."

"No? Who is he—and why not? The double cross I mean."

"Jim Addison. He wasn't at the lunch, out of town at the time, but I did tell him about my . . . project."

"Why?"

"Because it's the only way I could ever get it printed. Jim's the editor of the Sunday Section of the *Chronicle*."

"Okay. Why wouldn't he double-cross you?"

"I got him started in the newspaper game, from the time he was a copyboy. I was what is currently called his 'mentor.' A more honorable man never breathed than Jim Addison. He told me if I solved the riddle of the missing Fabergé and confirmed it—he would print it."

"And you'd get another Pulitzer Prize . . ."

"Possibly."

"And what would he get?"

"Satisfaction."

"You think he'd settle for that?"

"I'd stake my life on it."

"Maybe you have."

There was a knock on the door of Elliot's suite.

"Enter," Elliot responded.

The door opened and enter she did. What an entrance. On stage they call it Center Door Fancy. Subdued but sizzling. Everything about her. The way she stood. The way she moved. And especially the way she looked. The outfit she wore was not meant to conceal the configuration of her body. It didn't and couldn't. Nothing short of a suit of armor could—maybe not even that.

"Why, Sonja!" Elliot exclaimed. "This is an unexpected turn. Do come in."

She did and I was glad she did. Sonja was about twenty-five, an overwhelmingly beautiful creature with the greenest eyes and darkest hair on land or sea, an invitingly willowy body, the sort of body that any man whom she walked past would turn to make sure he saw what he saw.

The sight of her would make an old-timer think of Hedy Lamarr in *Comrade X*. For us younger fellows Catherine Zeta-Jones would come to mind.

She glanced over at me. I stood and more than glanced back at her.

She wore a form-fitting summer skirt that vacillated as she moved and matched her hair and a soft, serpentine green blouse that vacillated even more and matched her eyes. It was a safe bet that she neither needed, nor wore a bustier. Her voice was throaty and as inviting as her walk, almost.

"Elliott, so nice to see you again," she extended an alabaster-white hand. In the other hand she held an oversize black purse, Prada, I believe, but I wasn't paying much attention to the purse.

"Sonja Vladov," Elliot took the extended hand, then turned toward me. "This is Alex Night."

I was hoping she'd extend that hand in my direction and she did. I didn't waste any time taking it.

It felt just like I knew it would.

"How do you do, Mister Night?" she murmured.

"Swell," I think I said.

"And, Sonja," Elliot continued. "This is Charles Oliver Dash."

Old C.O.D. started to rise, but was preempted.

"Oh, please, Mister Dash, don't get up." She took her hand away from mine and greeted Dash in the same manner.

"Sit down, Sonja," Elliot pointed to the other empty straight-back chair with his crosier, "and tell us all about what it is you have to tell us."

Sonja smiled what I thought was a mysterious smile and crossed her legs.

She had the kind of legs that made you want to know more. I sat down to get a better look.

"This is an unbelievable coincidence," she said. Those green eyes swept across all three of us in Elliot's office.

By then I would have believed just about anything she said.

She opened her purse and removed three square, pink envelopes.

"I was on my way to see all three of you and here we are all together at the same place at the same time. By the way, Elliott, Grandfather sends you his warmest personal regards."

"You may return best wishes."

"Thank you, I will, but you can do that yourself at the reception."

"What reception? When? Where? And for whom?"

"Elliot," Dash grinned. " 'What? When? Where? Who?' You've just quoted the requirements of any good lead paragraph of any newspaper story."

"Quite by accident, I assure you. Please go on, Sonja."

"The reception this Friday at Grandfather's estate in honor of Serge Goncheroff."

"Who," Elliot arched an imperial eyebrow, "is Serge Goncheroff?"

"A friend of Grandfather's at the Russian Consulate, visiting here from San Francisco. Grandfather asked me to deliver the invitations to all three of you and this, Elliott, was my first stop."

She rose and handed an envelope to each of us.

I noticed that my name was calligraphied on the envelope she handed to me.

"May I inquire how it is that all three of you happen to be here together in Elliot's office?"

I picked up the folder from Elliot's desk and, for no particular reason, turned it over and placed it back on the desk.

Actually, I did have a particular reason. I wanted to see if she would react to it. Maybe she did and maybe she didn't. She didn't give much away.

"We were just going over some . . . well, it wouldn't be of any interest to you, but Miss Vladov . . ."

"Oh, please, 'Sonja.' "

"Yes . . . Sonja, two questions, if I may."

"You certainly may," she smiled that mysterious smile.

"From his greeting I surmise that Elliot knows your grandfather . . . but your grandfather doesn't know me, and I don't know him. Why do I get invited?"

"Why don't you ask him Friday evening?"

"I will . . . if I'm there."

"Oh, please be there," she said it as if she meant it. "And what was the other question, Mister Night?"

"Oh, please, 'Alex.' " I thought it was cute—repeating her phrase.

"Very well, Alex."

"The other question is—doesn't your grandfather trust the US mail system? Or do you do all his deliveries to save on postage?"

"No, no, Grandfather wanted to make sure you received the invitation and personally RSVP'd to me," she turned and looked at Elliot.

"Elliott, you'll attend, of course?"

"To coin a cliché, 'Wild horses couldn't keep me away.' "

Then she moved toward Dash sitting on the wingback and that gave me a great gander at the profile of her anatomy.

"Mister Dash? Will you attend?"

"Do we have to bring our own booze?"

"No, of course not."

"Then I'll attend."

"Very good."

She turned and stepped close to me, close enough to share her perfume, Joy by Patou, I believe it was.

"And you, Alex?"

"Consider me RSVP'd."

"Wonderful."

And then . . . and then—you could have knocked me over with a pussy willow—she reached up and touched my face with all four fingers of her right hand, touched my face and allowed those four fingers to linger a little longer than I would have expected, but not hoped.

"Did you have an accident, Alex?"

I nodded.

"Oh, I'm so sorry." She took her hand away.

"You should see the other car," I said.

She smiled and walked toward the door with those Angie Dickenson, *Police Woman* legs, then turned back as she opened the door. "Well, then," she said, "until Friday."

Maybe it was my imagination, but her last look before she went out and closed the door was right smack at me—and that, too, was an invitation.

When she left, Elliot tapped on the folder with his envelope and smiled toward me.

"Did you believe her story?"

"I believe her legs."

"Yes, I noticed that you noticed."

"Did you notice any reaction when I picked up the folder?"

"Hard to tell."

"Tell me what you know about Vladov that I don't."

"I will, as we have lunch at Massimo's."

"There's one more thing," Charles Oliver Dash said, "that you ought to know."

"What's that?" I asked.

"The guest of honor at the Press Center lunch was Vladimir Vladov."

Chapter XVII

Massimo Ormani is as Mediterranean as his name. He and his wife Daniella have been tenants on the ground floor of the Writers and Artists Building for just over three years, operating one of the most successful, and according to E. Elliott Elliot, one of the best restaurants in Beverly Hills.

Elliot, according to Elliot, is the definitive authority on epicurism, arts, wardrobe, music, literature, antiques, style, sculpture, Sanskrit, and several other subjects that escape my memory.

I can't vouch for his expertise on most of those subjects, but he sure as hell knows where to eat.

Massimo's is as good as I've ever eaten. Massimo and Daniella are both in their thirties, attractive, charming, enthusiastic and efficient.

And they sure do make a fuss over Elliot. He has a special table reserved against a mirrored wall in the second dining room that features a huge photograph of a smiling Massimo—on the ceiling.

At the table for four, Elliot and Dash sat next to each other and I sat across from them next to the empty chair.

I had brought the folder down with me after securing it again with rubber bands then tucking the pink invitation envelope inside the rubber bands. I set the folder on the table at my elbow intending not to let it out of my sight until Kinko's, even if I had to take it with me to the toilet.

Of course Elliot took it upon himself to order lunch for the three of us. Ministroni soup, endive belga salad, linguini carbonara, and for dessert, mele insabbiate—which is apple crumble. All to the accompaniment of a bottle of Antinori Guado Al Tasso, a 1999, which I happened to notice went for one hundred seventy dollars, not lira.

Before and during the course of the courses I went to work on Elliot to find out all he knew about our host for Friday, Vladimir Vladov.

"First," Elliot said, "tell me what you know about him."

"He was a producer," I shrugged. "Tits and sand, sword and shield, spectacle sort of stuff. I never went to see any of his pictures or watched them later on television, but a lot of other people did. He made a lot of money, even owned a studio once. That's my book on him. What's yours?"

"My 'book' as you so quaintly put it, is considerably longer, but I'll be as brief as possible. His forebears were of royalty or near-royalty, White Russians that survived the Revolution but had nearly all their assets confiscated by the Bolsheviks. Vladimir was born during Stalin's regime, too young to soldier during the German invasion. But after WWII, while still in his teens, he fled the Soviet Union. Do you recall another producer, Joseph E. Levine?"

"Yeah."

"Levine made a fortune bringing Hercules to the USA. Vladov made a bigger fortune bringing Odysseus to the shores and theaters of the US. He bought a shabby series of movies about the Odyssey made in Spain, added sex and sadism, dubbed them in English and ended up owning Paragon Studios which he later sold to a Mafia connection for over a hundred million dollars."

"A real Horatio Vladov story."

"Not without some setbacks, none of them financial."

"What sort of setbacks?"

"His wife along with their son and daughter-in-law were killed when Vladov's private jet crashed—but they had a young daughter who was not aboard . . ."

"And who grew up to be Sonja Vladov, the invitation bearer with legs."

"Correct. Vladov has spent his declining years collecting treasures of his native Russia."

"Uh, huh. Now then, among those treasures, is there a Fabergé egg?"

"Not that I know of."

"Well, if you don't know, nobody does."

"Probably also correct."

"But he'd like to get his hands on one . . ."

"Who wouldn't?"

"Mister Dash . . ."

"Yes, Mister Night."

"You said he was the guest of honor at that lunch."

"As Elliot would say, 'correct.' "

"Why would the Press Center honor Vladov?"

"Simple. Over the years he spent millions on publicity, treated the press to junkets all over the world, everything first class, even donated a hundred-thousand-dollar endowment to the Press Center—so the Press Center presented him with a lunch in his honor and handed him a seventy-dollar trophy in appreciation of past and present investiture."

"And that's where and when . . ."

Charles Oliver Dash pointed to the folder with his fork and nodded . . .

"My whiskey-soaked tongue took over."

"You think he overheard you?"

"I think everybody did . . . unfortunately."

"Knowing Vladov as I do," Elliot said, "nothing escapes him."

"How is it, Elliot," I inquired, "that you know Vladov . . . as you do?"

"Well," a sly smile came upon Elliot's face, "I've never admitted this before, and I do so now, providing I can swear you both to solemn secrecy."

"We both swear," I volunteered for myself and Charles Oliver Dash.

"The truth is that during Vladov's halcyon years, when he produced some original films, I wrote several of the scenarios . . . not under my name, of course, for obscene fees and healthy percentages, and for which I still collect considerable royalties and profits."

"Elliot," I shook my head, "you are a . . ."

"Yes, aren't I," he winked. "It was a much smaller town in those days, and Vladov was ripe for plucking, so I proceeded to pluck."

Sometime during our conversation—mostly Elliot's, a man and woman had entered Massimo's and sat at a corner table.

I was too much engrossed in what Elliot had been saying to notice them then, but I noticed them now. They were both very noticeable, especially the woman.

And they were both looking at our table. He rose, then she rose and followed him as he moved toward us.

He was lean, athletic, a six-footer, maybe fifty, with a long, sharp, handsome face, light complexion, deep-set blue eyes and a knife-blade mouth. He had a George Hamilton head of hair and not a hair out of place. He wore a well-tailored, double-breasted blue suit, a lighter blue shirt and a darker blue tie with pocket square to match.

I didn't waste much time looking at him because she was a

lot better to look at. Sharon Stone a decade ago, but silver blonde, lapis lazuli eyes, high cheekbones, beautiful sculptured nose, and a hospitable mouth mounted above a perfect chin with just a hint of a dimple in a heart-shaped face.

She was dressed mostly in white and mostly jersey—St. John, I think. The kind that clings. A white shoulder-strap purse reposed on the curve of her fluent hip.

And the way she walked. There are walks and there are walks. Some women give it all they've got, leaving little to the imagination. But this lady's walk; it was supple, not fluid—holding back just enough in reserve, private, yet provocative—and promising. It was an awful lot to take in in just a few seconds, but I took it in.

"Elliott, good to see you," the man said with just the slightest trace of an indeterminate accent.

"Andre Shenko," Elliot nodded. "Good to see you, too."

"Mister Elliot," Shenko smiled, "may I present Miss Linda Bundy. Miss Bundy is my Executive Assistant."

Elliot, Dash and I stood. Dash wobbled a bit.

"Oh, please sit down, gentlemen," Linda Bundy said in a cultured voice, maybe a little too cultured.

"This is Charles Oliver Dash," Elliot pointed to C.O.D.

"Oh, yes," Shenko nodded, "the renowned newspaperman."

"Renounced, nowadays," C.O.D. took a gulp of Antinori.

"And," Elliot said, "Alex Night here completes our luncheon trio."

"Please sit down," Miss Bundy repeated.

This time we did.

"Actually, Elliott," Shenko smiled, "another reason why we came over, besides to say hello to you, is because of Mister Night." He turned to me and smiled even more. "I thought I recognized you from your picture in the newspapers and wanted to confirm the fact that it is you."

"Confirmed," I said.

"The man who saved The Star of Good Hope at the premiere the other night, is that not so?"

"Well, that's not the way I'd put it, but I was there."

"You're too modest, Mister Night," Linda Bundy purred.

"You'd be surprised at how immodest I can be."

"At any rate," Shenko went on pleasantly, ignoring my remark, "we're grateful for what you did that night."

"Who is 'we'?" I asked, "and why?"

"We, is I," he shrugged. "And because I bought The Star of Good Hope the next day."

"From Mike Meadows?"

"Yes."

"You paid too much for it. A million and a quarter, wasn't it?"

"Yes."

"Too much."

"But I sold it this morning for a million and a half."

"That's a pretty fair turnover for twenty-four hours or so."

"I've done better," Shenko's blue eyes brightened.

"I'll bet you have," I said, glancing at Linda Bundy.

"Andre is in the import/export business," Elliot said. "Deals in antiques and he's also a collector."

I let that pass without glancing at Linda Bundy again.

"Well," Elliot said in a more or less dismissive tone, "it was good seeing you again, Andre . . . and meeting you, Miss Bundy."

"Oh, I think we'll be seeing you again soon," Shenko smiled.

"Really?" Elliot seemed surprised.

"Because of that," Shenko pointed to Dash's folder on the table near my elbow.

Needless to say, that surprised *me* even more.

"Linda . . ." Shenko nodded.

She opened her purse and removed a pink envelope that matched the one tucked under the rubber bands on Dash's folder.

"Linda and I will see you at Vlad's reception on Friday evening."

The son of a bitch was slick, slick as a snake's belly. Miss Bundy was on the slick side, too. She didn't say anything but there was something, something suggestive, about the way she placed the pink envelope back into her purse and ran her fingers along the side of the handbag.

"Oh, by the way, Elliott," Shenko said as he turned and looked back, "I hope you don't mind, but I asked Massimo to put your lunch on our check."

"I don't mind in the least, and congratulations on your Star of Good Hope transaction."

The two of them went back to their table and out of earshot.

" 'Renowned newspaperman' my ass," Dash smirked. "That Russkie's playing mind games."

"What's the book on Shenko?" I asked.

"He's a reformed character," Elliot said.

"Reformed from what?"

"The well-founded rumor is, that in the old days, in the old Soviet Union, during the Cold War, Andre Shenko was, under the reign of Vladimir Putin, a crack operative of the KGB."

"I didn't know that it paid that well."

"It did if you had several accounts squirreled away in Switzerland."

"Elliot, you know something? You're a better detective than I ever was."

"No, Alex, just a nosier gadabout. By the by, I have no book on Miss Linda Bundy."

"Yeah, well, on Friday night, as the song says . . . that's going to be a 'swellegant, elegant party!' And you know something, fellas . . . this has been one hell of a day . . . and it's only half over."

Chapter XVIII

After that lunch at Massimo's I felt like taking a snooze. I'm not used to a glass or two of wine during daylight, or during night-light, or anytime. I know that Greeks are supposed to be wine drinkers, but not this Greek. Gin man, after the sun's over the yardarm and an occasional Grand Marnier after dinner and before a bedtime adventure.

I bade adieu to E.E.E. and C.O.D., shook off the affects of the Antinori and the two belles that rang in the day, Miss Sonja Vladov and Miss Linda Bundy. I couldn't help asking myself which of the two I'd like to . . . let's just say it was a photo finish.

I walked around Beverly Hills a few minutes to make sure I wasn't being tailed, then, with folder, headed over to Kinko's and one of their replicating machines.

About an hour or so later I was at the Beverly Hills post of-fice addressing and mailing the replicate copy.

Back at the office I called my mother.

"Mom, I put a package in the mail for you . . ."

"I know what it is, Alex."

"You do?"

"Why sure I do. You finished your novel and want me to be the first to read it, right?"

"No, Mom. The novel's not finished . . ."

"It's not?"

"Well, not quite. This is something else and I want you to do me a favor . . ."

"For you, my only son, anything, just name it."

"When the package comes, don't open it."

"You've got secrets from your only mother?"

"No, Mom. I'll tell you all about it later, but for now just put it in a closet 'til I pick it up in a few days. Will you do that, please?"

"It's done. When are you coming over?"

"I'll let you know."

"Do that so I can make a nice dinner."

"I will, and thanks, Mom."

After the usual good-byes I hung up and couldn't help thinking about the time a couple of months ago when she made another nice dinner for me at her place over on Van Ness where she lives.

I could tell that there was something troubling her and not the usual "when are you gong to get married and settle down" stuff—It was during the coffee and Koluria that she began to open up.

"Alex, I think I'm getting old, so I'm thinking about selling this place and moving into an apartment or a condo. You know, one of those gated places . . ."

"But, Mom, what about the yard, the garden and the roses? You're out there most of the time. What would you do all day long . . . just vegetate?

"I got my soaps, and . . ."

"And what?"

"Well, I think it's just too much for me . . ."

"I don't believe that. That's not true."

And it wasn't. Suddenly she looked up and shuddered. I couldn't remember the last time I saw her react like that. She heard it before I did. Maybe that's because she was expecting to hear it. First it was a rumble, then it got louder.

"What the hell is that?" By the time I asked, there were more noises, racing, subsiding and then reverberating and reviving again. And I could hear voices from outside. I stood up. She didn't.

"They've been coming around almost every night," she said.

"For how long?"

"About a week. Three of them. On their motorcycles. Drunk. They'll go away after a while."

By now the motors were blasting and when they did ease up, the voices came again.

"Why didn't you call the police?"

"I did. By the time they finally get here," she motioned outside, "they're gone."

"Why didn't you tell me?"

She shrugged.

"Mom, why didn't you tell me!?"

"I don't know. I just thought, maybe they'd quit coming. Go someplace else . . ."

I started for the front door.

"Alex, leave them alone. They'll go away. Don't go out there!" I went. I opened the door and stood there. There were three of them all right, in a lot of leather, shirts that no self-respecting laundry would accept, and all three were wearing what looked like WWII German Army helmets. One of them was cracking about two feet of chain against the driveway.

They were surprised to see me, but I can't say that they were displeased. The odds were dominantly in their favor, particularly since I didn't have the .38 equalizer on me. They were big, dirty and drunk. But that was okay, because I was mad.

"Beat it," I said, "and don't come back."

First they laughed. No, not laughed. Cackled. A couple of them had cans of beer. "What're you doin,' layin' the old broad?" said the one with the chain.

Then they all said some things that got me madder. Things that nobody wants to hear about his mother.

"Step off that bike, asshole."

All three assholes stepped off their bikes. The one with the chain was the biggest and dirtiest. I walked down the steps and kept on coming. I learned a few things early in my dad's saloon. One thing was that whoever hits first usually wins, if he hits hard enough. They were going to taunt and talk some more. I wasn't.

Instinctively, the other guy usually looks for your right hand to make the first move. While he was looking I hit the big son of a bitch with a left, broke his nose and knocked a few teeth into his throat. He went back over his bike and both hit the pavement. That startled both the other two. Just enough for me to kick the second one in his leather crotch, grab the third one by his leather jacket and send the hard edge of my free hand into his Adam's apple.

The second one, the one with the sore crotch, started to recover, when out of the night my mother hit him on the side of his helmet with all her might with my old Louisville Slugger baseball bat she has saved for sentimental reasons from my Little League career.

All three lay motionless amid the spilled beer. "Call the cops now, Mom." I stooped and picked up the chain, just in case. "These guys aren't going anywhere."

She was shaking. But she smiled and nodded and walked toward the door. Lights went on next door and across the street. I guess the neighbors felt it was safe to come out.

"Mom," I called, when she got to the doorway. "Who says you're getting old?"

Since then, not another word from her about getting old.

I could have delivered the Kinko package in person, but I didn't want anybody to see me carrying it, just in case I did start getting tailed.

A. Night In Hollywood Forever

When I decided to become a mystery writer instead of a shamus my mother gifted me with a briefcase, I guess so people could tell the difference.

It was dark brown Moroccan leather and expensive, but nothing was too good for my mother's son, the writer.

I never had occasion to use it until now. It was just too damn conspicuous and inviting to carry around Dash's folder in plain sight. So I tucked the folder inside the Morocco. I wasn't going to leave the folder in the office after the rash of break-ins in the building. One break-in was one too many.

I got to my condo on Wilshire and Fremont at just about sunset, changed into something more comfortable, a pair of khakis and a short-sleeved terry cloth shirt, then headed for the refrigerator. I had stored a two-story steak in the meat compartment, but after the Massimo lunch I decided on something lighter.

A salami sandwich on rye filled the bill and my belly, washed down with a bottle of Bud.

The second half of the day hadn't been nearly as interesting as the first half but that was okay with me.

I poured out a snifter of Grand Marnier, opened up the briefcase, removed the folder and settled into the leather chair and ottoman to do a little more research.

That's when there was a knock on the door. Not only wasn't I able to do any writing lately, now I wasn't even able to do any reading.

I hadn't carried a gun since my retirement, but I still had a permit and the piece in the drawer in the stand near the chair.

The knock came again. I pulled the drawer halfway out.

"Who is it?"

"It's Linda, Alex."

I didn't know we were on a first name basis, but that was okay, too. I shut the drawer, went to the door and opened it.

She stood in beauty like the night. She had changed her outfit into a suit that was even more clinging, red, and wore just a touch more make-up. Illegally beautiful.

I couldn't remember seeing anything more fetching since I was too old to sing tenor.

"May I come in?" she asked.

"That's what doors are for," I answered and closed the door behind her.

"A very nice place you have here," Linda said as she looked around.

"It used to belong to a whore named Gilda, until she got murdered in that bedroom," I pointed, "that's why I got it so cheap. Nobody else wanted to buy it."

"You're kidding."

"No, and neither was the murderer. But don't let that bother you, I didn't do it."

"Alex," she smiled, "I don't know how to take you."

"With a grain of salt or maybe a beer chaser."

"I changed my mind about your being modest. You are the most intriguing man I ever . . ."

"More intriguing than Shenko? I hear he was with the KGB."

"I wouldn't know about that."

"How long have you been . . . with him?"

"I've been working for Andre for a couple of years . . ."

"As his . . . executive assistant?"

She nodded and looked toward the snifter.

"What are you drinking?"

"Grand Marnier. You like oranges?"

"Not tonight, thank you."

"What would you like tonight?"

"Actually, Andre sent me . . ."

"That was friendly."

"He instructed me to give you this."

She removed an envelope from her purse. It was a different purse and a different envelope. It was longer and thicker, quite a bit thicker. She handed it to me.

I took it.

"Do you know the contents?" I asked.

"Yes, I'm the one who put the contents in it."

"What are the contents?"

"A hundred and twenty-five hundred-dollar bills."

"Is this a bribe of some sort?"

"No. A sort of commission. Twelve thousand five hundred dollars, cash."

"For what?"

"For his profit on the sale of The Star of Good Hope. A profit he made thanks to you. Aren't you going to open it?"

"I'll take your word for it." I put the envelope on top of the folder. "What else did he instruct you to do?"

"My instructions from him ended when I delivered the envelope . . . the rest is up to you. I can stay or leave."

She moved closer, put her arms around me, and kissed me with all she had.

I didn't resist, but I didn't cooperate.

"It's even better when you help," she smiled and did it again.

"Sorry, but I'm booked for the night. I've got work to do."

She looked over at the folder on the table.

"What kind of work?"

"Homework."

She kissed me again.

"Strike three," I said.

"Maybe I'll come up to bat again, some other time."

"Maybe," I nodded. "It's not over 'til it's over."

She moved to the door in a way that would knock the sandals off a monk . . . and opened it.

"I guess that this is what doors are for, too. Good night, Alex."

"Good night, Miss Bundy."

"See you Friday."

And she closed the door.

I wanted to believe that she would have stayed because she wanted to . . . but I didn't.

Yeah, the second half of the day could have been a lot more interesting than the first half.

Chapter XIX

After Linda Bundy left I sat there with a page from Dash's folder in one hand and the snifter of Grand Marnier in the other.

I wondered how much Miss Bundy and Mister Shenko knew about Dash's folder and the missing Fabergé. However much they knew, I knew that they wanted to know more—and it was obvious that they would resort to bribes and other incentives to do it.

A twelve-thousand-five-hundred-dollar bribe and an incentive that included bedtime with Bundy.

Since neither was going to turn the trick, I wondered what they'd resort to next.

Whatever it was, it wouldn't be tonight.

It was useless to try to concentrate on Dash's folder.

My mind and thoughts were on something, someone else. A kiss, kisses, and Grand Marnier, not with Miss Bundy, but with Goldie Rose—and the first time she had invited me to her place for dinner and drinks. After dinner . . .

We both stacked the dishes and Goldie suggested that I remove my jacket, loosen the paisley and be more comfortable. I stripped to the degree she suggested.

She put on a King Cole tape—The Nat King Cole Story—and at her further suggestion we repaired to the sofa with the bottle of Grand Marnier and a pair of oversized snifters while the "King" serenaded the two of us.

"You like oranges?" She pointed to the bottle of Grand Marnier.

"If they're from your tree." I had read that somewhere.

"Well, go ahead," she said after smiling appropriately at my borrowed bon-mot.

"Go ahead," I repeated, "that's pretty damned dangerous on your part, 'go ahead' and what?"

"You promised to tell me why you quit being a private investigator."

"Oh, that, well that's no great shakes of a story. The real detective business, unlike the stuff you and everybody else write about, isn't what it's cracked up to be in fiction . . ."

"But I understand that you dealt mostly with people in show business, glamorous people . . ."

"There are no glamorous people, sister. There's just people. And nobody ever came to call unless he or she was in trouble. But usually it was pretty dull and dreary and when it wasn't I got tired of carrying all that extra lead in my system. Would you like to see my etchings? They're all over my body."

"Some other time," she said. "Maybe when we go swimming this summer."

That was promising. King Cole was singing "Blue Gardenia."

"So now your ambition is to be a novelist."

"No. My ambition is to get you on my boat."

"You own a boat?"

"Not yet, but I'll get one, a slow boat—like the song says, we'll take a slow boat to China. How's that sound?"

"Oh, I don't know. I'm pretty particular. What's the name of your boat?"

"I'm not particular. You name it."

"I'll tell you what. A boat's got to have two sides. You name one side. I'll name the other."

"Fair enough. You take starboard, I'll take port. You first."

"Okay. True Love. *That was Bing Crosby and Grace Kelly's boat in* High Society."

"Right," I said. *"And before that it was Cary Grant and Katharine Hepburn's in* The Philadelphia Story."

"What's the name of your side?" She smiled.

*"*Briny Marlin."

*"*Briny Marlin? *What's that mean?"*

"It's from another Cary Grant picture, Mr. Lucky. *It was set during WWII, and he played a draft dodging heel of a gambler with a Greek name, Joe Bascopolous, who had a gambling ship called* The Fortuna, *fell in love with a society girl played by Laraine Day. Their love, true love I guess, reformed him—so he renamed the ship* Briny Marlin *and risked his life taking a ship-load of goods to Europe for Greece and the other Allies."*

"But why Briny Marlin?"

"It's cockney rhyming slang—he used it all through the picture. 'Tit for tat' was 'hat,' 'storm and strife—wife,' 'fiddle and toot—suit,' 'lady from Bristol— pistol,' 'bottle and stopper— copper,' 'soft and fair—hair,' " I touched her hair.

" 'Sparkle and prize—eyes,' 'I suppose—nose,' " I touched the tip of her nose. " 'North and south—mouth,' " I touched her mouth, but not with my hand. I leaned close and kissed her.

She didn't pull back. So I kissed her some more. By then Nat King Cole was singing "Nature Boy" and nature was beginning to take its course.

Finally, she did pull back. I'd like to think reluctantly, but I let her. She looked at me and I looked at her, and nothing could be as it was before, not between us. I thought of all the other girls that I had kissed, and more. Never, never, never had I felt like this. I knew it and I think she knew it. I knew she knew it.

"What does Briny Marlin rhyme with?"

"Darlin'."

"I like the name of your boat."

"Want to take that trip to China?"

"Not yet, Alex."

Somehow, I knew she'd say that. I can't say that I wasn't disappointed. But I wasn't surprised. She just wasn't the kind to land in bed on the first bounce. But this time she kissed me. It was soft and tender and tasted of the sweetest oranges I had ever savored.

"Briny Marlin," I whispered, "I can't bear much more."

"I know. Me, too. We better call it a night." She rose.

"Goldie," I got up and put my arms around her.

"Alex, let's give it a little time."

"You're the skipper, mate."

I put on my coat and walked to the door. She followed.

"Thanks," she kissed me again, but I knew it was a good-night kiss.

"Good night, Briny Marlin," I said.

When I left Nat King Cole was singing "To the Ends of the Earth." But I didn't want to go to the ends of the earth.

All I wanted was a slow boat to China.

And now all I wanted was to look into her "sparkle and prize—eyes," touch her "soft and fair—hair," kiss her "north and south—mouth."

To hell with Linda Bundy and Sonja Vladov—to hell with Andre Shenko and Vladimir Vladov—to hell with William Randolph Hearst and Marion Davies, they were already dust—and damn Charles Oliver Dash and his Pulitzer Prize—and E. Elliott Elliot and his Academy Awards—and most of all damn Peter Carl Fabergé and all his Eggs that you could put in one basket . . . and while I was at it damn Frances Vale and Mike Meadows for making me break that date with

Goldie—no, wait a minute, I said to myself as I took a gulp from the snifter, *they* didn't make you break that date—that was your own doing—so damn you, too, Alex Night.

But most of all, damn somebody else—whoever it was, and is—that's doing harm to Briny Marlin, if she is in harm's way, I swear I'll track that son of a bitch to the ends of the earth and break the sixth commandment.

Chapter XX

Come hell or high tide, I swear I'm going to go to the gym to-morrow—so I said to myself the next morning when I took a look in the full-length mirror on the toilet door and the still swollen and bruised remnants of the contest with Ski Mask.

The truth is I just didn't feel like going. Of course that's the time you should go—but I didn't.

Instead I rustled up breakfast, three cups of coffee from my trusty and slightly rusty aluminum drip coffeepot which they don't manufacture anymore, a slice of pumpkin pie and a few dollops of yogurt, plain—I don't believe in those fancied up flavors—banana/cherry—avocado/lemon—strawberry/cinnamon. I like it just the way it came from the goat.

Having taken a look at those bruises and the fact that my ribs still ached reminded me of something. My gun.

Whoever it was who came after the folder from C.O.D. and me had something besides a ski mask. A gun.

He, or somebody else, might try again, so I decided to leave the pocket watch and tote an equalizer. I hooked the holster onto my belt and slid in the .38. It felt right at home.

I got to Rodeo Drive about a half hour later. I was running low on Luckies but Kramer's wasn't open yet, so I proceeded into the Writers and Artists Building with briefcase in hand where I met the brothers Bernstein, Bruce and Bernie.

I was surprised that they were there so early, and I was further surprised at the way they were both dressed. While, up to now, they hadn't been in the same league with E. Elliott Elliot in the wardrobe department, the Bernstein brothers always had been middle-of-the-road, blazer-and-striped-tie types. That morning they were costumed in jeans, denim shirts, and WWII leather bomber jackets.

"Morning, Alex . . ." Brother Bruce.

". . . how are you this morning?" Brother Bernie.

"Fine. You two sleep here?" A. Night.

"No, we were rehearsing . . ." Brother Bruce.

". . . a pitch we're doing this morning." Brother Bernie.

"Pitch?" A. Night.

"Yeah, at a cable network . . ." Brother Bruce.

". . . for a reality series." Brother Bernie.

"Didn't think you two did television." A. Night.

"Hard times . . ." Brother Bruce.

". . . call for reality dollars." Brother Bernie.

"I see." A. Night.

"You might have noticed . . ." Brother Bruce.

". . . we're dressing down for the occasion." Brother Bernie.

"I did notice. What kind of a series?" A. Night.

"It's great. We call it . . ." Brother Bruce.

". . . *The Last to Die*." Brother Bernie.

"Sounds exciting." A. Night.

"Nothing like it on television!" Brother Bruce.

". . . we get ten terminal patients . . ." Brother Bernie.

". . . and monitor them . . ." Brother Bruce.

". . . for however long it takes . . ." Brother Bernie.

". . . family of the first to die . . ." Brother Bruce.

". . . gets ten thousand bucks." Brother Bernie.

"The second gets twenty grand . . ." Brother Bruce.

". . . the third gets thirty." Brother Bernie.

". . . right down the line . . ." Brother Bruce.

". . . each gets ten Gs more . . ." Brother Bernie.

". . . fourth, fifth, sixth . . ." Brother Bruce.

". . . seventh, eighth . . ." Brother Bernie.

". . . the ninth gets ninety . . ." Brother Bruce.

". . . the last to die . . ." Brother Bernie.

". . . gets the grand prize . . ." Brother Bruce.

". . . one hundred thousand dollars!" Brother Bernie.

"Ever see anything like that . . . ?" Brother Bruce.

". . . on television?" Brother Bernie.

"No, I haven't." A. Night.

"Damn right . . ." Brother Bruce.

". . . you haven't!" Brother Bernie.

"But isn't that a little disheartening to watch?" A. Night.

"Hell, no . . ." Brother Bruce.

". . . the audience participates." Brother Bernie.

"How?" A. Night.

"They get to bet . . ." Brother Bruce.

". . . on who's *The Last to Die!*" Brother Bernie.

"Fellas, I still think it's a little depressing." A. Night.

"We've got a back-up pitch . . ." Brother Bruce.

". . . more upbeat." Brother Bernie.

"What's that?" A. Night.

"A doozy. It's called . . ." Brother Bruce.

". . . *Homeless on the Range.*" Brother Bernie.

"We get ten homeless people . . ." Brother Bruce.

". . . old people, young people . . ." Brother Bernie.

"Good luck, fellas. I've to get to work." A. Night.

"Adios, Alex . . ." Brother Bruce.

". . . have a nice day." Brother Bernie.

As I walked up the stairs I wondered whether television was ready for the Bernstein brothers—and vice versa.

After I got to the office and lit a Lucky, I checked for messages from Goldie or Garter.

Neither.

A. Night In Hollywood Forever

So I opened the briefcase and dove into Dash's folder. I thought I'd find out more about what all the fuss was about—the missing Hearst-Davies Fabergé egg—The Tear of Russia.

Dash had done his research all right, from first to last with a description of each Imperial Egg, when it was made and where it ended up—except for the ones that were missing.

Dash's list of Fabergé Eggs and current whereabouts:

1885	Hen Egg	Forbes Magazine Collection, New York★
1886	Hen Egg w/Sapphire Pendant	Missing
1887	Blue Serpent Clock Egg	Collection of Prince Rainier III of Monaco
1888	Cherub Egg w/ Chariot	Missing
1889	Necessaire Egg	Missing
1890	Danish Palaces Egg	New Orleans Museum of Art
1891	Memory of Azov Egg	Kremlin Armoury Museum, Moscow
1892	Diamond Trellis Egg	Private Collection
1893	Caucasus Egg	New Orleans Museum of Art
1894	Renaissance Egg	Forbes Magazine Collection, New York★

1895	Twelve Monograms Egg	Hillwood Museum, Washington, DC
1895	Rosebud Egg	Forbes Magazine Collection, New York★
1896	Revolving Miniatures Egg	Virginia Museum of Arts, Richmond
1896	Alexander III Egg	Missing
1897	Mauve Enamel Egg	Missing
1897	Coronation Egg	Forbes Magazine Collection, New York★
1898	Lilies of the Valley Egg	Forbes Magazine Collection, New York★
1898	Pelican Egg	Virginia Museum of Arts, Richmond
1899	Bouquet of Lilies Clock Egg	Kremlin Armoury Museum, Moscow
1899	Pansy Egg	Private Collection
1900	Cockerel Egg	Forbes Magazine Collection, New York★
1900	Trans-Siberian Railway Egg	Kremlin Armoury Museum, Moscow
1901	Basket of Wild Flowers Egg	Kremlin Armoury Museum, Moscow

1901	Gatchina Palace Egg	The Walters Art Gallery, Baltimore, MD
1902	Clover Egg	Kremlin Armoury Museum, Moscow
1902	Empire Nephrite Egg	Missing
1903	Danish Jubilee	Missing
1903	Peter the Great Egg	Virginia Museum of Arts, Richmond
1904	Unknown	Japan-Russian War
1904	Unknown	
1905	Unknown	Massacre of Bloody Sunday
1905	Unknown	Czar Nicholas Assents to Constitutional Monarchy
1906	Moscow Kremlin Egg	Kremlin Armoury Museum, Moscow
1906	Swan Egg	Edouard and Maurice Sandoz Foundation, Switzerland
1907	Rose Trellis Egg	The Walters Art Gallery, Baltimore, MD
1907	Cradle with Garlands Egg	Private Collection

1908	Peacock Egg	Edouard and Maurice Sandoz Foundation, Switzerland
1908	Alexander Palace Egg	Kremlin Armoury Museum, Moscow
1909	Standart Egg	Kremlin Armoury Museum, Moscow
1909	Alexander II Commemorative Egg	Missing
1910	Alexander III Equestrian Egg	Kremlin Armoury Museum, Moscow
1910	Colonnade Egg	Royal Collection, Her Majesty Queen Elizabeth II
1911	Bay Tree Egg	Forbes Magazine Collection, New York*
1911	Fifteenth Anniversary Egg	Forbes Magazine Collection, New York*
1912	Czarevich Egg	Virginia Museum of Arts, Richmond
1912	Napoleonic Egg	New Orleans Museum of Art
1913	Winter Egg	Private Collection
1913	Romanov Tercentenary Egg	Kremlin Armoury Museum, Moscow

1914	Grisaille Egg	Hillwood Museum, Washington, DC
1914	Mosaic Egg	Royal Collection, Her Majesty Queen Elizabeth II
1915	Red Cross Egg with Imperial Portraits	Virginia Museum of Arts, Richmond
1915	Red Cross Egg with Triptych	Cleveland Museum of Art
1916	Steel Military Egg	Kremlin Armoury Museum, Moscow
1916	Order of St. George Egg	Forbes Magazine Collection, New York*
1917	THE TEAR OF	PURCHASED BY RUSSIA W. R. HEARST – CURRENTLY MISSING

NOTE: The Forbes Collection was purchased at auction in 2004 for $100,000,000 and is now in the Kremlin Armoury Museum, Moscow.

The Tear of Russia was the last and most ornate—and probably the most valuable of the lot. By 1917 Russia was in chaos. The revolution was successful and the days of the Romanov dynasty numbered. So Peter Carl Fabergé outdid himself.

The Imperial Egg was four inches high, oval, representing a tear like no other—containing a replica of the royal crown embedded with diamonds and a perfect red ruby in the center, trellised with bands of gold; the surface, an enameled translucent pink applied to a golden field of starbursts. The oblong base was crested with panels of blue sapphires and six brilliant-cut diamonds.

As I read Dash's description of The Tear of Russia I couldn't help thinking of its tragic legacy—from the decadent opulence of the Romanovs to the ruthless reign of Lenin and Stalin to the star-crossed, unsanctified love of William Randolph Hearst and Marion Davies. I wondered . . .

I wondered who was at the door knocking.

There was one way to find out.

"Come in."

She did, and closed the door behind her. Sonja Vladov stood on those same Angie Dickenson legs, with the same Hedy Lamarr–Catherine Zeta-Jones face and that same feline figure that would stop a stampede—or start one. She was wearing a different outfit, but I didn't bother much studying it because I was busy imagining what was underneath it.

Those green, green eyes framed by that dark, dark hair swept around the office, then settled on me.

I stood up—gentleman that I am.

"Yeah," I said, "this one's a little different than Elliot's. It's what they nowadays call . . ."

"Eclectic?" She smiled.

"Close enough. I was going to say 'thrift shop.' "

"I think it's charming."

"So are you. Why don't you sit down?" And cross your legs, I thought to myself.

Sonja sat down and crossed her legs. That had a very salutary effect.

"Say," I inquired, "you don't happen to have some cigarettes on you, do you? I'm down to nuts and butts . . ."

"Sorry, I don't . . ."

". . . don't smoke?"

"That's right."

"Well, as Joe E. Brown said in the movie, 'nobody's per-fect.' But this is a swell surprise, I didn't expect to see you 'til Friday."

"Well, I have some very good news that couldn't wait . . . and besides, it's private."

"Should I lock the door?"

"Oh, I don't think that's necessary. Alex." She leaned for-ward. "You're quite famous, you know."

"I am?"

"You certainly are, as a private investigator with all those adventures, and the latest one especially, The Star of Good Hope . . ."

"Oh, that."

"Getting your picture in all the papers and on televi-sion . . ."

"That was another life. I'm retired."

"Yes, as a private investigator, but now you're a writer."

I am? I was going to say but I didn't.

"Well, yes," I *did* say, "I am working on a couple of things."

"That's why I'm here with the good news."

"And that is . . ."

"My grandfather, who is also retired, from production, but still has many investments, just invested in another enter-prise and you'll never guess what it is . . ."

"No, I won't. Suppose you tell me what it is."

"A book publishing company that specializes in mysteries, in fact it's called Four Star Mysteries."

"Is that a fact?"

"It is, and he's appointed me President and Senior Editor."

"Oh? I didn't know you had experience in the publishing racket."

"Well, I took some courses in college."

"Uh-huh."

"And I'm here to make you a proposal."

"Any proposal from you would be hard to ignore."

"I hope so. I thought with your background as a private investigator and as a writer, you'd have a story to sell."

"I do. Would you like to hear a synopsis?"

"I'd love to."

"Well, this private investigator is in his office one night and a big fellow, call him Brute Benson, comes in. Brute's been in jail for seven years and when he gets out he finds that his girlfriend has disappeared and wants to locate her so he hires the PI, who discovers that the girlfriend is now married to a rich, old man and is also in cahoots with a quack—a pseudo-psychologist who is blackmailing her and getting her to steer other rich women to him who provide him with enough intimate details so he can also blackmail them. You know, an extortion racket. The PI tracks her down, there's an exciting climax where Brute and the girlfriend are both killed and the PI wounded, but he ends up with the rich, old man's beautiful daughter and they live happily ever after. What do you think of it?"

"I think it's splendid and I'm prepared to give you a fif-teen-thousand-dollar check in advance and another fifteen thousand when you finish it. Is that satisfactory?"

"It would be except that you're a little late."

"You mean you've already sold it?"

"No. But Raymond Chandler did. He called it, *Farewell, My Lovely.*"

"Oh."

"I think you ought to get a little more experience before

you go around waving checks at strange writers."

"I'm afraid you're right." She uncrossed then crossed her legs again. "Perhaps I should hire you as a story consultant or something."

"I do have another story you and your grandfather might be interested in. Maybe you already are."

"What story is that?"

"A mystery." I pointed to Dash's folder on the desk. "It has to do with a missing Fabergé Imperial Egg. How much would he be willing to pay for that story?"

It was obvious that she was surprised and pleased.

"Well, I'd have to consult with him, or better yet, you talk to him, but I believe you could name your own figure . . . if you solve that mystery."

"Why don't we let it go at that . . . for now. That story doesn't have an ending . . . yet."

"Do you mind if I mention our conversation to my grandfather?"

"Go ahead, but I've got a feeling he already knows part of it, and that's the reason for the invitation and for your visit here today."

"Alex." She rose and extended her hand. "I'm glad we had this little visit."

I took her hand for a moment, then gave it back to her.

"I'm glad you're glad."

She turned toward the door.

"Just a minute," I said. "Your grandfather is a very rich man, right?"

"Very, *very* rich."

"I stand corrected. Millions?"

She nodded.

"Hundreds of millions?"

She nodded again.

"Then why all the fuss about an egg?"

"Well, I think . . ."

"Yeah, what do you think?"

"I think you ought to ask him."

"Let me tell you what I think."

"Go ahead."

"Suppose somebody, say an ex–private eye, had pertinent information, say in a folder, information written by a certain newspaperman, and somebody else or maybe a couple of somebody elses wanted access to that information. Say that first they'd try to get it from the ex-newspaperman. That didn't work, so they'd try to snatch it from the ex–private eye. Say that didn't come off, either. The next step would be to try to bribe the ex–private eye . . . wouldn't you say?"

"I wouldn't really know."

"Somebody tried to bribe the ex–private eye last night. Somebody else tried this morning. Only last night they were willing to throw in a little sex in the bargain. I'm not talking about the principals, I'm talking about their representatives."

She took a step closer, in more ways than one.

"Is that what it would take?"

"Well, it didn't work last night, but . . ."

"But what?"

"But I'm a little disappointed that the second representative didn't give it a shot this morning . . ."

I was just stringing her along, but I wondered how far I could string. I didn't find out because somebody knocked on the door.

Sonja looked at the door, then back at me and shrugged.

"Come in," I said.

He did.

E. Elliott Elliot, freshly barbered and elegantly attired in a dark blue double-breasted blazer, severely creased charcoal trousers and the inevitable gold-crowned walking stick.

"Good morning, Alex, I . . . oh, excuse me, I didn't know you were entertaining. Good morning, Sonja."

"Hello, Elliott. That's quite all right, I was just on my way out. See you both Friday night."

"Are we dressing?" Elliot inquired. "The invitation didn't specify."

"Business attire will be fine."

Sonja Vladov went to the door and left, but didn't quite close the door behind her.

"What is it, Elliot?" I asked.

"I just wanted to tell you that I spoke with Tyler . . ."

"Tyler?"

"Tyler Cassity, the owner of Hollywood Forever. He'll have a couple of people waiting with the keys to the mausoleum at ten in the morning Saturday."

"Saturday?" While Elliot was talking I strolled to the door and opened it wider.

"Oh, Alex," Sonja said, "I forgot my . . ."

"Purse," I smiled and handed it to her.

"Thank you."

She took it and this time went on her way.

This time I closed the door.

"Alex," Elliot said. "You know she heard . . ."

"That's all right, Elliot, I don't care who knows. That's one way to ferret out all the rats."

"My friend," Elliot pointed his walking stick at me, "I think you're playing a dangerous game."

"You got me into it . . . my friend."

Chapter XXI

Nothing much happened between then and the Vlad Vladov reception Friday night.

Except that I applied a little Arthur Conan Doyle–Sherlock Holmes deductive reasoning to the mystery of the missing Hearst-Davies Fabergé Imperial Egg.

It would have been impossible and useless to hie up to San Simeon and try to search the joint. First of all, the joint was too big, and second, they left the place long before either of them died so it wouldn't be there anyhow.

The same logic applied to their Wyntoon Castle near the McCloud River.

The Beach House had been demolished long ago.

The Bungalow had been moved to Benedict Canyon and sold.

The house in Beverly Hills where Hearst died had long since been occupied by several different owners.

Marion Davies would have held on to her precious memento as long as she could . . . maybe to the grave and beyond.

So Charles Oliver Dash was right. The logical place to start would be the Douras Mausoleum.

And that would have to wait until Saturday morning.

Elementary, my dear Watson.

What wasn't elementary was that Goldie was still missing and nobody knew why—where—who? With every tick of the clock and yes, damn it, beat of my still-cop heart, I felt that whatever had happened was not something Goldie and I were going to laugh about later.

So, one other thing did happen.

I made a damn fool out of myself and, thanks to that damn Greek temper . . . I don't like to think about it, but it went something like this . . . I called my best friend Myron Garter . . . he was in bed . . . with his wife . . . and they weren't sleeping . . . in fact he was breathing pretty heavy.

". . . Jesus, Alex, do you know what time it is?"

". . . yeah, I do, Myron, but I'm not so sure Goldie does . . . and I got a feeling both of us should be doing a hell of a lot more than sitting back on our heels and waiting . . ."

"Just a minute, pal, speaking for the department, we're not sitting back on our heels, on our asses, or anyplace else."

"You're not?"

"No, we're not! We've got every available . . ."

"Don't dish me any of that cop shit . . ."

"Is that what you think I'm dishing you?"

"You're home in bed and . . ."

"Where the hell would you expect me to be at one o'clock in the morning?"

"I'm telling you this . . . I'm going to start knocking down some doors and . . ."

"Try knocking some sense into that stupid head of yours . . ."

"Myron!"

I could hear Rhoda in the background.

"Myron, take it easy on him. You know how he feels about Goldie."

"Don't tell me what to do, Rhoda."

"You're both hotheads and you know it, and you both love each other and you know that, too."

"You hear that, boychick?" Garter said into the phone. "We love each other."

I could tell that he was muffling a laugh, and by that time I'd started to cool down and come to my senses.

"Yeah, Myron, I heard. The great love story that's never been told."

"Look, pal, give us the weekend to go through what we've got to go through . . . after that, legal or not, we'll knock down every door there is . . . together. Okay?"

"Myron."

"What?"

"That crazy son of a bitch who called you a couple of minutes ago . . . ?"

"What about him?"

"He doesn't exist anymore. Good night."

"Good night . . . sweetheart."

Other than that, nothing much happened until the Vladov reception Friday night.

Chapter XXII

Saturday night a couple of hours before post time at the Vladov's, I was just stepping out of the shower when the phone rang.

After grabbing a towel, I picked it up from the nightstand next to the bed on the fourth ring.

"Hello."

"How's my knight in shining armor?"

"Franny, your knight's not in shining armor. He's just stepped out of the shower dripping wet."

"Did you say dripping or drooping?"

"Both."

"We used to take quite a few showers together, remember, Alex?"

How could I forget? But I didn't say it.

A significant silence.

"Alex, are you there?"

"I'm here."

"Alone?"

"Like the song says 'all alone by the telephone.' Any other questions?"

"No, I just called to tell you that things are going great. Mike called. He's set up some more interviews, so I'll be away for a while more . . . *Oprah* in Chicago and . . . I won't bore you with the details . . . he also told me that he sold The Star of Good Hope."

"Did you know that he owned it?"

"I know everything. What are you going to do with the twenty-five thousand?"

"I bought a new suit."

"For twenty-five thousand dollars?"

"I got back some change. Going to wear it tonight to a party."

"You going with your writer girlfriend, what's her name, Goldie?"

"That's her name, but I'm not going with her. She's . . . out of town. Going solo."

"Where?"

It was none of her business, but I thought I might find out something if I told her. I did.

"At Vladimir Vladov's. You know him?"

"Who doesn't? He tried to get me to do pictures for him, first schlock, then when he got culture, he wanted me to do something by Chekhov, naturally there was a nude swimming scene in it. So much for his brand of culture. What does he want from you?"

"What makes you think he wants something?"

"Because I know Vladov. Be careful, Alex."

"Do you know his granddaughter?"

"I do. Be even more careful. Sonja's smooth, but those curves are dangerous . . ."

"I'll fasten my safety belt."

"She's liable to unfasten it, along with . . ."

"I get the picture, thanks, pal."

"No, I thank you, pal. I won't say it again, but . . ."

"Then don't."

"Who was it that said 'there are no second acts'?"

"Fitzgerald."

"Ella?"

"No. Scott."

"He was wrong. Thanks to you I . . ."

"There you go again."

"No more, but if you don't mind, I'll call again before I come back."

"I don't mind. Happy comeback. Good night, Franny."

"Good night, sweet shamus."

I slapped on some Brut and slipped into my new Chester Barrie suit that I'd bought at Carroll and Co. yesterday. Since Dick Carroll died a few months ago, his son John took over completely and started carrying a lot more sports attire and outerwear, but he still sold the Chester Barrie and Oxxford lines that went for more than two grand per suit. I popped for a dark blue pinstripe, 42 long, which they cuffed in a hurry so I could wear it to the Vladov party.

I looked in the mirror and only wished that Goldie could see me now. Maybe I'd wear it at our wedding.

Maybe.

I tucked Dash's folder under the mattress, then thought about packing the .38 but decided that it would spoil the cut of the pinstripe. So, instead, I slipped the Elgin pocket watch into the watch pocket.

Besides, what could happen at a hoity-toity party in Beverly Hills?

Top up, I drove the Sebring through Beverly Hills with the CD playing Cole Porter's *Night and Day* disc. I cut up Benedict Canyon, past the Beverly Hills Hotel through Lexington and Summit Drive to the really hoity-toity neighborhood. Ten-, fifteen-, twenty-million-dollar mansions.

At the gate of one of the mansions stood two sober-faced security persons, but courteous. One asked my name. I told him, the gate opened as if by magic and I drove into Shangri-

La while the CD played "Love for Sale." A couple of other cars came up behind me. One was a limousine, the other a Bentley.

I parked, snapped off the CD while another sober-faced fellow opened the door. I walked toward the Taj Mahal as he drove the Sebring into the night, I know not where.

Before I could knock, one of the huge, twin ornate doors opened, again as if by magic, and I sauntered into the house that Vladov had built.

The Romanovs would have felt right at home.

The place was a glittering monument to extravagance—wall-to-wall extravagance—ceiling-to-carpet extravagance—and the furniture was right out of the ballroom scene in *The Prisoner of Zenda*.

I was greeted by the chatelaine. I got the feeling the chatelaine was waiting in the wings just to greet me. She fairly flew toward me as if I was the guest of honor—or the object of her affection.

Sonja Vladov took both my hands in hers and kissed me on both cheeks, barely missing my mouth both times. She wore a low-cut something that must have cost twenty times my Chester Barrie. And she smelled like a garden after the rain . . . the Garden of Eden. If she had been an apple, I would have taken a bite.

She ignored the other guests who were arriving, slipped her right arm through my left and led the way along the Primrose Path.

"Come on, Alex, I'm so anxious for you to meet Grandfather and so is he."

She led me into another room that was even larger and more ornate, where people were mixing and munching from the sumptuous buffet. At least a dozen in help were attending to the beverage requirements of the guests from two bars strategically set up. Music was coming from an orchestra composed of about a dozen players. Nice romantic music from some romantic Russian composer.

A gentleman I took to be the host was at the center of a small group that included E. Elliott Elliot and Charles Oliver Dash.

Elliot was his elegant self with his elegant walking stick and Dash was his usual self with a tall glass of milk slightly discolored so I assumed it was liberally laced with Scotch.

"Grandfather," Sonja fawned. "This is the gentleman . . ."

" 'You were so anxious to meet,' " I finished Sonja's earlier quote.

I wasn't going to find out anything by being coy, so I decided to be blunt . . . for the rest of the evening.

"Mister Night," Vladimir Vladov extended his hand. "I've heard so many good things about you."

"I've heard a lot about you, too, Mister Vladov."

"They can't prove a thing," he quipped.

In my former occupation I'd met quite a few Hollywood producers, but none quite like Vladov. There was a quiet strength about him. Not a big man, but militarily straight as a Cossack . . . although I'd never met a Cossack. Crudely handsome, a melodious voice and a serpent smile. I wouldn't trust him any farther than I could toss the grand piano in the orchestra. Whatever his age, he looked ten years younger.

"Oh, Mister Night," Vladov nodded, "I'd like you to meet Serge Goncheroff, our guest of honor. Serge is with the Russian Consulate in San Francisco. Trade Commissioner."

We shook hands. Goncheroff was a little fellow with big eyes and spoke with just a tad of an accent. In the olden days he would have been played by Peter Lorre.

"I, too, have heard many things about you, Mister Night," he said.

"They can't prove a thing," I re-quipped.

"Mister Night," Vladov nodded toward Elliot and Dash. "Of course you know Mister Elliot and Mister Dash."

"Sure," I said. "We're in business together."

"You are?" Vladov seemed surprised.

"Yeah. The writing business. The difference is they've got Academy Awards and a Pulitzer Prize and I've got writer's block."

"But you, Mister Night," Goncheroff said, "are a hero."

"I am?"

"I'm referring to the affair of The Star of Good Hope."

"You also interested in jewels . . . say, what do I call you 'Commissioner' or . . ."

"Serge, if you please."

"Speaking of The Star of Good Hope," Elliot said, "here comes the recent owner of that particular gem."

Andre Shenko had heard what Elliot said. So did Linda Bundy who was alongside him.

Linda and Sonja stood next to each other. They both inspired lust. It was hard to tell who was the lustier.

"Good evening, all," Shenko smiled.

"Well, the gang's all here," I said. "There's only one thing missing."

"What's that?" Linda Bundy inquired, but it was evident that everybody in that little cluster wanted to know.

"This." I pulled the thick envelope out of the inside pocket of the Chester Barrie and handed it to Miss Bundy. That put a slight dent into her composure, "I don't accept tips. It's un-heroic."

Actually that put a slight dent into everybody's composure . . . and that's just what it was meant to do. Everybody didn't know exactly what was in the envelope, but they had a pretty good idea.

"I think I need another drink," Dash said. "I *know* I need another drink, a double." He headed toward a bar.

"I must say, Mister Night," Vladov said, "you certainly are . . ."

"Blunt?"

"I was going to say 'surprising.' "

"You ain't seen nothin' yet, Mister Vladov. And I ain't seen anything quite like this spread. You certainly do surround yourself with . . ." I let my gaze sweep around the room and settle on Sonja. ". . . Granada and not Asbury Park."

"I'm not sure I . . ."

"Oh, it's just part of a lyric to a song called 'At Long Last Love.' Isn't it, Sonja?"

"Cole Porter," she nodded.

I motioned at some of the paintings on the walls and at other objects in the room.

"Some of these pieces look like they came from a museum."

"Some did." Vladov nodded. "From several museums . . . and other places. You never know from where you're going to add to your collection, do you, Andre?"

"Never," Shenko replied.

"Yes," Elliot said, "some *objects d'art* turn up in the most unlikely places. Welcome back, Charlie."

Charles Oliver Dash had returned with a refill.

"Shall we repair to the library and continue this conversation in more secluded surroundings?" Vladov suggested. "Ladies, would you excuse us?"

"Why don't you invite them to come along? They'll find out everything anyhow." I suggested.

"Very well. Serge, you, too. We couldn't do without the guest of honor."

Within minutes Elliot, Dash, Goncheroff, Shenko,

Vladov, Sonja, Linda and I were within the paneled walls of the luxurious library and had been served beverages by one of the staff who disappeared discreetly after serving.

Both ladies sat down and crossed their legs, everybody noticed. Goncheroff sat down and crossed his legs, nobody noticed. Serge probably felt more comfortable sitting instead of standing in a room where all the men were taller. Even the women were taller, so the chair served as a sort of equalizer.

" *'Nasdrovia,'* " Dash saluted with his glass.

" *'Peesbogyan,'* " Elliot returned the salute.

"Here's looking at you, kids," I said and took a sip of gin and tonic. "By the way, Mister Vladov, it wasn't you who bought The Star of Good Hope from Andre, was it?"

"No, Mister Night, when you get to be my age you become much more selective in adding to your collection . . . although in the past I have purchased one or two items from Andre."

"What about you, Mister Shenko," I said, "how selective are you in adding to your collection?"

"Very. Collecting is a sideline. I'm mainly in the import-export business."

"You used to be in the spy business, didn't you?"

That didn't seem to faze the Bolshevek one bit. Not so with some of the others in the library. Goncheroff almost spilled his vodka.

"One must adjust with the times and circumstances," Shenko said and sipped his wine.

I knew that neither Vladov nor Shenko would put up with my arrogance unless they thought I had or knew something that they wanted to have or know so I thought I'd push as far as I could and maybe find out a few things myself.

"It is ironic," I pushed, "both of you coming from the same country and from different backgrounds, one from royalty, the other a . . ."

"Peasant," Shenko smiled.

"I was going to say commoner, but nevertheless, different backgrounds, and here you are both highly successful in your fields and both collectors. Have you ever competed for the same . . . item?"

"No, I don't think so," Vladov said. "Have we, Andre?"

"Not yet."

"Does either of you collect eggs?"

"Eggs?" they both repeated.

"Yes, eggs, as in Imperial Fabergé, I understand some of them are still missing, or didn't you fellows know?"

"Those missing eggs . . ." Serge Goncheroff stood up, ". . . are the property of my country, Mister Night."

"Not as long as they're missing, Mister Goncheroff," I said.

"That's not the opinion of my country."

"Yes," Elliot smiled, "but the possessor of each of those eggs undoubtedly has a different opinion."

"There's an old saying," Dash said, "possession is nine-tenths of the law."

"Different countries," Goncheroff replied, "have different laws."

"But we happen to be in this country," I added. "And it's all academic so long as each of those eggs is missing. But what if one were to be found?"

"Yes," Elliot grinned, "to whom would the egg and the ten million dollars belong?"

"There are some collectors," Vladov said, "who don't care about the notoriety, they only care about possessing the art object . . . at least while they are alive."

"I repeat, gentlemen, history dictates that the eggs are the property of the government of Russia." Goncheroff gulped the rest of his vodka.

"Which government?" Dash remarked. "Russia has had several in the last century. Makes for a hell of a story."

"What do you think, Mister Shenko?" I asked.

"I think that's a bridge too far . . . until each egg is found."

"Mister Goncheroff," I asked, "how many Imperial Eggs did you say are missing?"

"I didn't say, and there is some doubt, probably eight. But some may have been destroyed during the Revolution, inadvertently, of course. No one would purposely destroy anything of such beauty."

"Not even the revolutionaries?" Elliot prodded.

"Especially the revolutionaries." Shenko parried. "Not just because they were so beautiful, but because they could be sold for eggs that could be eaten. The Soviet Union was in dire need of food, and the leaders were pragmatists."

"Is that what they were?" Dash grunted. "Pragmatists usually win wars . . . hot or cold."

"Were you in favor of *glasnost?*" I pointed at Shenko.

"I was in favor of . . ." Shenko paused.

"Whatever you were told to be in favor of . . ." Vladov smiled. "Isn't that so, Andre?"

"Yes . . ." Shenko shrugged, ". . . and no."

"Oh, by the way," I turned toward Vladov, "congratulations."

"On what?"

"On being honored by the Press Center. Mister Dash tells me it was a very interesting lunch."

"Oh, yes, very interesting. The 'Press' has always been very good to me."

"And vice versa," Dash added.

"Well, this has been very interesting, too." Vladov rose. "But I think that the others are beginning to wonder whatever happened to our guest of honor." He nodded toward Goncheroff. "Shall we get back to the reception?"

We did.

Back at the reception, the reception was in full bloom.

If the guests had missed the guest of honor it didn't show. They were occupied in conversation, and in the consumption of food and drink, while the orchestra concertized.

Elliot, Dash and I managed to drift away from the rest and moor in front of a French window.

"I thought I had a big mouth," Dash spoke just above a whisper, took another sip of his milk and Scotch, and looked directly at me. "But it appears to me that you spilled just about all the beans and you're not even drunk."

"Not *all* the beans," I said.

"That's true," Elliot smiled. "You failed to mention The Tear of Russia by name."

"I was just tossing out a little chum to see if any one of *them* would mention it, but the sharks didn't bite . . . at least not yet."

"You think one of them will?" Dash queried.

"I wouldn't bet against it. Did *you* mention it by name at The Press Center?"

"I don't remember," Dash said.

"Which of them do you think hired Ski Mask?" Elliot wondered.

"I don't know," I said, "but having failed with that ploy, both Vladov and Shenko tried a slightly more subtle approach . . ."

"Are you referring to the female of the species?" Elliot smiled.

"Both ladies paid me a visit. Separately, of course. Miss Vladov offered a book deal with a publishing company her grandfather just happened to buy . . . and Miss Bundy brought over an envelope bulging with pictures of my favorite printer, Benjamin Franklin. And both ladies more than intimated that there would be . . . fringe benefits."

"Why don't you take both deals," Dash grinned, "and double-cross the sons of bitches?"

"I think the stakes'll get higher."

"And more dangerous," Elliot added.

"After we find the egg . . . if we ever do," I added. "In the meantime, as the song goes, 'ain't we got fun?' "

"What about tomorrow?" Elliot asked.

"What about it?"

"Do you want us to go with you to the . . . resting place, or is it *nesting* place?"

"I don't think so, fellas. But I am going to take a friend along."

"What friend?" Dash inquired.

"A special friend. A .38 Police Special."

Just then the orchestra struck up a couple of chords of what sounded like "The Volga Boatman" and Vlad Vladov stepped up to a microphone, hailed by a round of enthusiastic applause from the invitees.

He introduced himself, which was not necessary, then introduced "our guest of honor, the Trade Commissioner from the Russian Consulate in San Francisco, Serge Goncheroff."

For the guest of honor the microphone had to be lowered about a foot. Both Vladov and Goncheroff tried, but failed to succeed. Sonja Vladov appeared and with a deft twist or two brought the stem down to the appropriate level, triggering applause from the audience along with a few "bravos!"

I didn't hear much of what Goncheroff had to say because I was too occupied watching Sonja Vladov walk to the sideline and stand like a queen of lilies, flawless and serene.

To me, out of the whole crowd, she was the only thing in

focus. And damn if she didn't know I was looking at her, because she looked right back with those *ocho chornias*.

I do remember hearing the guests clap a couple of times during Goncheroff's speech, but don't ask me what he said. He might as well have been talking Russian.

After staring at Sonja for a few minutes I noticed something else—someone else—two someone elses.

Andre Shenko and Linda Bundy standing near Sonja.

Linda and Sonja both gave the lie to Kipling's definition, "a rag, a bone and a hank of hair" and truth to G. B. Shaw's "O fairest of creation! Last and best of all God's works." Even though they were studies in contrast; one, dark and sensuous and the other fair and composed, but alluring.

Linda leaned and whispered something to Sonja. Sonja responded with that Mona Lisa smile. Whatever Linda said, I hoped it was about me. But not likely.

Serge Goncheroff finished with what he had to say, bowed stiffly and walked away to polite applause as the orchestra went on with the show.

Having concluded that I'd learned just about everything I was gong to, I wasn't very anxious to stick around for what was left of the soirée.

I bade good night to Elliot and Dash who had come to the reception in Elliot's Bentley. Elliot assured me that he would keep a brood eye on Dash and that he and Carstairs would make sure C.O.D. got home in close to an upright position.

But the proceedings were not quite over yet. On the way to the goal line I was intercepted.

First by Shenko and Linda.

"Mister Night," Shenko smiled. "You're not leaving so soon . . ."

"I'm not?"

"What I meant . . ."

"I know what you meant, but, yes I am. I've got a date in the morning . . . with some ghosts."

I thought there was a glance between the two of them, but I couldn't swear to it under oath.

"Mister Night," Shenko said, "I do wish you'd reconsider."

"Reconsider what?" I did glance at Linda.

"The commission Linda delivered to you. You earned it, and more."

"I've got a feeling the stakes might get higher, so I'd just as soon leave it in the pot until the next hand is dealt."

"And when might that be?" Shenko asked. "Soon?"

"You never can tell. It might be a long time. Or it might be as soon as tomorrow."

Linda smiled.

"You could have been a little more discreet about returning it."

"Yeah, I guess I could have. Maybe next time. Good night, you two."

I walked away to let them think things over.

I didn't get very far before I found Serge Goncheroff looking up at me.

"Mister Night."

"Yes, Mister Commissioner."

"It was a pleasure meeting you."

"Thank you."

"And may I remind you, sir, about the Imperial Eggs."

"What about them?"

"If one is found . . ."

"That's a mountain of an 'if.' "

"Nevertheless, if one is found, my government considers that egg our property, but . . ."

"But what?"

"We would make a generous payment, very generous, for the return . . ."

"Ten million dollars?"

"Let's not negotiate . . . yet."

"Why doesn't your government try to find the missing eggs?"

"My dear sir, we *are* trying."

"Good luck and good night."

The next and last encounter was with the host and chatelaine.

"Thank you for coming," Vladov smiled. Sonja was already smiling, yes, that Mona Lisa smile.

"Thank you for inviting me. Both of you."

"If you change your mind," Vladov said, "about the deal . . ."

"What deal?"

"The mystery you're working on, the one you're trying to solve."

"Oh, yeah, the one about the Imperial Egg . . ."

"You'll never get a better offer."

"I've been told that before."

"Mister Night, please take a moment and look around you."

I did.

"Nice people, nice party," I said, "nice place."

"I have everything that a man could want. And it will all belong to my granddaughter when I . . . depart. All my life I've gotten everything I've wanted. Against all odds . . . no matter what the cost."

"Congratulations."

"There is only one thing left that I want. Not because of its value in money."

"No?"

"No. There is another value. A heritage . . ."

"Mister Vladov, don't oversell." I looked at Sonja, then back to her grandfather. "I'd say you've got a pretty good horse in this race."

"Alex . . ."

"Yes, Sonja?"

"Do you mind if I . . . stay in touch?"

"Touch all you want," I said.

As far as I was concerned, the party was over.

Chapter XXIII

On the way home from Vladov's house in Beverly Hills, I couldn't help thinking about the time I left another party also in Beverly Hills.

Only that time I hadn't left alone. I had a date with Goldie. We had had other dates before, but I think we both knew that this one would have a different ending—make that a beginning.

For some time we both knew it was going to happen. We just didn't know when.

Somehow that night we knew.

We knew from the way we looked at each other when I picked her up earlier that evening. From the way we walked next to each other, touched each other, danced together.

Somehow we just knew.

I had been to her apartment before.

But this time was different.

This time I did see her bedroom.

Only it wasn't a bedroom. It was a magic carpet. It was all the love songs ever sung. All the poems ever written. All the movies ever made.

A trip to the moon on gossamer wings: Dancing in the Dark. How Do I Love Thee? Heaven's Gate. The Great Love Story that's Never Been Told. Do It Again. Something to Remember You By. Love Is a Many Splendored Thing. Grand Illusion. There's No Tomorrow.

★ ★ ★ ★ ★

And as I drove home, I wondered if, for Goldie and me, there ever would be a tomorrow.

Chapter XXIV

During the 1920s, '30s, '40s, '50s and '60s the places to be seen in Hollywood were the Coconut Grove, the Brown Derby, the Clover Club, the Trocadero, Ciro's, Mocambo, Chasen's, Perinos, Romanov's, Santa Anita, Hollywood Park, the Polo Lounge and Schwab's.

The place to be buried was Hollywood Memorial Park.

Just ask Rudolph Valentino, Elmo Lincoln, Adolph Menjou, Peter Lorre, C. B. DeMille, Harry Cohn, Janet Gaynor, Nelson Eddy, Paul Muni, Bugsy Siegel, the Ritz Brothers, Clifton Webb, John Huston, Peter Finch and dozens and dozens of other celebrities.

Hollywood Memorial Park is now known as Hollywood Forever Cemetery.

Since I had a date with some of those tenants Saturday morning, I decided to delve into Dash's folder when I got home after Vladov's party and get acquainted with some of the cast and plots . . . while getting reacquainted with a jug of Gordon's Gin.

According to C.O.D., Hollywood Memorial Park was established in 1899 by Isaac Lankershim and Isaac Van Nuys, when they bought a hundred acres in the heart of Hollywood, then sold off about forty of those acres on the south side to what became Paramount Pictures in 1920.

As the old saying goes, "people were dying to get in."

For half a century business grew, and so did the buildings

165

on the property . . . from the original Bell Tower to the Cathedral Mausoleum to the Columbarium, to the Sanctuary of Memories to the Abbey of the Psalms to the Hall of David, the Hall of Solomon along with the sections of land known as the Gardens; The Garden of Eternal Love, The Rose Garden, The Garden of Israel, The Garden of Legends—that's the site of the Douras-Davies Mausoleum—and a half dozen other gardens where the flowers of show business were and are planted.

But in 1939 the cemetery was sold to a debonair ex-con named Jules Roth, who owned it until the 1990s.

During that span he succeeded in looting the once-glamorous cemetery of over nine million dollars by all sorts of schemes, leaving it in disrepair and bankruptcy.

But before that, among his other schemes and scams, Roth managed to sell off two long strands of the cemetery's Santa Monica Boulevard frontage for over eight million dollars to a strip mall developer. Nobody knew where that money went. Nobody but the high-living snake oil salesman who kept a bevy of beautiful, adoring females, as well as himself in obscene luxury while the cemetery sank into a sea of disuse.

Yes, Jules Roth was not an altogether honest man. He was an altogether rascal.

The place was about to be shuttered when a twenty-nine-year-old white knight rode to the rescue with a sealed bid of $375,000 for the entire bundle.

That was in 1995.

Since then Tyler Cassity has changed the name to Hollywood Forever and pumped seven or eight million more into renovations and improvements—the mausoleums no longer leak, crypts are stain free, the grass is green, formerly potholed roads have been repaved, tombstones are polished—until it has once again become a desirable status symbol with some of the highest priced plots per square foot of any bone-orchard in Hollywood or any place.

In fact, it has become such a desirable status symbol that even his eminence E. Elliott Elliot has chosen it as his permanent address.

Through it all, since 1961, Marion Davies has resided in the Douras Mausoleum on section eight aside the lake in the Garden of Legends, and tomorrow morning through the good offices of E. Elliott Elliot and Tyler Cassity, I would pay my respects to the lady in the sepulcher and do a little snooping.

But for tonight I took another slug of gin, and as the inscription on Mel Blanc's tombstone says, "That's all folks!"

Chapter XXV

Saturday morning as I breakfasted on my third cup of coffee and second slice of rye toast with marmalade, spooned out a dollop of yogurt and tried to decide whether to go to the YMCA, swim and workout before heading for the Hollywood Forever Cemetery, fate intervened via the telephone.

"Good morning, Mom."

I knew that by the time I got off the phone with my beloved mother, it would be too late to get in a workout at the gymnasium.

"Good morning, Alex. How's your weekend so far?"

"Fine, Mom. How's by you?"

" 'How's by you?' What kind of English is that? And you a college graduate . . ."

"It's just a saying, Mom."

"Well, don't say it anymore. It sounds unrefined . . . undignified."

"Okay, Mom. From now on dignity will be my escutcheon."

"What's that escutcheon stuff? Don't get too fancy schmancy . . ."

"I won't."

"What are you doing today, Alex?"

"I'm going to do some more . . . uh, research."

"Research . . . again? What're you writing, history or mystery?"

"Some of both, I guess."

"Well, concentrate on the mystery part. History don't sell . . . and throw in some you know what."

"What?"

"Sex. What else?"

"Okay, Mom, I'll sprinkle it liberally with sex."

"Not too liberally . . ."

"Just like you always say, Mom, *Pan—Metron—Ariston* . . ."

"That's it, moderation. Alex, you going to the library for research?"

"Uh, yeah."

"Alex, you've got to get modern. Get on the Internet. You can find out anything you want there . . ."

"I don't know how to work those computers, Mom."

"I'll teach you. It's easy. As a matter of fact I'm going to e-mail my cousin as soon as I get off the phone. You remember my cousin Irene Poletes, don't you, Alex?"

"I do, Mom. Well, I won't hold you up. Give cousin Irene my best regards."

"She always gives regards to you, too, Alex. You want to come over for dinner tonight?"

"No, thanks. I'll call you tomorrow."

"Have a good weekend, son."

"You, too, Mom."

I took a fast shower and shave, slipped on a pair of khakis and a field jacket, I left the Elgin pocket watch on the dresser, packed in the .38 Police Special and drove off to do some research.

I didn't mention the word "cemetery" to my mother because she didn't like to talk about such things. The few times I tried to get her to make plans she'd always wave me off, saying that she wasn't ready to think about it yet. Maybe next year.

My dad had died in Florida, three months after he retired from the saloon business in Akron at the age of fifty-six. Never sick a day in his life. He had survived three landings in the not-so-Pacific during WWII. These days they would have given him a new pump, or repaired the old one. But he couldn't wait for medical science to catch up.

I didn't know whether my mother wanted to be buried next to him in Akron, or bring him out here so they could be together in one of the . . .

Just then I spotted the Hollywood Forever sign and turned right into the entrance off Santa Monica Boulevard.

The guard at the gatehouse waved me in, and I parked the Sebring close by and walked into the Administration Building.

A sunny-faced young lady with a willowy build standing next to the reception desk introduced herself as Samantha Eden Tibbs and asked if I was Alex Night. I told her I was Alex Night.

"Andy and Annette are expecting you," Samantha smiled.

Just then a young man and woman appeared from around the corner of one of the hallways.

He was a tall, dark, handsome, wavy-haired fellow and she was a handsome, sharp-featured young lady, both less than forty. He wore a dark gray suit, probably Brooks Brothers, a light blue button-down shirt and rep tie. Her trim figure was encased in a tan pants suit and maroon blouse. They both looked like they worked in a law firm rather than a cemetery.

"Mister Night?" the handsome fellow extended his right hand.

"Alex," I replied as we shook.

"I'm Andy Martinez and this is Annette Lloyd. Annette is our celebrity historian."

I didn't know there was such a thing at a cemetery, but we shook, too.

"Tyler's out of town," Martinez smiled, "but he asked us to cooperate with you any way we can."

"I appreciate that and I guess we can start by visiting the Douras Mausoleum."

"Understand you'd like to go inside," Andy said.

I nodded.

"We can take a golf cart, it's not far."

"Fine."

"If you have any questions, just ask Annette. She'll probably know the answers."

I knew she didn't know the answer to one of the questions, but I just nodded again.

"I've got the key right here."

Martinez held up a key and we headed outside.

"Is it true that you're a private investigator?" Miss Lloyd asked.

"Past tense. Was. I'm . . . writing a book now."

"About Marion Davies?"

"Partly." I wanted to change the subject. "Say, you two don't look like you belong in a cemetery. What's your background?"

"I've done a lot of things, including writing a few books. But nothing as unusual as Andy here."

"Annette," Andy said, "don't bore Mister Night . . ."

"I'm not bored. Go ahead, Annette."

"Andy was a Marine, then he was a monk."

"Yeah? What rank? In the Marines I mean."

"Corporal," Martinez said.

But I got the feeling he also wanted to change the subject.

"That *is* unusual," I remarked.

"Not only that," Annette added, "he knows more about old movies than anybody."

"Is that so?" I said. "What was John Wayne's name in *Sands of Iwo Jima*?"

"Stryker. Sergeant John Stryker."

"Very good, Mac."

"Marines don't much call each other Mac anymore."

"No?"

"Nope, not much."

"They still say *Semper fi*, don't they?"

"Always," Martinez smiled. "Let's take this cart."

There was a row of golf carts parked outside the Administration Building.

Martinez drove. I sat next to him and Miss Lloyd had the backseat all to herself. We proceeded east along the Pantheon, the Pathway of Remembrance and Griffith Lawn for about the length of three football fields adorned by hundreds of markers. That Saturday morning there was a scattering of visitors with flowers at the sites of graves.

Martinez struck me as an enigmatic sort of fellow. Didn't say much, there was a marked strength about him, and still, a gentleness.

We turned right on Nelson Eddy Drive.

This section, the Garden of Legends, was without doubt the most glorious portion of the cemetery, the center of which contained a beautiful lake with floating lily pads and live swans. And there were gaggles of geese along the shoreline.

As soon as we made the turn and moved south, the celebrity historian, who was a bubbly sort anyhow, commenced to give me a history lesson in departed celebrities.

Annette pointed to twin crypts in the distance.

"That's where Cecil B. DeMille is entombed, his wife is

next to him and members of the DeMille family have graves all around."

"Uh huh."

"Janet Gaynor and Adrian are right there," she motioned, "nearby are Jayne Mansfield, Lady Sylvia Ashley, who was once married to Douglas Fairbanks, then to Clark Gable. And right now we're passing by Adolphe Menjou directly under that cypress tree."

We were still moving along the lakeside.

"There's John Huston," Annette Lloyd pointed.

"You ever get any homeless people who sneak in here to sleep?" I asked.

"Not anymore," Martinez said, "since we've increased security. But years ago they did. Jim Morrison used to hop over the wall and flake out."

"Is he buried here?"

"No. He OD'd in Paris and that's where he's buried."

We turned left on Lydia Lomonsow Lane past a mausoleum marked Boettger and proceeded past the Douglas Fairbanks reflecting pool and tombs for swashbuckling father and son on our right.

Martinez slowed down and parked the golf cart near the curb opposite the Cathedral Mausoleum, one of the largest and most ornamental Italian Renaissance structures in Hollywood or anyplace.

"We walk from here on," Andy Martinez said. "It's not far."

We debarked and started across the tomb-laden lawn.

As we approached a white marble twin crypt I stopped for a better look.

"Hey, that looks like the DeMille tomb."

"Right," Andy said. "They're practically identical."

"That's where Harry Cohn is," Annette nodded.

"Not the most popular man in town, was he?" I noted.

Martinez stopped, so we did, too.

"I'll tell you something," he smiled, "something that Annette won't tell you. I wasn't here at the time, of course, but for a few months after he was entombed, there were quite a few visitors to the gravesite and the maintenance people had to clean the urine off the tomb after some of those visitors left."

"Payback time," I commented and we proceeded.

After about a hundred feet, Annette paused in front of a white bench.

"You'll want to see this," she said.

"I will?"

"Yes. Tyrone Power's grave."

I took a couple of steps closer to Jesse James, Zorro, and the Captain from Castille, and pointed to the flowers in a vase at the head of the grave.

"Yes," Annette said, "there are almost always fresh flowers here . . . from fans who haven't forgotten. There's an inscription on the bench."

I took a moment to read it.

> *"Goodnight, sweet prince,*
> *And flights of Angels sing thee to thy rest."*

"Well, here we are," Andy Martinez pointed with the key to a magnificent marble mausoleum just a few feet away from the lake. Above the iron doors a one-word carved inscription.

DOURAS.

We approached and stopped just in front of the gleaming structure.

A. Night In Hollywood Forever

At the base were three grave markers.

George Barnes Van Cleve
1880–1949
Maitland Rice Lederer
1896–1934
Louis Aldon
1908–1947

"Relatives," Martinez said. "The immediate family is inside."

"Right," the celebrity historian added. "Marion Davies bought this mausoleum when her father died in 1935, as a Douras family crypt. She didn't intend to be buried here. She hoped it would be with Hearst after they got married."

"But they never did," I said.

"No, they didn't," Lloyd went on. "And the Hearst family whisked his body away from the house where they lived and buried it back east. They wouldn't even let Marion attend the funeral."

"But Miss Davies did get married," I said. "Didn't she?"

"Yes, after Hearst died she married a fellow named Horace Brown who looked amazingly like a young W. R. Hearst. Both Brown and Marion ended up here at the Douras Mausoleum."

Martinez walked up the five marble steps that were flanked by two large cement planters out of which grew clusters of marigolds.

We followed.

There were huge twin iron doors. A strong chain secured by a Brinks lock was looped between the handles.

"Ready to go inside?" Martinez asked.

"That's what we're here for," I nodded.

Chapter XXVI

Andy Martinez inserted the key and unfastened the Brinks lock. He pulled the chain out of one of the door handles, then opened both of the heavy doors.

He stepped in and indicated for us to follow.

We did.

The inside of the mausoleum looked like nothing I had imagined. But then I had never been inside of a mausoleum before.

I had imagined a kingdom of darkness. But even if the doors had been closed there would have been light within. The light came from the twelve-foot ceiling where there were nine small skylights. One of the skylights was slightly open.

The interior was 15' by 15'. All of white marble except for the floor that was composed of inlaid Italian marble with black and gray squares and triangles.

I expected the place to be cold as an igloo, but it was not at all icy. The three of us, Annette, Andy and I, looked at each other for a moment or two then at the crypts.

Alongside the north wall there were four crypts from the ceiling to the floor, all occupied. At the top, Patricia Van Cleve Lake—daughter of Davies and W. R. Hearst; died October 3, 1993 at 70.

Then Horace G. Brown, Jr.—husband of Marion Davies; died November 9, 1972 at 67.

Josephine Rose Douras—sister of Davies; died June 11, 1935 at 25.

Arthur William Lake—husband of Patricia Van Cleve Lake, son-in-law of Davies; died January 9, 1987 at 77.

Alongside the south wall the top crypt was unoccupied.

Then Rose Douras Adlon—sister of Davies, widow of Louis Adlon; died September 20, 1963 at 60.

Ethel Frances Douras—sister of Davies; died July 18, 1940 at 46.

Reine Douras Lederer—sister of Davies; mother of Maitland R. Lederer; died April 2, 1938 at 45.

And on the east wall the top crypt was unoccupied.

Then Marion Douras Brown aka Marion Davies—died September 22, 1961 at 64.

Rose C. Douras—wife of Bernard, mother of Davies, died January 25, 1918 at 56.

Bernard J. Douras—husband of Rose, father of Davies, died April 26, 1935 at 82.

But there was only one crypt that I was interested in.

And it had two distinguishing characteristics: near each end of Marion Davies' crypt were two crosses.

And in the lower center there was attached to the crypt a white marble container, probably attached by cement.

It was just about the right size.

Six inches high. Five inches across. Five inches deep.

The Tear of Russia Imperial Egg was four inches high and three and a half inches at the base.

"Annette, Andy. Do you know anything about this?"

I ran a forefinger along the top of the marble container.

"No," Annette shook her head.

Andy shrugged.

"Isn't there a record of what might be inside? Or some instructions from the time of interment?"

"Not that I know of," Annette said. "All that took place when Jules Roth ran the cemetery and he purposely didn't keep very detailed records . . ."

"The better to steal by," Martinez added.

"Well, this thing . . ." I tested the marble container. It didn't budge. ". . . seems to be cemented and sealed tight. Permanent."

"You want to tell us what all this is about?" Andy asked.

"Not yet."

"Well, then . . ."

"But maybe it's inside . . ."

"What's inside?"

"A piece of history . . . and valuable. Very valuable."

"That helps," Martinez said.

"Look. How could we get this open?"

"That's up to Tyler. He'll be back this afternoon. Without his okay we can't do anything more."

"Yes, we can," the voice came from the doorway.

From one of the two men standing there. Both their faces covered by stocking masks. Both holding guns fitted with silencers in hands fitted with surgical gloves.

Gunman #1 who made the remark had a slight accent, detectable even though his mouth was muffled.

"You fellows are trespassing," I said.

"Shut up!" Gunman #2 ordered. "Don't need your funny stuff."

His accent was even a little more detectable.

"What do you want, boys?" I asked, as if I didn't know.

"You!" Gunman #1 pointed his gun at me. "Get over against that wall." Then he pointed the gun toward the north side.

I took a couple of steps northward.

"Face the wall."

I did.

Neither of the two men was built like, or sounded like Ski

Mask. These were new players, but they were in the same game with the winning cards pointed right at us.

"All right, the two of you . . ." Gunman #2 said to Martinez and Lloyd. ". . . against the other wall."

They complied.

Both gunmen walked toward Marion Davies' crypt.

I could make out that Gunman #1 was applying pressure to the small marble container, trying to loosen it.

It didn't loosen.

"Step back," Gunman #1 said to Gunman #2.

He stepped back.

Gunman #1 put his weapon alongside Marion's crypt and squeezed the trigger twice.

Two *pop-pops*.

The marble container fell into his waiting palm.

But the container was still sealed. Bullet scarred, but unbroken.

They didn't care. They got what they wanted.

"All right," Gunman #1 said, "you all stay where you are. You're going to be locked up here for a while."

What would John Wayne do? I said to myself. What would Sergeant Stryker do?

Then I did it.

"Gung Ho, Mac!" I hollered and whirled.

"*Semper* . . ." Martinez' left hand sprang, palm out, the hard edge chopped into Gunman #2's Adam's apple. ". . . *fi!*"

His gun went *pop* and a bullet slammed into the iron door.

"Get on the floor," I hollered at Annette.

"Bet your ass!" she said and did.

But before that the .38 Special was in my hand.

Both Gunman #1 and I fired at the same time.

He missed. I didn't. He was hit below the left shoulder.

Gunman #2 had one hand at his throat and was pointing

179

his weapon at me. I leaped at the floor and shot twice. Both shots hit his chest and he collapsed, the gun still in his hand.

Martinez went for the gun and I turned toward Gunman #1, but he had the marble container in his left hand and his gun in the other, heading toward the door.

He fired back without looking and both Martinez and I ducked while he flew down the marble steps and past Tyrone Power's bench.

The son of a bitch was leaking blood but running like his spine was on fire.

"Stay here!" I said to the ex-marine/monk, and followed as fast as I could.

"I'll call security," Annette had a cell phone in her hand.

Gunman #1 turned back, took aim and fired.

The bullet hit a tombstone right in front of me. I dodged behind it and saw where he was headed.

The Jeep, a green Grand Cherokee SUV, was parked along the curb not far from Harry Cohn.

It was pointed west.

Gunman #1 scrambled inside and slid over to the driver's side.

I fired again and glass shattered but he had started the engine.

I ran as fast as the Lucky Strikes would let me and leaped onto the back of the Jeep as it roared away.

Lucky for me the Jeep was fitted with luggage racks. I grabbed hold with one hand, the gun still in the other, and crawled topside while the Jeep picked up more speed.

He knew I was up there and tried to shake me off, swerving the Jeep from left to right and back again.

He almost succeeded.

Almost.

The Jeep almost tipped over but didn't.

A. Night In Hollywood Forever

I crept along the luggage rack toward the front of the Cherokee. The closer to the front I got the madder I got. My Greek blood was boiling with stubborn Greek pride. I wasn't just Alex Night anymore. I was the mighty Macedonian, Alexander the Great, conqueror of Persia, India, Egypt and the world—I was a Spartan at Thermopylae—winner of the marathon—hero at Vardar Valley, WWII. I wasn't gong to let this hooded creep shake me off this Jeep.

At the intersection of Lomonsow Lane and Nelson Eddy Drive he took a sharp right, gunned the motor, and headed north past John Huston toward Adolphe Menjou.

The son of a bitch drove with his right hand and stuck his left out the window and fired back and up at me.

Not close.

He swerved some more. Left, then right again.

This time the Jeep jumped the curb and headed across the Garden of Legends, markers, tombstones and benches, tearing up grass and granite, still going plenty fast with me still on top. It was evident that the bullet in his body was taking effect on the driver and he was losing control. The Jeep did a swan dive off the ground and into the lake.

The last thing I have a clear recollection of is swans scattering and geese honking and the sound of a splash.

I must have hit my head on the roof or the hood or someplace, because the next thing I knew I was underwater and so was most of the Jeep with the gunman still in it.

I surfaced, brushed away a lily pad, took a couple of breaths and dove back down.

I had lost my .38 but I didn't care. By now I was mad enough to choke the bastard to death.

And I wanted to get my hands on that marble container.

The grill and hood of the Jeep were stuck into the bed of the lake with the rear end just above the surface.

The driver's door had sprung open and the gunman was slumped over the wheel.

I grabbed a hold of his stocking mask and pulled it off. Ugly bastard. His head plopped back against the seat, his eyes open. Vacant.

I didn't know if he was still leaking blood.

But he was dead.

It was pretty murky down there but I could make out the marble container next to him.

I reached across, picked it up, bade the former gunman good-bye and swam toward the surface.

Like the Count of Monte Cristo, the world was mine.

Chapter XXVII

Sopping wet, I wobbled out of the lake on monkey legs.

But what cared I? In my grasp, one of the great treasures of the past century.

I didn't know who it was going to end up belonging to, but at that time and place it belonged to me—and with it, my place in history secured.

The events of the next few hours remain hazy due to the punishment my head and body had absorbed, but I recollect that Martinez and Annette were at the lakeshore to help me out. So were a few members of the Hollywood Forever security squad—and also some police officers of the LAPD, Hollywood Division, led by Lieutenant Frank Rodriquez.

And in the next few hours I recall a few other things that transpired, not necessarily in their order of occurrence or importance.

I got a change of wardrobe, most of which had been destined for recumbent clients of the cemetery. The Jeep got towed out of the lake, so did the body of Gunman #1. Gunman #2 was also carried to someplace in the cemetery. Neither cadaver carried any identification.

I had asked Martinez to call Elliot and tell him what happened.

In a short time both E. Elliott Elliot and Charles Oliver Dash arrived . . . and so did the young ladies and gentlemen of the media.

Lieutenant Rodriguez recognized me from the events at the Kodak Theatre involving The Star of Good Hope . . . and so did the young ladies and gentlemen of the media. Of course none of them recognized C.O.D., who had won a Pulitzer Prize . . . a prize none of those young ladies and gentlemen of the media would ever attain.

It was a replay of the Kodak Theatre media blitz with questions and cameras, but Lieutenant Rodriguez cut it short.

"Two unidentified gunmen were killed in a gunfight at the cemetery. Mister Night and security personnel were involved. The motive of the gunmen is unclear. Probably robbery. There will be no other statements from anybody until further investigation is completed. We will proceed without members of the media present. You are all dismissed until that statement is forthcoming."

The young ladies and gentlemen of the media were escorted off the immediate premises by officers of the LAPD.

"It seems," Lieutenant Rodriguez said to me, "whenever you show up in my territory bodies start to pile up. Now what really happened?"

I told him.

Both Annette and Martinez confirmed my account.

"The two of you," Lieutenant Rodriguez motioned toward Andy and me, "took on two goons with guns?"

"The *three* of us," Annette corrected.

"Yeah," I said, "and I'm glad the Marine showed up instead of the monk."

The lieutenant didn't know what the hell I was talking about, but he let it pass.

In the meantime my clothes had been dried in a dryer and I changed back into them. They were all wrinkled, but I felt more comfortable in them than in the duds for the deceased.

And most important, Tyler Cassity showed up. He looked more like a leading man in a soap opera than the bossman of a cemetery.

The cops left and that's when we got down to the business at hand in Cassity's office.

We were gathered around the small scarred marble container on his desk. Cassity, Martinez, Lloyd, Elliot, Dash and I.

For a time Cassity seemed uncertain of just what was the proper thing to do regarding the dingus.

E. Elliott Elliot was his usual logical, persuasive self.

He told Cassity about the lost Hearst-Davies Fabergé Imperial Egg and briefly summed up the events to this point.

"Tyler, my friend. This object—" Elliot pointed with his walking stick to the container on Cassity's desk. "—is in no condition to be replaced in the crypt from whence it came—if that is its ultimate destiny. Correct?"

Cassity nodded.

"What is the harm in opening it and determining its contents before deciding the next step? I will underwrite any costs involved."

Cassity concluded that there was no harm and great potential benefit—and publicity—in proceeding with Elliot's suggestion.

Bossman Cassity called for a workman with proper implements to come and unclose the container.

While we waited we all began to tremble, Charles Oliver Dash a bit more noticeably than the rest of us.

"Is there any booze around here?" he inquired.

"Hold on for just a little longer, Charles," Elliot said. "If The Tear of Russia is in there, I'll buy you a carload of the best Scotch in the world . . . and milk to go with it."

"If it is in there," Dash wiped at his mouth, "I'll quit drinking . . . the hell I will!"

The workman arrived and proceeded with his work. He cleaved open the top of the container, revealing within it another container.

All that was left to do was pull it out.

"Charles?" Elliot inquired.

"I'm too shaky," Dash replied.

"Then I'll do the honors." Elliot placed his walking stick on Cassity's desk, reached in, unwedged the container and lifted it for all of us to see.

"Son of a bitch!" Charles Oliver Dash's fist pounded onto the top of Cassity's desk.

There was an inscription on the side of the smaller vessel.

'Gandhi'

"The ashes of her goddamn dog!" Dash growled.

Chapter XXVIII

The good news was that the cops had retrieved my .38 Police Special.

The bad news was that I'd probably need it again.

Sometime later E. Elliott Elliot, Charles Oliver Dash and I were seated in corner booth twenty-eight at Musso and Frank's after I had stopped by and changed into more suitable attire, attire which still included the .38 Special. While I was home I put in a call to my mother. I didn't want her finding out about the dust up at Hollywood Forever on television or from some neighbor. Unfortunately, or fortunately, she wasn't in, so I left a message that I and everything was okay and I'd talk to her later.

As usual the employees at Musso's—Manuel the maitre d', Manny the bartender and Fernando the waiter—made a fuss over Elliot. We were drinking and dining, except for Dash who was just drinking.

Elliot had ordered sand dabs, and looked askance when I opted for a hamburger. But I partially made up for his disdain by complying with his beverage selection. Tanqueray Gin martini.

"Well," I said, "those two gunsels were real pros. They left nothing behind but their bodies."

Lieutenant Rodriguez had told us that the Jeep was stolen and so was the set of plates they had attached. There were no fingerprints on anything and the serial numbers on their guns had been acidized.

"One thing we know," I said, "with those accents they weren't born in Texas."

"Possibly in Georgia?" Elliot smiled.

"If you mean in the former USSR, you could be right."

"What about our friend in the ski mask?" Dash wondered. "You think they're all part of the same outfit?"

"I don't know," I said. "But it's a cinch they were all hired hands. More brawn than brains . . . like me, or I wouldn't be involved with you two geniuses."

"Some of it might rub off," Elliot noted.

"Before I get rubbed *out?*"

"My friend," Elliot turned serious. "You make a valid point. This thing has become deadly and neither we, nor others, have the right to expose you to further danger. It might be better all around if we drop the matter . . ."

"Maybe you're right, 'my friend,' " I said. "But will the matter drop us? Or will it and they—whoever the hell *they* are—keep coming?"

"Alex," Elliot sipped his martini, "you make another valid point."

"They probably think," I said, "that we know a lot more than we actually do."

"Yes, thanks to me," Dash nodded, "and that damn folder."

"What if," Elliot—I think in jest-suggested, "we issued a statement to the reporters proclaiming our ignorance in the matter and declaring that we are all going off on holiday, say a yearlong safari on the Serengeti?"

"You call these colonials reporters?" Dash said. "They couldn't find their bunghole with a funnel. The reportorial breed is extinct. Hecht, MacArthur, Hovey, Winchell, and out here Jack Mathews, Ted Thackrey, Paul Coates. Everybody's dead and buried."

"Except you," I said.

"I'm just not buried."

"And you're not dead, either," I said. "Not with the story you've got in that folder."

"A story's no good without an ending. Ol' Thackrey, he was a two-fingered typhoon on the typewriter. He would have made up an ending, he often did. But I can't take any chances, not after that John Wayne interview. I've got to be able to back up everything I write. Every paragraph. Every sentence. Every word. Check and double-check . . . hey, I'm running out of milk . . . and Scotch."

Fernando had heard and forthwith replenished Dash's supply of milk . . . and Scotch.

"Gentlemen, pardon the intrusion. I won't be long."

He couldn't be long. He was short.

Serge Goncheroff, all five-feet-five of him materialized at the open end of the table.

"This is no intrusion," I said, "compared to the one earlier today."

"Yes," Goncheroff nodded, "we heard about what happened at the cemetery. Everybody has. How unfortunate . . ."

"Unfortunate for those two comrades."

"Comrades?"

"Yeah. Like you, English wasn't their first language. Sit down Mister Goncheroff. You're probably on an expense account. You can pick up the check."

"No, thank you." He glanced at his wristwatch. "I can't stay. I have an appointment."

"Too bad. Say. Is this a coincidence?"

"I beg your pardon . . ."

"You eat at Musso's all the time or were you tailing us . . . like those two comrades this morning?"

"You are correct, Mister Night. This is not a coincidence. But I assure you I had nothing to do with those two . . ."

"Dead comrades? Then how do you happen to be here?"

"Let's not go into that . . ."

"All right. What do you want to go into?"

"I merely wanted to report that the Imperial Eggs . . ."

"Are the property of your government."

"Correct again, and we are prepared to . . ."

"Make a generous payment for the return of same."

"Yes."

"Mister Goncheroff, you *are* getting repetitious."

"And we will take any measures, legal, of course, for the return . . ."

"You're at a disadvantage, Mister Commissioner . . ."

"I don't understand."

"There's a certain other party—or parties, that don't give a damn about *legal measures.*"

"I see what you mean."

"You've got a hell of a lot better chance with us than with them. So I strongly suggest you don't get in our way. Report that to your government . . . unless you intend to double-cross them and grab the Egg for yourself."

"I have no such intention, I ass . . ."

"Assure us. Okay. We're assured. Now do you mind if I finish this hamburger?"

Goncheroff bowed, did a one-eighty and went on his way.

"Do you believe the little bastard?" Dash watched him leave.

"I, for one," Elliot said, "believe none of the bastards, big or little."

"You said it before, Elliot," I went back to the hamburger, "you're a wise, old party."

"Yes, I am. But what's the next step?"

"I'm not sure. Mister Dash, your first suggestion was the

Douras Mausoleum. That didn't pan out. What's your second suggestion?"

"I don't know. Let me think about it. But I did remember something else."

I looked at Elliot, then back to Dash.

"What's that?"

"Bacon."

"Bacon?"

"Yes," Dash nodded, "James Bacon. Another two-fisted, hard-drinking newspaperman. He's still alive . . . and so is Frank Barron."

"Would they know anything about the Egg?"

"No."

"What then?"

"Nothing. Just happened to remember them. Ought to call Jim and Frank up sometime and have a drink or two together. By the way, ol' Paul Coates, he's buried at the Hollywood Forever Cemetery."

I looked at Elliot again.

This conversation was getting us nowhere.

There was no sense in going to the office. There'd just be a lot of irrelevant messages on the machine and maybe a few reporters on the stairs, plus, of course, the usual tenants with their predictable wisecracks.

At home there were a couple of messages.

The first from Lieutenant Myron Garter.

"Congratulations, boychick, on still being alive. No news on Goldie. I'll talk to you tomorrow . . . if you're still alive."

The second message was from my mother with instructions to call her "right away."

"Hello, Mom."

"Alex, what the hell were you doing in a cemetery?"

My mother seldom cursed.

"Well, Mom . . ."

"Were you looking to buy a plot for your mother? I told you I'm not ready . . ."

"No, Mom, I wasn't . . ."

"Then what? For yourself? It's bad luck to . . ."

"No, that wasn't it, either."

"Then what was *it?*"

"I was doing . . . research."

"That again? What kind of research do you do with a gun and shooting at people?"

"They shot first."

"That's no excuse."

"It isn't?"

"How does it feel to go around shooting people?"

"I don't know. They didn't say."

"Now you're making jokes."

"No, I'm serious and so were they."

"Alex, are you going to tell me what this is all about?"

"I promise I will, Mom, when I see you, but right now I'm a little tired and I'm going to get some sleep."

"Good idea. You didn't get hurt, did you, Alex?"

"No, Mom . . ."

"Not this time, you mean."

"Right, Mom."

"What about next time?"

"There won't be a next time. It's all over." I lied.

"I've heard that song before. Alex, tell me something."

"What, Mom?"

"That cemetery. Is it a nice place?"

I didn't expect that one.

"Yes, Mom. A very nice place."

"Well . . . we'll talk about it sometime . . . but I'm not ready yet, you understand."

"I understand. Good night, Mom."

"Good night, son, and God bless you."

I was pouring another Gordon's Gin on the rocks when I heard the knock on the door. Somehow I could tell it was a feminine knock and I wondered if it was Linda Bundy back with another offer of money or something more interesting, but I picked up the .38 anyhow.

"Who is it?"

"It's Sonja."

Brunette time. Green-eyed, long, lovely legged brunette time. I put the gun in a drawer and opened the door.

Maybe it was the lighting, maybe it was my imagination. She looked like one of those killer tomatoes out of the RKO and Universal *noir* movies in the forties and fifties. A blend of Jane Greer, Ava Gardner and Yvonne DeCarlo. I asked all three of them to come in.

"Just happen to be in the neighborhood?" I inquired.

"No."

"Want a drink?"

"No."

"What do you want? Besides the Egg, I mean."

"I don't want the Egg, Alex . . ."

"Your grandfather does. Same thing."

"Not exactly."

"But he knows you're here."

"I just wanted to tell you something."

"They've invented the telephone."

"The telephone is so . . . impersonal."

"Well, here we are person to person. Go ahead and tell me."

"I wanted to say that my grandfather had nothing to do

with those two . . . men at the cemetery today."

"No?"

"No, Alex. You've got to believe me."

"I do . . . and I don't, but let's say I do."

"Thank you."

"You're welcome. Now what?"

"I don't know what you mean."

"I told your grandfather he had a pretty good horse in the race. Are you here for a trial run?"

"That's a low thing to say. But would it make a difference?"

"Not tonight. Anything else on your mind, or your grandfather's?"

"My grandfather might have done some questionable things in business, but . . ."

"But what?"

"He's not a criminal. He didn't hire those two gunmen today."

"You said that before, but what about that fellow in the ski mask who tried to swipe Dash's folder?"

"I don't know anything about that. There is something I do know."

"Spill it."

"Andre Shenko."

"Ah, yes. Comrade Shenko, late of the KGB."

"There's a rumor that some of the people who work for him in the import-export business as agents and couriers and . . . in other capacities . . ."

"What about them?"

"They were also in the KGB and their tactics are sometimes . . ."

"Like those two gunmen?"

Sonja Vladov shrugged.

"Well, that's nice to know," I said. "And if it's true he's going to have to get a couple of replacements."

For a minute I thought she was going to come close, put her arms around me and kiss me like Linda Bundy did when she came to see me.

But she didn't.

I can't say that I wasn't a little disappointed.

"One more thing, Sonja."

"Yes?"

"Tell your grandfather that if he did hire that fellow in the ski mask, to call him off, because if he doesn't . . . there's going to be another cheap funeral."

This time I went close to her, put my arms around her, and kissed her.

It was good. Too good.

A piece of fruit out of Hell's orchard.

I knew it was time to say good night.

"So long, Sonja."

"Good night, Alex."

So ended that night.

Chapter XXIX

Like cheese chips falling off the moon I saw faces floating downward through the space of my dreams. Female faces. Male faces. Beautiful faces. Ugly faces. Happy faces. Solemn faces. Gracious faces. Greedy faces. Deceitful faces. Dead faces.

Like an MGM montage by Slavko Vorkapich.

Goldie Rose. Frances Vale. Mike Meadows. James Glazer—the Bogus Priest. Myron Garter. E. Elliott Elliot. Morgan Noble. Wes Weston. The Bernstein Brothers. Henry Fenenbock. Judy Kirk. Charles Oliver Dash. Sonja Vladov. Vladimir Vladov. Linda Bundy. Andre Shenko. Serge Goncheroff. Ski Mask. Andy Martinez. Annette Lloyd. Tyler Cassity. The hooded cemetery gunmen—both dead.

The faces of W. R. Hearst and Marion Davies.

Peter Carl Fabergé whose face I never saw. And all those damn Imperial Eggs. Hundreds of millions of dollars' worth of Eggs.

And of course, Euridice Night—my mother.

The Good. The Bad.

The Quick and the Dead.

And Alex Night in between.

I had been slugged, sapped, shot at, bounced around, and nearly drowned.

I knew I was still alive but my body felt like it was dying

196

one piece at a time—until I could feel the sunlight on my face and knew it was past time to get up.

And it was past time for me to go to the YMCA to swim and work out—or maybe too soon, my aching body told me. "Wait another day or two" was the message the muscles and bones sent to the rest of me. I obeyed the message.

I stopped in at Kramer's Tobacco Shop for a few decks of Luckies and little Marsha who still looked like she could play Wendy in *Peter Pan* took up the anticigarette crusade where her mother had left off.

Marsha had read the newspapers and watched the television accounts of what had happened at Hollywood Forever.

"Alex," she said, "I don't know which is going to get you first, cigarettes or bad guys."

"Marsha, I'm cutting down."

"On what? Cigarettes or bad guys?"

"Both, I hope. See you later."

"The later the better if you're going to buy more cigarettes."

I didn't try to come up with a reply.

Morgan Noble was standing by the directory in the hallway reading Elliot's copy of *Variety*. She, too, knew about the Hollywood Forever encounter. She whacked Elliot's *Variety* against her trousered hip.

"Good for you, Night. Wipe out all those bastards!"

"What bastards?"

"The criminal bastards. Save court costs. Today's juries wouldn't convict Hannibal Lector."

Up the stairs I went. Wes Weston was coming down. He held out an imaginary .44 and squeezed the trigger.

"Bang! Bang! Good shootin', Pardner."

Weston smiled and winked.

I nodded and headed up another flight.

On the second floor I noticed that the door to office 205 was open and Henry Fenenbock, Jr. noticed me, and so did his splendorous assistant, Judy Kirk.

"Oh, Alex," Fenenbock called out, "would you come in for just a minute?"

I knew that Henry was a benevolent landlord, but couldn't help wondering if he was about to raise my rent. If he doubled it, I was still going to stay.

"Sure. 'Morning Judy, 'morning Henry."

"Do you know how much you've increased Judy's work-load?" the usually affable Henry Fenenbock, Jr. didn't seem quite so affable . . . until he smiled.

"How's that?" I looked at Judy who sat near the telephone.

"Well," she also smiled, "I used to get one or two calls every day inquiring about renting space in the building. Not anymore . . . on account of you."

"Have I jinxed the joint?"

"Just the opposite," Fenenbock said. "She's flooded with calls from all kinds of people—writers, private eyes, inventors, lawyers, promoters—who want to be in the famous building where that gun-toting private eye–writer has his office."

"Ex–private eye, yet-to-be-writer," I corrected.

"Jack Nicholson didn't cause this much commotion when he rented an office," Judy said.

"Yeah, but he causes more commotion at the Lakers' games," I smiled humbly.

The phone rang . . . and rang.

"Aren't you going to answer it?" I inquired on the third ring.

"The machine will pick it up," Judy said. "I'll call 'em back later."

"I've even had three offers to sell the building. Fantastic offers."

"Are you going to . . ."

"Never. Take care of yourself, Alex."

I nodded and headed up another flight.

Both Bernstein brothers, still dressed for *Twelve O'Clock High*, were coming out of the toilet. I didn't give them a chance to make any opening Ping-Pong remarks.

"How did *The Last to Die* pitch go, fellas?"

"Great!" Brother Bruce.

"Sensational!" Brother Bernie.

"All they want is . . ." Brother Bruce.

". . . a few changes." Brother Bernie.

"Instead of *The Last to Die* . . ." Brother Bruce.

". . . they suggest *The First to Breed*." Brother Bernie.

I kept on going.

E. Elliott Elliot, that elegant, old fox, was peering with eyes of prey, out of his suite, waiting to pounce.

"Good morning, Alex."

"You bet, Elliot."

It was my notion to keep on going.

E.E.E. had a different notion.

"Please come in, Alex. I want to share something with you."

"What kind of something?"

"An idea . . . triggered by something you said."

The old fox knew how to bait, all right."

In I went.

"You know, Alex, I fear for old Charlie Dash . . ."

"Yeah, well, I fear for all of us, 'specially me."

"No, I mean his health. Diabetic, you know . . . and he has a heart condition."

"He ought to quit soaking it in Scotch."

"Yes, I know . . . and so does he, but . . ."

"But what's your idea?"

"Yesterday at Musso's you said that his first suggestion about the Douras Mausoleum didn't work out."

"It didn't."

"Not quite, but I'm going to make a phone call and I want you to listen."

I nodded.

He clicked on the speaker and got Tyler Cassity on the line.

"Tyler, I'm here with Alex Night."

I could almost see Tyler Cassity beaming over the phone.

"Alex, Elliot, our tour business is booming. Everybody wants to see where the shoot-out and car chase took place. People are inquiring about, and buying plots and crypts left and right. Annette is adding a new chapter to the history of Hollywood Forever. Andy Martinez is a celebrity . . ."

Between the Writers and Artists Building and the cemetery—I thought to myself—I ought to be working on commission.

"Congratulations, Tyler," Elliot said. "I wonder if you'd do something for us?"

"Anything that I can."

"We were inside the mausoleum, but not inside the crypt and the casket . . ."

"Just a minute, Elliot. I said 'anything I can.' I'm afraid what you just suggested goes beyond that."

"Think of the publicity if we find that ten-million-dollar Fabergé Egg nestling with Marion Davies. Think hard, Tyler."

A pause.

"Tyler . . ."

"I'm thinking."

"Tyler . . ."

"Elliot, I want to help you and Mister Night, but there's also an ethical matter to consider. The privacy of our clients."

"Tyler, your clients are dead."

"They're still entitled to privacy."

"Tyler . . ."

"No, Elliot, I have to think about this, talk to Andy and our lawyers . . ."

"Tyler, we don't want the whole world to know about this . . ."

"I have another idea," Cassity said, "something I've been investigating anyhow. I'll get back to both of you."

"When?" Elliot asked.

"As soon as I can. And, Mister Night, thanks again."

"Anytime."

Elliot clicked off the speaker.

"Think you laid an egg, Elliot."

"Don't be so sure. Tyler Cassity is a bright, young fellow. He may come up with something."

"What if he doesn't?"

"We'll cross that bridge when we come to it."

"Elliot."

"Yes?"

"How could you cross a bridge *before* you come to it?"

Chapter XXX

I spent the next couple of hours filling my office and lungs with smoke from a pack of Luckies.

I played and ignored all the messages on the machine.

I walked across the hall and stood in front of Goldie's office for I don't know how long, then started back to my polluted palace to call Myron Garter, when the phone rang.

It was Myron Garter.

"Alex, I've got news on Goldie."

"Good news or bad?"

"It could be a lot worse . . ."

"Go ahead."

"They found her car."

"Where?"

"San Bernardino."

"Wrecked?"

"No."

"What then?"

"Abandoned."

"What the hell does that mean?"

"It means she's alive. She was seen . . . with a man. We're having the car checked out for prints and anything else."

"Who saw her?"

"A fellow named Richard Joseph, owns a gas station . . ."

"Did you talk to him?"

"Yes, and I'm going to talk to him some more, that's why I'm calling you."

"Go ahead."

"Mister Joseph has some business in LA today and he's coming to see me and make a statement. I thought you'd want to be here . . ."

"You bet your ass!"

"Then be here. Three o'clock."

"Myron . . ."

"What?"

"About Goldie . . . was she all right? And don't shit me."

"I wouldn't, Alex, not about this. She seemed to be. Got into another car with the man. But they stopped at the gas station first. The rest we'll find out from Mister Joseph when he gets here . . . and from her car. But, pal, like I said, it could be a lot worse . . ."

"Yeah."

"She's *alive*, Alex. That's the most important thing. She's alive. I was afraid . . . well, we can all breathe a lot easier."

"You're right, pal. Thanks."

"Sure."

I did breathe easier . . . and lit another Lucky.

I did some deep inhaling until my lungs didn't want anymore, stubbed the cigarette in an ashtray that was already full of stubbed cigarettes, and went out the door to tell Elliot the news about Goldie.

"That's grand, Alex! Our luck is on an upward arc. I feel it in my bones."

"We haven't found her yet."

"We will . . . and you can praise me later. Isn't it time for lunch?"

"I couldn't eat anything. I'd just throw it up."

"Please, must you be so graphic? I intend to enjoy a hearty meal, I . . . well, I see one of us has company. Guess which one?"

Sonja Vladov stood in the open doorway.

She was a female chameleon. Now she looked like Isabella Rossellini, at least to me she did.

"Alex, may I talk to you?"

"Sure. We've got a lot to catch up on. It's been hours."

"Thank you. Nice to see you, Elliott."

"Yes."

"Let's go to my office."

I led the way and when I opened the door it was like looking through a smoke screen and it smelled bad, too.

"You stay out in the hall. I'll open a window, then we can walk over to the park and do it *al fresco*."

Right across the way from the Writers and Artists Building is a park right out of Green Pastures, fourteen blocks of trees, shrubs, flowers and grass, fronting along Santa Monica Boulevard. Beverly Gardens is a haven for joggers, picnickers, readers, writers and just plain benchers.

We found an empty bench close to one of the fountains.

The sunlight played tricks with her green eyes and her green eyes played tricks with me.

"Alex, about what you said last night . . ."

"I don't remember what I said. I only remember what I did . . . and didn't."

"You could have taken advantage . . ."

"Oh, I'm not so sure . . . you look like a pretty good screamer."

"I wouldn't have screamed."

"Hmmm. What was it that I said?"

"About Grandfather . . ."

"Oh, yeah. The guy who's got enough money to buy anything that's for sale—except the Egg isn't—so he might try to get it some other way . . . like with some hired help."

"That's what I wanted to talk to you about."

"Talk."

"I told you he didn't have anything to do with the two gunmen at the cemetery."

"So you did."

"Then you asked about . . ."

"Ski Mask."

"Yes, and I said I didn't know anything about that."

"And now you do?"

"Yes."

"Go ahead."

"I asked him last night and he admitted that he . . ."

"Had hired Ski Mask?"

"Yes, but only to get the folder, not to harm anyone."

"But it didn't work out that way. Not with Dash and not with me. So now what?"

"Grandfather has promised . . ."

"You? Or me?"

"Both of us, if you don't press charges against . . ."

"Ski Mask and your grandfather . . ."

"You'll never be bothered again and, Ski Mask, as you call him, will vanish. All Grandfather wanted was information as to the whereabouts of . . ."

"The Tear of Russia. Doesn't he want it anymore?"

"Of course he does. It's a symbol to him of a faded way of life, just as it is to Andre Shenko. Only in a different way."

"How?"

"Shenko's way of life was defeated along with communism and the KGB. He wants the Fabergé as a form of personal victory for his side."

"Seems like he's done pretty well on *this* side."

"He has, but . . ."

"Once a comrade, always a comrade."

"At least in his case. He's got everything but a soul."

"And The Tear of Russia."

"Alex, what about my grandfather?"

"Who now wants to play nice."

"He'll take his chances with the Imperial Egg, when and if it's found."

"Do you believe him?"

"Yes, Alex, I do. But the important thing is . . . do you?"

"Well, as I said before, I do . . . and I don't."

"What does that really mean?"

"It means I won't press any charges and neither will Dash. Probably couldn't prove anything anyhow. But tell Mister Vladimir Vladov, his friend Mister Ski Mask better disappear off the face of the earth or he'll end up under it."

"Thank you. I'll tell him, and Alex . . . when all this is over . . ."

"Look, baby, don't tempt me with any low-hanging fruit. I was sorely tempted last night, but it's like this, I already met the girl of my dreams."

"Dreams don't always come true, but you know something, Alex?"

"What?"

"You're a very nice man and I hope things work out the way you want."

"I'll remember that, Sonja, no matter how things work out."

I walked her back to the entrance of the underground garage where her car was parked and started toward the tunnel with her.

"Alex."

"Yeah?"

"Let's say so long here in the sunlight. I don't trust myself with you in the dark."

"Yeah."

I turned and headed toward the Writers and Artists Building.

And much to my surprise—or was it—who do I meet coming out of the Massimo Café but Andre Shenko and his faithful companion, Linda Bundy.

They greeted me with smiles. Shenko's smile reminded me of a scimitar.

"What a startling coincidence," I innocently observed.

"We stopped up to see if you cared to lunch with us," Shenko said, "but you weren't in your office."

"No, I wasn't, was I."

Just then Sonja Vladov drove right past us in her Mercedes convertible, waved and headed west on Santa Monica Boulevard.

"Oh," Shenko still smiled, "did you lunch with Miss Vladov?"

"Right," I nodded. "We do every Thursday."

"How quaint," Miss Bundy remarked.

"Well," Shenko buttoned the middle button on his perfectly tailored single-breasted blue suit. "I've got to stop in at the tobacco shop. I'll leave you two to visit for a bit."

"Swell, by the way, Mister Shenko, how many employees do you have working for you . . . currently?"

Nothing fazed this satin-skinned son of a bitch.

"Oh, I don't keep track of such matters. I believe Linda does. Why do you ask? Are you looking for employment . . . currently?"

"I'll let you know if and when."

"Excellent. We can always use a good man."

"Or woman?" I looked at Linda.

"That depends on the kind of work . . . in the import-export business . . . of course."

"Of course," I said.

Shenko proceeded toward Kramer's.

"You keep track of all of Shenko's business?"

"That's what I'm paid to do."

"Among other things."

"What 'other things' are you talking about?"

"Dirty laundry . . . you wash stocking masks like those two gunsels were wearing at the cemetery?"

"I'm only involved in his import-export business."

"Unless he says otherwise."

"This conversation is becoming unpleasant."

"So were those two gunsels. Where would you draw the line for what he's paying you, Linda? Robbery? Murder? Or something else?"

"I don't have to listen to this."

"No, you don't. There's a price no man will pay . . . or woman. Maybe it hasn't come to that, yet."

"I can take care of myself. I wasn't to the manor born. I had to claw my way up—"

"Congratulations, kid. You're on top of the world, for now. Shenko's world. But I've got the feeling he should've been choked in his cradle."

If we weren't in the middle of the street, she probably would have slapped me and maybe I deserved it. Maybe not.

I saw Shenko coming out of Kramer's.

"You better get a move on, Linda. You don't want to keep your comrade waiting. Maybe we can visit again sometime."

Linda Bundy walked toward Shenko who was still smiling. But then he didn't know our little visit hadn't turned out the way he expected.

When I opened the door to the office the room was still

smoky and smelled stale and the phone was ringing. I intended to let it ring and have the machine pick up the message but then thought it might be Lieutenant Myron Garter with something to do with our three o'clock meeting or some other word about Goldie.

"Hello."

"Mister Night, this is Clara in Mister Meadows' office. He's been trying to reach you for some time, will you please hold?"

Good ol' efficient, persistent Clara.

Mike Meadows was on the phone in less than four seconds.

"Alex, a couple more escapades like The Star of Good Hope and the cemetery and somebody'll make a movie about you, or at least a television series."

"Not you, Mike, that's not your kind of movie. You've got too much class."

It wasn't at all like Meadows to schmooze, but I figured he was feeling expansive what with the profit from The Star of Good Hope and his hit movie *When Winter Comes*.

"Listen, Alex, I know what's going on with you and that booze-soaked reporter . . . with Vladov and all those other Russkies."

"Tell me about it."

"The Fabergé worth millions that once belonged to Hearst and Marion Davies . . ."

"You know more than I do."

"No, I don't, but I've got spies everywhere in this town."

"And out of town."

"That, too. But you and I've always been on the level with each other . . ."

"Yeah, it's a great love story."

"Quit cracking wise. I want to make a preemptive strike . . ."

"You want the Fabergé, too, huh? You in the jewelry business now?"

"I don't give a shit about the Fabergé."

"What then?"

"Look, I've got Frances Vale's next picture all lined up, but what about after that?"

"Mike, I don't know how that mind of yours works. I don't know what the hell you're talking about."

"I'm talking about the movie rights to the story of Marion Davies and that goddamn Fabergé with Frances Vale playing Marion Davies. That's what I'm talking about."

"Jesus Christ!"

" 'Jesus Christ' is right. She'd be sensational as Davies. The part's got everything. Love. Humor. Suspense. Triumph and tragedy. She'll get an Academy Award and not as a supporting actress, as the star. And, Alex, that *is* my kind of picture!"

"I don't believe this."

"Well, I do. I'll pay you fifty thousand dollars up front . . ."

"For what?"

"For the exclusive movie rights . . ."

"Mike, I don't know how this thing is going to turn out."

"It doesn't matter. You've got the inside story, you and that boozer. I'll get a hot writer to do the screenplay. No matter how it turns out there'll be plenty of publicity and a great part for Frances."

"Look, Mike, save your fifty thousand. But I'll give you my word . . ."

"That's good enough for me . . ."

"You haven't heard what I'm going to say."

"Say it."

"I'll do what I can for you and Frances on one condition."

"Name it."

"No publicity. Not a word about the Fabergé."

"Bullshit!"

"Not until Charles Oliver Dash writes his story . . . no matter how it turns out. Then I'll do all I can."

There was silence . . . for less than three seconds.

"That makes sense, Alex. I don't want some other asshole producer jumping in anyhow. You've got a deal. About the money . . ."

"I'll leave that up to you, Mike. Like you said, you and I have always been on the level with each other. Deal?"

"Deal."

Producers always hang up first. Mike Meadows was no exception . . . in that department.

I wasn't carrying my pocket watch because I was still carrying the .38, but I knew it was getting pretty close to three o'clock.

The Beverly Hills Police Department is part of the recently renovated Civic Center complex on Rexford Drive between Santa Monica and Burton Way, just a few blocks from the Writers and Artists Building. I decided to take my time and walk over instead of driving.

As I walked along Santa Monica, I couldn't help thinking what a good friend Myron Garter had been ever since we met at the Police Academy all those years ago, how he had gone out of his way in trying to trace Goldie, and some of the good and not so good times he and I had been through together.

I especially remembered that night at Cedars Emergency. I was with him when he got the call that his wife, his ex-wife, had OD'd . . . her chances didn't look good.

* * * * *

"Alex, I got to tell you something . . ."

"Sure."

"What happened to Rhoda . . . it's my fault . . ."

"Myron . . ."

"No listen. I saw her last night. We had dinner together. I swore I'd never see her again after what she . . . what happened. But when she phoned I never heard her like that before. There was something about her, something . . . desperate. She promised she'd never bother me again if I'd see her just one time. So I said okay, I'd meet her.

"Jesus Christ, Alex, I barely recognized her—my own wife of eighteen years—and I barely recognized her. If I'd have passed her on the street I probably wouldn't have known her. You think I'm fat? She must have put on over a hundred pounds. You remember how slim and beautiful she was.

"I could hardly look at her and she knew it. I could tell she had her hair done and got all made up, but she looked terrible.

"She started crying and told me how sorry she was, said she'd do anything—all that crap about what a good man I was and she didn't deserve me—but she'd do anything if we could get back to-gether—if we could just try.

"All the time she was crying and talking all I could do was think of that day when I found her and that son of a bitch in bed to-gether, my bed, our bed, with him and his naked ass on top of her. How I never killed them both that day I'll never know—killed them and myself—well, I didn't. But something else died.

"She kept on talking and I kept on thinking about that day and how many times it must've happened before, even though she swore it never did.

"But it happened since, 'til he left her, the son of a bitch, for some young dame in the office. She went to hell, Alex, straight to hell after that. You know Rhoda, she never could drink, so she

started eating, I guess. Just like I did only a lot worse. Popping pills. Pills to lose weight. Pills to sleep. Pills! Pills! Pills! Morning, noon and night. She's a wreck. A bloated wreck.

"I sat there and listened to her spill her guts out and I didn't do or say a damn thing to help her. I can't excuse what she did and neither can she. But I wasn't any prize package as a husband either. All those years after we lost the baby, I was hardly ever home. I was a big hero with the department. I was a one-man band. Stick a broom in my ass and I'd clean up the joint. And I was also a real shitheel as a husband.

"The point is, that no matter what happened before, I didn't do or say one word last night that could have helped that woman in there. I just sat there and let her humiliate herself, whip herself to pieces, maybe to death—and I sat there holier than God Almighty and let her do it.

"If I had just given her one word of encouragement, one glimmer of hope . . . but I didn't. I let her fall apart. So here she is in there, maybe dead for all I know. The door opened and a young Korean or Philippine doctor came in from the emergency room.

"Are you the husband, sir?"

"Yes, well . . . I'm Myron Garter . . . we're not . . ."

"You'd better come in."

"How is . . . is she alive?"

"Please follow me, sir."

I waited for Myron Garter to come out of the emergency room. It seemed like hours, but when I looked at my Elgin I realized that it had only been six or seven minutes. Still, it was too long. But then I thought to myself, the longer the better. The doctor wouldn't let him stay in there all that time with a dead woman. I felt better.

So did Myron when he came out. He was almost smiling.

He just stood there for a couple of seconds, then he nodded. I went up to him, pumped his hand and whacked him on the shoulder.

"It was close, Alex. Too damn close. She swallowed every pill ever invented. I guess she's taken so damn many of them she built up a resistance. Would've killed anybody else."

"Maybe she just wanted to live, Myron. Just to see that ugly kisser of yours."

That wasn't the end of our beautiful friendship—not by any stretch—but since Myron and Rhoda got back together I saw less of him—there was a lot less to see. He had lost quite a few stones and so had Rhoda.

Ten minutes after I left my office I approached the Spanish Baroque architecture dominated by the stately tower. The complex houses the Beverly Hills City Hall, Public Library and the new Fire and Police Departments.

The detective cubicles are located on the span that bridges across Rexford connecting the Police Department to City Hall. Garter's cubicle is smack in the center of the span, but Officer Cal Woodward at the reception desk told me that Garter said he'd be in Interview Room B.

So he was and so was an imposing black man, and Chief Dave Snowden was just coming out the door as I started to walk in.

"Hello, Alex," Snowden smiled.

"Hi, Dave. You working on this case, too?"

"No," his smile broadened, "just poked my head in to keep track of things. Go right in."

"Thanks, and Dave, I appreciate all the help of the department."

"That's what cops are for."

He left the room and closed the door.

"Alex," Garter said, "you'll want to meet Mister Richard Joseph. I told him you were a close friend of Miss Rose. He's been very helpful."

Richard Joseph stood up and extended his hand. It was a big hand, strong. He was well over six feet, with an athletic build fitted into a dark green sport coat, white shirt open at the collar, and a pair of unpleated tan trousers. He reminded me of another athlete who became an actor, Woody Strode.

"Pleased to meet you, Mister Joseph."

"Hope I can be of some help," he said.

We both sat at the table near Garter.

"Mister Joseph," Garter said, "would you mind summarizing for Mister Night what you told us earlier in your statement."

"No, of course not."

"Alex, Mister Joseph is the owner of a gas station just off the freeway in San Bernardino. Go ahead, Mister Joseph."

"There's an empty lot across the street from the station. I don't know who owns it but people who work in the area leave their cars there during the day. The owner never complained. But a few days ago I noticed one of the cars was there for a couple of days . . . and nights. A brown PT Cruiser.

"Didn't think much about it until I was opening up at dawn and I saw a man and a woman in a BMW drive up right next to it. They both got out and got into the Cruiser. He was close by her all the time.

"The Cruiser drove over to our air pump. The back tire was awfully low. I had to go over and unlock the pump for him, so I got a pretty good look at both of 'em.

"He was about six feet, sandy-haired and light-complexioned, wearing one of those safari-type jackets. She was on the passenger side with a bandana over her head and kept looking straight ahead.

"I told him I'd be glad to change the tire if he wanted me

to, but he said he'd change it later. He took the hose out of my hand and went to work filling the tire with air.

"He had left the driver's door open so I asked the lady if she wanted some coffee to take along and she said something I didn't understand but he cut in saying they were in a hurry. He was wearing gloves. He took 'em off, put 'em in the jacket pocket and asked me if he owed me money for the air. I said no charge . . ."

"Excuse me, Mister Joseph," I interrupted, "you said she said something you didn't understand."

"That's right."

"Can you remember anything about it? About what she said?"

"Uh . . . something about a bottle . . . a bottle . . . bottle, maybe topper."

"Bottle and stopper!?"

"Yep . . . that could be it. Does it mean anything?"

"It sure does, Mister Joseph. It's cockney rhyming slang from a movie called *Mr. Lucky*. It's a sort of code Goldie and I use. 'Storm and strife' is wife. 'I suppose' is nose, and so on. 'Bottle and stopper' is copper. Police."

"Police?"

"Yeah. Please go on."

"Well, that's about it. He was in a hurry, all right. He got in, slammed the door and drove off."

"In which direction, Mister Joseph?" Garter asked.

"Hard to tell. From where we are, he could have taken any freeway or road in any direction."

"Yes, you did mention that in your statement. You also mentioned something else. Something that may be very important, about the license plate."

"Right. I don't remember all the numbers or letters, but the plate, California, started with the numbers eight and nine. Eighty-nine, that was my jersey number when I played football at USC, eighty-nine. I remember thinking that at the time."

I looked at Garter.

"We're already on it, Alex, but checking out a partial takes some time."

"Yeah, I know."

"And we dusted the car. No prints on the wheel or driver's side, he wasn't that dumb."

"Mister Joseph," I asked, "this might be a dumb question, but could you tell, I mean, well, could you tell if he might've been carrying a gun?"

"Hard to tell, under that safari coat. It was loose fitting. He could have been. In some ways he seemed more . . . nervous than she did. We got that notice from the Beverly Hills Police about the missing car. It matched the Beemer they left in the lot so I called."

"You did just fine, Mister Joseph. Well, I know you have to get back to work," Garter said as he stood up. "We appreciate all your cooperation."

Mister Joseph and I also stood. He reached out his hand. So did I.

"I hope you find your friend," he smiled. "She seemed like a fine lady."

"If you think of anything else," Garter added, "please call." Garter handed him one of his cards.

"I sure will."

After Richard Joseph left, Myron and I stood silent for almost a minute.

"We'll find her, Alex."

I just nodded. I felt weak in the knees and other places.

"I'll call you when we make that partial."

"Thanks, pal."

Chapter XXXI

I don't know whether the walk back to the office cleared my head or cluttered it. But when I got back I sat at the swivel chair, put my elbows on the rolltop and buried my face in both palms.

I don't know how long I stayed that way, but when I looked up I remembered. I could almost see Goldie Rose standing there on that day after we had spent our first night together.

She looked as if she had been racing against nature all day. Her hair was windblown, her face a little red from the sun. She wore no lipstick or eye makeup. She looked like the fire of Spring—and beautiful.

"Alex, put your arms around me. Hold me for just a minute."

I kept my mouth shut and did what I was asked to do. She felt good, very good, and in those few seconds it brought back all of last night. I thought that maybe that's what she wanted. To be re-assured that it happened and that I still felt the same way. I still didn't say anything.

She pulled back just a little. I let go. She walked to the window then turned and looked at me. She was framed against the window and backlit so her face was almost in shadow.

"Alex, right after I got up this morning I went for a ride. I just got back."

"Where did you go?"

"Geographically, up along the coast, up to Santa Barbara. I even stopped at an old Spanish mission. I went inside. There was nobody there. I mean . . . there were no other people.

"For the first time in a long while, I guess since my mother and father died, I knelt and prayed. I didn't pray to be forgiven of my sins. I don't believe in that. I think that God, if there is a God, doesn't listen to that 'I'm sorry' stuff and 'I'll never do it again.' You don't show that you're sorry by mumbling a few words and crossing yourself. If you're sorry you show it in other ways. By what you do, or don't do from then on.

"Don't get me wrong, Alex. I'm not sorry about last night. Not one bit. It was the sweetest, the best, the most wonderful thing that's happened to me since, well since I grew up and lost my childhood faith.

"It's not because of what happened, at least not what happened between us. It's because I'm afraid of what might happen if I let go and let it happen again. I made a mistake with a man once before. He was sweet and gentle and thoughtful. Until we were married.

"I was just starting to be successful and he wasn't. So I guess he had to show me and himself that he could be successful at something else. The first time it happened, I left him. He followed me and told me he was sorry, promised it would never happen again. For some reason I believed him. I wanted to believe him. The next time it was worse. He was drunk, and afterward he left me bleeding and unconscious and went to sleep.

"He kept a gun. When I came to, I got the gun out of the drawer, walked over to the bed, held it an inch from his head and squeezed the trigger.

"But I just didn't squeeze hard enough to pull the trigger. Looking back, maybe I didn't want to squeeze hard enough. At the time I thought I did. But I came that close. And so did he. That close to changing my life and ending his.

"I haven't touched a gun since. Or a man. Until last night.

Alex, I never thought I could put all of that behind me, but I did. You did it for me. And I'll never forget it, and I thank you for it, no matter what happens. And no matter what happens we'll have last night. But I'm still a little afraid to let go.

"*In spite of last night I don't know that much about you. What I do know, what I have seen, I like very much. Very much. But I also know there's been a lot of violence in your life. I can't take any more violence. I can't have it turned toward me. I don't know what I'd do if that ever happened again.*

"*Alex, can you understand that?*"

I understood. And I understood the tears that she was trying to hold back and couldn't. I walked close to her and put both of my hands on her face as gently as I knew how. And then I kissed her as gently as I knew how.

"*Before I'd hurt you, Briny Marlin, I'd . . . I don't know what I'd do.*"

But there was someone who had hurt her. Someone who was capable of hurting her again . . . and worse.

I should have thought of it, of him before, but I had tried to shut him out of my mind and succeeded . . . until now.

I got Garter on the phone and told him about Goldie's ex-husband.

"What's his name?" Garter asked.

"I don't know. She never told me and I never asked her. But there's got to be a marriage record somewhere or something you can trace."

"Probably."

"Forget probably. Do it, this guy's beat the hell out of her. There's no telling what he'll do . . ."

"Alex . . ."

"Don't tell me she can take care of herself, not against some son of a bitch like this . . ."

"Okay, Alex, okay. We'll get right on it. Does Goldie have any relatives?"

"No. Mother and father are dead. No other family. Myron . . ."

"I said we'd get on it. I already put out an APB on the Cruiser. He can run Alex, but he can't hide, not for long."

"Thanks."

What Garter said was some consolation . . . but not enough. If this son of a bitch meant to hurt Goldie, how long might it take? He could've done his dirty work right in her condo . . . but anything short of killing her and he knew she'd report him to the police. And he must have had a gun otherwise she never would have gone with him.

I wished that I had asked her more about him that day when she told me about him. But I didn't want to know. I didn't want to know anything except that she and I were together and I wanted us to stay that way.

But we didn't.

I got up and walked to the window.

God, I was mad. I felt like smashing my fist through the window, through anything, but mostly through him.

There was a knock at the door. I turned and Elliot walked in.

"Alex, I talked to Tyler again. He's working on something for us, but I'd like to take a look at that folder, there might . . ."

"Elliot, shut up!"

I might just as well have poleaxed him. In a way, I did.

His lips quivered and so did the rest of him.

I opened the briefcase, pulled out the folder and whacked it into his chest. He managed to take hold of it in the hand that wasn't carrying his walking stick.

"You can take the folder and the Fabergé and shove 'em. I

don't give a shit about them or about you right now. I just want you to get the hell out of here and leave me alone. You understand that?!"

He didn't say anything.

He couldn't.

He just turned and walked out, with the folder in one hand and the walking stick in the other, through the open door, and left it open.

I have to admit that I was quivering a little bit, too.

I had to take it all out on somebody and poor Elliot walked in at the wrong time.

That damn Greek temper. I should've tempered it. No, I should have squashed it instead of squashing Elliot, a man who had been a friend when I needed one. A man who some thought to be caustic and cynical, but a man who I knew to be sensitive, vulnerable, and unselfish.

Now I felt like smashing my stupid head through the window.

Instead I walked out the door, through the hallway and into Elliot's suite without knocking.

He was sitting at his desk with both hands covering his face.

"Elliot . . ."

He looked up and there were tears in his eyes.

"Elliot, there was a crazy man in that room just a minute ago. He's not crazy anymore. Please forgive me."

He still couldn't say anything, so I did.

"Goldie's been taken by her ex-husband who used to beat the living hell out of her . . ."

"Oh, Alex . . ."

"They were spotted in San Bernardino. Garter's got an APB out, but, well . . . I'm sorry, Elliot, I didn't mean to flare up like that . . . 'specially at you . . ."

He took the handkerchief from his breast pocket, wiped the tears away from his eyes and smiled through his quivering lips . . . but it was a different kind of quiver.

"I should have known it was something like that," he said. "I'm the one who ought to apologize, bursting in as I did, I . . ."

"Elliot . . ."

I stuck my mitt out and we shook hands. The first time we had ever done that. His hand was a lot firmer than it looked.

"You're right, Alex. To hell with the Fabergé. To hell with everything until we know that she's safe."

I nodded, turned and walked out.

I drove over to Saint Sophia's, lit a candle and drove home.

Chapter XXXII

I hadn't eaten all day. After leaving Saint Sophia's I should have stopped by C & K, the Greek delicatessen across the street from the church, and picked up some dolmas, olives, cheese and other stuff from Chris Papacristos to bring home but I just didn't think about it at the time. I did drop over to the Larchmont Deli and had Emile fix a Mediterranean sandwich to take with me.

I built a tall gin and tonic, unwrapped the sandwich and brought the phone over to the kitchen table to listen to messages. I drank and ate and didn't intend to call back on any of them until I came to one from my mother to "call me right away."

I took another bite of the Mediterranean and a deep swallow from the tall glass and dialed her number.

"Hello."

"Hi, Mom."

"Never mind the olive oil, I knew something was wrong. I could tell the last few times we talked. What is it that you can't even tell your own mother? Alex, are you there?"

"I'm here."

"So?"

"Mom, what makes you think anything's wrong?"

"You can't fool me. I know you think that I'm getting old and my mind's not sharp like it used to be, and my face is all wrinkled and . . ."

"Mom, that's not true. I know your mind's sharper than it ever was and you're not at all wrinkled, you're beautiful . . . you're as beautiful as Gene Tierney ever was . . ."

"What? Wasn't he the fighter who beat Dempsy?"

"No, Mom, that was Tunney, Gene Tunney. Gene Tierney was a movie star . . ."

"Don't change the subject. Tell me what's wrong. Are you sick?"

"No, Mom."

"What then? I know it's something."

"How do you know?"

"I can tell by your voice lately . . . and besides Gloria Moulopolous called and told me she saw you at Saint Sophia's, so now tell me what it is."

I was licked.

"It's just that Goldie's been away for a few days and I . . ."

"You miss her. Is that it?"

"Yeah, Mom. That's it."

"Well, I knew it was something like that. Alex, I'll give you some advice."

"Go ahead."

"Get married. You'll either be very happy . . . or it will make a philosopher out of you."

"Good advice, Mom. I'll get right on it as soon as she gets back. Good night."

"Good night, son."

I finished the Mediterranean and poured more gin into the tall glass, but no tonic. I did that a couple of times then went to bed.

I've always been an early riser but that morning I rose even earlier because the phone rang.

"Alex. This is Myron."

Garter calling this time of morning, I thought it must be bad news.

But it wasn't.

"NCIC came through. We ID'd the son of a bitch, Alex. You want the details or the bottom line?"

"Skip the details."

"They were married in 1999. Goldie Rose and Thomas J. Farrell. Divorced 2001. Tom Farrell was released from Atascadero two weeks ago . . ."

"Atascadero . . ."

"Yep. Mucho mental problems, but here's the bottom line. He still owns property, land and a cabin near Big Bear."

"You got an address?"

"Got a pencil?"

"Go."

"77200 Tiger Tail Road. It's pretty isolated. We're getting a search warrant and . . ."

"You do that Myron, but I'm not waiting . . ."

"Alex, goddammit . . ."

I hung up.

If you've ever driven east on the 10 when the sun is rising you know that it's rising right into your eyes.

And that's just what it was doing for about seventy-five miles while I drove toward San Bernardino.

I had the top up, the visors down, the sunglasses on and my .38 in its holster. During those seventy-five miles, mile after mile, I broke law after law. Speeding. Passing. Tailgating. Changing lanes and everything in the book. The cops must have been looking the other way.

Most of the traffic was moving west into LA, but there was enough moving east to keep me cursing and trying not to think of Goldie with that nutcase just out of Atascadero.

Atascadero.

A. Night In Hollywood Forever

Halfway between San Francisco and Los Angeles. In my former occupation as a private eye I had occasion to come across a few other graduates from ASH—Atascadero State Hospital, whose purpose was to design and provide treatment for mentally ill and disordered forensic patients. To provide professional evaluations and recommendations to the courts and other agencies and to maintain security and control of patients in a safe, therapeutic and supportive environment. To provide an environment for success. Sometimes the program works and other times it doesn't. That's why they call it recidivism. If I got hold of Thomas J. Farrell the odds were he wouldn't be going back.

But I tried not to think about that.

I thought about all those people in all those cars, station wagons, SUVs, pickups, and vans, driving to work every day in a tangle of traffic, some of them for an hour or more . . . listening to the same morning shows, going to the same job, with the same routine . . . every day, five days a week, the same dull, dreary workaday drudgery . . . then driving back through the same knotted traffic every night.

The poor, musty bastards.

How I envied them that morning.

Whatever they had on their minds, it wasn't as heavy as what was on my mind.

But I tried not to think about that.

I thought about what a horse's ass I was. First I'd flared up at Elliot, then this morning when Myron Garter called—I don't know how long he'd been working on it, maybe through the night with the NCIC—I didn't even thank him or wait for whatever else he had to say. The NCIC is the National Crime Information Center, a computerized index of criminal justice information; criminal record history information regarding fugitives, stolen properties, missing persons, convicts and ex-convicts, and is operational twenty-four hours, three-hun-dred-sixty-five days a year.

I just hung up, got dressed and bolted out the door. I didn't even shave. I just packed the .38 and tore off.

For all I knew Lieutenant Garter was on his way to Big Bear, but he'd have a hell of a time beating me there.

The truth is I didn't want him with me, not him or any other policemen, because then we'd have to do it their way. The legal way.

But I wanted to do it my way, without any warrants or writs or waiting around for court orders while something could happen to Goldie Rose.

When I got to San Bernardino, I swung north, grabbed the 15 and started the crooked climb. Not until then did it occur to me that I hadn't lit a Lucky.

I wasn't going to light one now. My lungs would have to settle for the fresh mountain air coming in through the low-ered window on my left.

I had been to Big Bear more than once. A few times to fish and relax with and without companions—male and female—and once on location to shoot a couple of scenes for a Robert Mitchum movie called *The Old Dick*. Mitch was playing a re-tired private detective and I had been hired by the producer, who was a client of mine, to act as technical advisor.

Robert Mitchum needed a technical advisor on how to play a private dick like Custer needed more Indians. But the producer owed me money and this way he could charge off my fee to the budget.

Needless to say, I never presumed to give Mitchum any pointers on how to play a private eye, but we got to be pals on that picture and stayed pals 'til he bought the farm.

Countless other movies and TV shows have been shot at and around Big Bear—from the early silents to Cinema-

scope—from B Westerns to scenes in *Gone with the Wind*—
with actors like Roy Rogers in *Trail of Robin Hood* to Fred
MacMurray in *Trail of the Lonesome Pine*. Some of the biggest
stars, including John Wayne, Kirk Douglas, Ginger Rogers,
Ray Milland, Eddie Murphy, Lee Marvin, Elvis Presley, Ann
Sheridan, Dick Powell and hundreds more, had filmed scenes,
chases—horse and car—made love—on and off screen—and
knocked off bad guys amid the rugged landscape.

But there was only one bad guy that I was interested in—
and if I ever got my hands on him there wouldn't be any "take
two's"—and my gun wasn't loaded with blanks.

In less than half an hour I was at Big Bear Village and
spotted the sign at 630 Bartlett Road—BIG BEAR LAKE
VISITORS CENTER.

I parked in front and walked to the entrance. The door was
locked and on the glass a lettered sign. Hours—
Monday–Friday 8 a.m.–5 p.m. Saturdays, Sunday and Holidays 9 a.m.–5 p.m.

But they were very accommodating, because next to the
door was a wooden container with a sign. MAPS—TAKE
ONE.

I did.

I unfolded it and finally found Tiger Tail Road. Back in
the Sebring with the map on my lap, I was on my way.

It took another twenty minutes and I didn't break any laws
because I was searching for signs while I drove.

Tiger Tail Road, according to the map, was to the left off
Crescent Drive. Crescent Drive wasn't hard to find. Two
twisting miles later I spotted the marker for Tiger Tail Road
and turned left.

It was isolated all right. After another mile or so I saw the
post with the mailbox on top. No name, but an address.
77200 Tiger Tail Rd.

The post with the box was just off the road at the side of a flimsy chain-link fence and double gate. The gate had a chain through it with a lock holding it together.

On the other side of the gate there was a dirt road through a pine-studded field with a cabin about two hundred yards away. At the side of the cabin a brown PT Cruiser was parked.

I pulled off the road near the gate and shut off the motor.

For the first time since Garter called that morning I had to think about what I was going to do next.

Chapter XXXIII

I lit a Lucky.

It was time to think. But not for long. I didn't know what was happening inside. Or what had already happened.

In only as long as it took to inhale the first drag, let it settle into my lungs, then leak out, I conjured up images of that dirty bastard—I didn't even know what his face looked like—with Goldie during all those hours since he had taken her. What he had done to her and what motivated that debased mind of his.

But I didn't want to think about that. I had to think about what I had to do in the next few seconds.

I sure as hell wasn't going to wait for Garter and the police. That was out. My combat/cop training kicked in in less than a heartbeat. The options:

A) Climb the fence—make my way to the cabin—take a chance of being seen—if he spotted me I knew he had a gun, a hostage and a car—I'd be on foot and hesitate to shoot for fear of hitting Goldie—if he drove off with her I'd have to get back to the car—he'd have a hell of a start.

B) Bust the lock or chain—if I shot it off he'd hear the gunfire—I had a tire tool in the trunk—neither the lock nor chain looked very strong—get the gate open, drive through and smash into the front of the cabin—I knew that Goldie would do whatever she could to help—if she was able.

I decided on Option B or some variation thereof. Try to take him by surprise and if he spotted me and got into his car with Goldie I'd be right on his heels.

The tire tool turned the trick on the lock. I opened the gate, got into the Sebring, took off the sunglasses, and drove through on the dirt road toward the cabin, picking up speed.

But it was too late. He was already on his way to the Cruiser with Goldie and a gun. He fired twice. The second shot hit the windshield of the Sebring on the passenger side and I instinctively veered to the left and ducked.

By then the Cruiser was on the dirt road and heading toward the gate. I made a one-eighty, almost ripped the bottom out of the Sebring on some rocks but started after him.

The Cruiser raced through the gate, knocked part of it off its hinges, turned right on Crescent leaving a wake of blinding dirt and dust that I blasted into and through until the windshield cleared and I could see the Cruiser again widening the distance between us.

But not for long.

I slammed my foot onto the accelerator and the distance diminished.

By now there were a few other cars on the road but neither he nor I let that slow us down. He swerved and passed a pickup and trailer and so did I.

He charged through an intersection with a stop sign and so did I.

The road twisted and he twisted with it. Ditto.

On the way up I had barely been aware of the climb with all the bends and sharp turns but it was different gunning down at sixty, seventy miles an hour. It was different chasing a madman who drove like he didn't care whether he lived or died. I didn't care whether he did either. But I cared about my beautiful Goldie next to him. No matter what she'd been through she was still alive and I wanted her to stay that way.

I had to keep him in sight but there wasn't much else I could do. It was too risky to try to force him off the road and even if I wanted to try there were razor sharp edges on the mountainside and steep craggy drops on the other side.

And then I saw them. Two cars approaching uphill. One a sheriff's black and white. The other an unmarked BHPD Chevy sedan.

The sheriff's car passed both the Cruiser and me and so did Myron Garter in the Chevy.

They each did a one-eighty on the narrow road and came back after the both of us.

If the driver of the Cruiser had any sense at all he'd've known that the jig was up. He'd've pulled over and faced the music, the cops, and the consequences. But he was an alumnus of Atascadero and it was obvious that he had no such notion.

I don't know what he said to Goldie at that moment but I was close enough to see her make a move. She lunged at the wheel and spun it.

The Cruiser jerked to the right, scrapped along the chiseled mountainside, skidded to the left and scudded off the cliff, plunging down along the jagged slope ripping at the Cruiser until it smashed into an overhang and caught fire.

I swerved to the left, hit a post and my head crashed into the windshield. I wiped at the blood dripping into my eyes, opened the door, staggered and slid down through the brush and rocks.

The Cruiser seemed infinitely far away and as I made my way toward it, it appeared to retreat into the distance at the same rate I approached. I almost gave up, but somehow I reached the Cruiser and managed to pull open the passenger door. Through the smoke I could see both of them slumped and twisted, his head battered into the broken wheel, her body embedded into the dashboard. I grabbed Goldie. Her face was bruised and bloody and so was the rest of her.

I got her out of the car and dragged her away as far as I could before the Cruiser exploded.

The last thing I remembered was Myron Garter coming toward me and the sound of a helicopter. It occurred to me that I never saw the son of a bitch's face . . . then I passed out.

Chapter XXXIV

What happened after that comes back to me through a hazy vinculum only parts of which I remember—because I was going in and out of consciousness—and the other parts were told to me later by dear ol' Myron Garter.

The sheriff had called in the rescue helicopter. I half remember being lifted aboard along with Goldie as paramedics worked on her.

We were taken to the emergency hospital at Big Bear, her condition was stabilized, and they gave me something to make me even dopier while they stitched up my skull.

I woke up at Orthopedic Hospital in Los Angeles. Garter had called ahead, not about me, about Goldie. He knew Dr. James V. Luck who had operated on hundreds of injured policemen and countless civilians, from indigent patients of the inner city to movie stars from Beverly Hills. Years ago his father, Vernon Luck, had pioneered hip replacement and severe bone damage procedures and now James V. was regarded as one of the best orthopedic surgeons in the city or anywhere.

Dr. Luck had asked Garter about Goldie's next of kin. Myron told him to talk to me.

I was still laid up and woozy and only understood part of what he said, ". . . displaced comminuted fracture of the femoral head and neck ball of her left hip joint . . . open fracture of tibia and fibula on the right side necessitating external fixator pins and external clamp to hold bones in position . . .

bladder laceration . . . high risk of infection . . . even if the operation is successful, results indeterminable . . . possible loss of ability to walk . . . slow healing at best . . ." He said some other things that I don't remember.

Dr. Luck spoke calmly, professionally, but not dispassionately. He looked like a kinder, gentler Donald Rumsfeld and there was a quiet strength in his voice and bearing. He reminded me of a field doctor in combat.

No hesitation on my part. I looked at Garter then back at Dr. Luck.

"Thank you, doctor. I know you'll do everything you can."

He nodded, smiled, and left the room.

Garter started to say something, but a nurse came in and gave me a couple of pills and a cup of water to wash them down. I saw her motion to him. Garter nodded.

He moved closer, made a fist with his right hand and in slow motion arced a punch to the left side of my chin.

"Go to sleep," he said.

I did.

The operation lasted over nine hours. So I was told.

When Garter came back he brought me a change of wardrobe. He had taken my keys and gone to my place. He told me the Sebring had been towed to LaBrea Chrysler-Jeep to be repaired. I felt that I had been repaired as much as I needed to be. I got dressed and we went to the waiting area.

Dr. Luck came over and said Goldie had been moved to Intensive Care. She was conscious, barely, and the sight of a familiar face might be reassuring.

On the way I asked him if the operation was successful.

"She survived, Mister Night. As for the rest, we'll have to wait and see."

That was good enough for me . . . for now.

She was hooked up to all sorts of contraptions, IVs and monitors.

But her eyes were open. I wanted to touch her but I was afraid to. I did lean over and whisper.

"Briny Marlin."

She closed her eyes for just a second or two, maybe remembering, then opened them and smiled.

Her face was discolored, swollen and bandaged but it was the most beautiful smile I'd ever seen.

I put my hand into her open palm. Her fingers moved, ever so slightly at first, then tightened for just a beat. It probably took all the effort she could muster, but she did it.

The look in Dr. Luck's eyes told me it was time to go. I drew my hand away.

"See you later," I said to her.

Still smiling, Goldie Rose closed her eyes and slept.

Outside in the hallway Dr. Luck said her reaction was a good sign.

"Doctor, I want to stay with her as much as possible."

"Not a good idea," he said. "She needs rest and time to get back her strength. Check in as often as you like, Mister Night, but give her a chance to recover some of that strength. Let her get out of Intensive Care first."

"He's going to do exactly what you said," Garter nodded at the doctor, then at me. "Come on, boychick, we go now."

I'll say one good thing about Lieutenant Myron Garter—actually starting years ago at the Police Academy, then together at LAPD, then me as a private eye, and him switching to BHPD, and now me switching to mystery writing at the Writers and Artists Building, even though I hadn't written anything yet—through shoot-outs, fistfights, car chases and assorted mayhem—through all those adventitious adventures—I could say many good things about Lieutenant Myron Garter, but one of the things I appreciated most was that on certain occasions, such as on the drive away from Orthopedic Hospital, he kept his mouth shut.

He just smoked his El Producto and didn't mention how dumb I was and what a stupid stunt I pulled by tearing up to Big Bear and busting in without back-up.

But I knew what he was thinking and I couldn't blame him, besides, maybe he was thinking that he'd do the same thing if Rhoda were in the same spot.

I was amazed at the change in him since he and Rhoda were back together—actually the change in both of them. While she wasn't exactly svelte, she had gone on a diet and to a gym and could be considered *zoftig,* instead of fat. He quit noshing all day long and dropped over forty pounds, his clothes no longer looked like dirty laundry bags, and fit him reasonably well. He even smelled better. Must have switched aftershave lotion.

I looked over at him and smiled.

"Thanks."

"What for?" Garter asked *dégagé.*

"For sticking out your neck for me . . ."

"It wasn't for you."

"Okay."

He drove on, got off the freeway at Crenshaw, turned left on Wilshire and pulled up in front of my condo.

"Myron."

"What?"

"Who ever you stuck your neck out for . . . thank you. You gonna get in any trouble?"

"Who, me?"

"Okay."

"Will you get the hell outta here? I got a cold beer and a warm woman waiting for me."

I started to get out.

"Oh, by the way," he said.

"Yeah."

"Here are your keys."

By the time I got inside, unpacked the .38, and changed most of my clothes, I realized that I was not fully repaired. My head ached, and other parts—arms, legs, ribs and joints—made known their protests.

I whacked down a Gordon's on the rocks, poured out another one and punched in my mother's number to answer the message she had left on the machine.

"Hello, Mom."

"Hello, Alex. Did you have a nice day?"

Where to start?

"Well, yeah, Mom, but . . ."

"But what? Why are you hesitating?"

"I . . . just took a drink."

"Of what?"

"Milk."

"Oh, a glass of milk before you go to bed. That's good. Makes you sleep better. So what happened?"

"Well, remember I told you that Goldie had gone away . . . for a few days?"

"Of course I remember. Is she back?"

"Well, yes, but . . ."

"*But,* again. Is she all right?"

"She had an accident . . ."

"A car accident?"

"Yes . . . and she's in the hospital . . ."

"Which hospital? I'll go see her tomorrow."

"No, Mom. She had an operation and the doctor says no visitors for a while."

"That sounds serious, Alex."

"Pretty serious, Mom."

"I'll go to Saint Sophia's and light a candle tomorrow."

"Yeah, that'll be good, Mom."

I thought that telling her about one accident was enough for one phone call so I didn't mention anything about the Sebring and me.

"Alex, let me know how Goldie's doing and when I can go see her."

"I will, Mom."

"Have another glass of milk and go to bed, son."

"I will. Good night, Mom."

I poured out another portion of Gordon's milk and sipped. I looked at the .38 on the table. At least I didn't shoot anybody today. God, I was tired. I could have stayed in that chair for the next week. But I didn't.

I got up and walked to the bedroom, drink in one hand, gun in the other. And I thought about what Dr. Luck had said, ". . . even if the operation is successful, results indeterminable . . . possible loss of ability to walk . . . slow healing at best . . ." it wasn't right, it wasn't fair, it wasn't just. All because of that son of a bitch who burned in that car and may he burn forever in hell.

I put the gun on the bed stand, swallowed what was left of the gin and got into bed.

Before I fell asleep it occurred to me that for the first time in a long time I hadn't even thought about the Fabergé Imperial Egg.

Chapter XXXV

The way I felt and looked the next morning I sure as the turning of the earth wasn't going to go to the YMCA—besides I didn't have wheels. I decided to do something about that. Being without a car in LA is like The Lone Ranger without Silver.

I called a cab and got dropped off at LaBrea Chrysler-Jeep where I intended to get a loaner until the Sebring was repaired.

"How long before it'll be ready?" I asked Maurice Claff from whom I had in the past decade bought a couple of Sebrings and before that a couple of LaBarons.

"On the twelfth of never," Claff grinned.

"What the hell does that mean?"

"It means," Claff grinned broader, "totaled."

"It doesn't look so bad," I evaluated.

"Neither do you, but how do you feel inside?"

"Lousy."

"So's the Sebring. Radiator wrecked, engine block cracked, frame all bent, et cetera, et cetera, et cetera. The insurance company totaled it. But look on the sunny side . . ."

"I'm looking . . . and listening."

"Alex, sign it over to us and I'll put you into another one I've got on the lot just like it, only blue instead of gray—if you'll just write out a small check."

"How small?"

"Say . . . ten grand."

"Say . . . seven."

"Say . . . nine five."

"Where is it?"

"Right there. I had it all picked out for you."

Claff pointed to a sparkling blue convertible with a bluer top parked right outside the showroom.

I was licked and I knew it . . . but not quite.

"How soon can I get it?"

"You can drive it off the lot as soon as you sign the papers . . . and the check."

"I'll sign the papers . . . and the check . . . for nine thousand."

"Deal! Done and done!" Claff said. "And here's your handicap certificate. I took it off what was left of your windshield."

Fifteen minutes later I was driving a sparkling blue Sebring with top down toward Beverly Hills.

I looked at it this way; the balance in my bank account was piling up anyhow, and I wasn't used to significant solvency.

The reception at the Writers and Artists Building was gratifying.

Lieutenant Myron Garter had phoned E. Elliott Elliot with the news about Goldie Rose and within minutes ol' News Bee E.E.E. had spread the word to Henry Fenenbock and all the tenants.

The ensemble greeted me with congratulations on the rescue and with concern about Goldie's condition. I gave them as optimistic a report as I could summon and assured them all I'd keep them posted.

I noticed several men with clipboards wandering about the halls and offices making notes and discussing anchors, bolting and sheer walls. I asked Henry what all that was about. He said they were from the Beverly Hills Planning and Engineering Department to determine whether the three-story building would have to be upgraded to comply with the newly enacted earthquake requirements which might require a considerable monetary outlay on his part and probably a slight raise in rents. Just one of the imperatives in living on the shifting landscape of the left coast. Beats the hell out of floods, hurricanes, cyclones, typhoons and tornadoes—or does it? Yes, it does.

Besides, I had other things on my mind. Just one other thing.

I called Dr. Luck's office, spoke with his assistant, Martha Munoz, then with Dr. Luck. Goldie's condition was satisfactory, seemed to be making some progress, but still sedated and still no visitors. Two of the men from City Hall with clipboards came in and wondered if I would mind if they checked the walls and windows for their report.

No, I wouldn't mind. I told them I was going out for some fresh air and cigarettes . . . "Just close the door when you're finished."

When I went out into the hall two detectives that I knew from BHPD, Bernie Kowalski and Mike Caffey, were removing the crime scene tape from Goldie's door. They had been sent over by Garter.

"How's she doing?" Kowalski asked.

"Going to be okay," I tried to smile.

"Good," Caffey said. "Tell her . . . well, you know what to tell her."

"Sure I do, and thanks, fellas."

I wondered if she'd ever be able to make it up those stairs and knock out another novel in eleven days. I wondered a lot of things.

At Kramer's, Jim and Marsha Keller (*née* Kramer), like just about everybody in our neighborhood, had heard about

243

Goldie and Big Bear. Goldie didn't smoke but she'd stop by and buy mints. They both wanted me to give Goldie their regards and asked which hospital she was at so they could send flowers.

"Orthopedic Hospital," I said, "and I'll take a carton of Luckies."

"Keep smoking these things and we'll be sending you flowers," Marsha remarked.

Just what I needed, a pep talk. I plunked down forty-five dollars for the cigarettes and went about my business, even though at that point I didn't know exactly what my business was.

When I got back to the office the clipboard boys had left and closed the door. I went inside and lit up. Two Luckies later I heard the knock.

"Come in."

E. Elliott Elliot came in with his walking stick and with his face as somber as I've ever seen it.

"Elliot, what's wrong?"

"Plenty. I don't know where to start . . . I guess with Charles."

"What about him?"

"He's in the hospital. Good Samaritan."

"Ski Mask again?"

"No. Heart attack."

"Bad?"

"Well, I've never heard of a good heart attack, but not fatal. As a matter of fact I've just talked to him. Yesterday morning he felt severe pains, called 9-1-1. They took him to Good Sam. A Doctor Fay Lee performed an angiogram then angioplasty, opened up three arteries . . . stents . . . you know the procedure."

"Sort of . . . go ahead."

"I'm going to go down to see him but there's more . . . I don't know if you want to hear it . . . It's about the Fabergé . . . maybe . . ."

"Elliot, you're talking in code . . . what about the Fabergé?"

"First of all, Dash's folder that I got from you . . . it's gone."

"What do you mean 'gone'?"

"I thought I might have left it at home . . . called Carstairs . . . it's not there . . . and not in the office . . . and, Alex, I had a call from Tyler Cassity . . . do you want to hear about it or not?"

"Keep talking."

"He and a fellow who works for him, a fellow named Homer Alba who's been there since the time Jules Roth hired him years ago, have been going over Roth's records and papers . . . all they could dig up."

"And?"

"And you know this Roth was a slippery fellow, pulled a lot of shenanigans and bilked the place out of millions. They uncovered a file designated 'Hold for Roth,' and in that file, a notation of the sale of two crypts in one of the corridors—crypts that were never used."

"So?"

"The initials on Roth's records were W.R.H. and M.D. . . . the crypts are still sealed and still empty. The date of purchase was 1948, three years before Hearst died and when Marion Davies still thought Hearst would marry her and they would . . ."

"Be buried together?"

"It's possible. Davies could have been there when they were sealed and . . ."

"Put something inside."

Elliot shrugged.

"The corridor was damaged during one of the earthquakes and deemed unsafe. It has been recently renovated along with the rest of the cemetery."

"Jesus Christ."

"Amen. You know that Hearst's family whisked his body away while Davies was still sleeping. Wouldn't even allow her to attend the funeral."

"Why wasn't she buried in the crypt?"

"She probably thought she was going to be but her family wanted her with them and Roth certainly wasn't going to say anything. He pocketed the money and was probably going to sell it again—then the earthquake hit."

"So now what?"

"Tyler doesn't want to do anything in broad daylight with a lot of people around, but he's going to unseal the crypts tonight at midnight."

"Midnight?"

"That's what he said. He also said that you and I—and only you and I—could be there to witness the unsealing and whatever is—or is not, inside. Not even Martinez or Lloyd will be there. So, Alex, will you?"

"Will I what?"

"Be there? I seem to recall your saying that I could take the folder and the Fabergé and shove 'em . . ."

"Elliot, do you also recall that I was a little upset at the time . . . about Goldie . . . and that I came in and apologized?"

"Oh, yes," the suave bastard smiled, knowing he had me hooked. "I do seem to remember something to that effect."

"I'll be there."

"Grand."

"Appropriate."

"What is?"

"Right out of an old RKO movie, you know that RKO used to be right behind the cemetery."

"Know it? Hell, yes, I wrote several pictures there."

"You didn't write *The Body Snatcher* did you? Or *Isle of the Dead*?"

"Neither."

"Well, that's the kind of pictures they made—what could be more appropriate than a cemetery at midnight."

"Indeed. And I must admit that the image of a cemetery at midnight scares the liver out of me, but right now I'm going to visit Dash and tell him about it. Do you want to come along there, too?"

"Indeed."

I wanted to drive my new Sebring to Good Samaritan, but Elliot insisted that Carstairs chauffeur us in the Bentley.

We compromised.

We went in the Bentley but Elliot agreed that on our midnight ride to the cemetery that night I would drive and he would come along in the Sebring—with the proviso that I keep the top up.

Good Samaritan has the reputation of being one of the best hospitals in the state with a state-of-the-art heart care facility. But there's something unhealthy about the smell of any hospital. Undertakers use flowers to cover up the odor of death. Hospitals use antiseptics to cover up the odor of sickness. But somehow the true effect comes through in both places.

And it seemed that lately I had been spending too much time in both places.

Dr. Fay Lee, who had performed the angioplasty on Dash, was in the room with him. She was a small, handsome woman with tiny, but obviously capable, hands that had probably saved C.O.D.'s life.

Dash, who looked pale and fragile, introduced her to us as his guardian angel.

"Unless your friend changes his way of living," Dr. Lee said, "he's going to meet some different kinds of angels. He's got to stay on his medication and off the booze. You can stay for a few minutes, but don't get him too excited. He can go home in a couple of days. Nice meeting both of you."

She was small, but oh, my.

"You didn't happen to bring any Scotch with you?" Dash inquired after Dr. Lee left. "Did you?"

"No, nor strychnine," Elliot replied, "which would probably have the same effect."

"I'd die happier with the Scotch. And speaking of happy," he pointed to a vase of flowers on a bed stand, "see them flowers?"

"I see them," Elliot said.

"So do I," I said.

"At first I thought they might be from one of you."

"Not me," said Elliot.

"Nor me," said I.

"I know that. They're from an admirer who happens to be the editor of *The Sunday Chronicle*. Listen to this." He took a small card off the bed stand and read.

" 'Dear C.O.D., Get well and start typing. You write it—and I'll print it. Signed, Jim Addison.' " He set the card back on the table. "So all right, fill me in. What's the latest on the outside?"

"We're not supposed to get you excited, remember?"

"My friends, the sight of a naked, enchanted Lorelei would not excite me, howsomever any good news regarding our endeavor would have a most salutary effect," he managed to tap his chest a couple of times, "on the old pump. Lay it on me."

We laid it on him, but with a little editing. We didn't mention the missing folder—we had a back-up anyhow. But we did tell him about the "Hold for Roth" file, the W.R.H.-M.D. crypts and our forthcoming midnight expedition to Hollywood Forever.

"Boys, we may have hit the legendary jackpot. It's not unlikely that Marion would want to be interred forever with W.R.'s gift to her. Ah, just the sight of the fabled Fabergé inside that precious presentation box and I'd die happy—after I wrote the story . . ."

"You're in no condition to write a postcard." Dr. Fay Lee was back and her Asian eyes weren't smiling. "And I think it's time you two made an exit."

"Yes, m'am," we two said and started toward the door.

"Keep me abreast," Dash smiled. "Good-bye and good hunting."

On the way down in the elevator Elliot suggested that we stop in at the Pacific Dining Car across the street, have a drink, a bite to eat, and mull things over. Since the Pacific Dining Car has excellent, expensive food and since I knew Elliot would pick up the check, I saw no reason to refute his suggestion.

The Pacific Dining Car was established in 1921 and originally was just that—a dining car—a counter and stools, a small short-order kitchen and little else. It has changed through the years—the roaring twenties, the depression thirties, the warring forties, and the next half century, and today it sprawls over a quarter of a square block with plush, red-leather booths, private dining rooms and two or three noble bars, along with an extensive and pricey menu—so pricey that mostly those on an expense account or filthy rich patrons like

E. Elliott Elliot can afford to dine there . . . and, of course, their guests, like A. Night.

Elliot ordered a New York Steak—$45. Lowlife Night ordered a hamburger steak—$25.00. The meat was preceded by a martini for each, Tanqueray Gin for Elliot. Gordon's for Night. Price unknown. I didn't look at that part of the menu. The service was splendid. The beverages and food superb. Elliot was in his glory. While the last couple of decades had been financially rewarding due to his real estate investments, he had become more and more the dilettante, due to the fact that no one would employ him in a literary capacity, so no matter how much he strove to conceal his disappointment, there was an air of uselessness about him which he tried to make up for by way of cynical witticisms.

But lately—ever since his involvement in the Fabergé affair—it was evident that his outlook had changed for the better. Even if he wasn't a writer, he was a player in a game that was challenging and even dangerous. For a change he was doing *something*.

"Alex, whom among the usual suspects do you suspect the most?"

"Of what? They all want the Egg. Vladov and his granddaughter. Shenko and his hatchet lady, Linda . . ."

"And don't forget the diminutive Mr. Goncheroff. Whom, for instance, do you suspect of purloining the folder?"

"I don't know. You can add Mike Meadows to the list. Did I tell you he wants to buy the motion picture rights to Dash's story—when and if there's a story—to star Frances Vale as Marion Davies?"

"I'll be hanged."

"There's somebody else who might have wanted that folder, somebody we haven't met."

"Who? Pray tell."

"The flower sender, himself. Jim Addison. Maybe he wants to write the story himself, or have somebody besides Dash do it . . . somebody more *au currant.*"

"My, my. You are a suspicious critter."

"Just covering all the bases . . . like any self-respecting ex-private eye. By the way Sonja admitted that Vladov hired Ski Mask, but swears he had nothing to do with the business at the Douras Mausoleum."

"I don't believe anything that any of those people swears to."

"You echo my sentiments precisely. We don't know who knew what—or when. But one thing we do know."

"What's that?"

"Nobody among them knows that tonight at midnight you and I have a *rendezvous*—at the Isle of the Dead."

Chapter XXXVI

I still had a couple of hours to kill before midnight.

Elliot via Carstairs and the Bentley had dropped me off at the Writers and Artists Building after we left the Pacific Dining Car.

It's strange how much a part of me the building had become. Partly—maybe mostly—because this is where I met Goldie, where it started between her and me.

And there were the other people I met there—from Henry Fenenbock and Judy Kirk to all the tendentious tenants—Wes Weston, Morgan Noble, the Bernstein brothers, E. Elliott Elliot and all the rest.

At first Elliot had seemed the most standoffish, aloof and distant, but lately my opinion of him had changed—maybe he had, too. It reminded me of some lettering I once saw in a large glass box on the lawn in front of a church. *"I do not like that man. I must get to know him better."*

The people in this building had almost gotten to be a second family and the place a second home.

There was something warm about the cold, old, creaking structure, an architectural anomaly among the newer, more elegant buildings in Beverly Hills. I thought about the stories that must have been written here. Poems, plays, novels, movies and television pilots and episodes. Comedy and drama. Heartbreak and triumph. Hope and despair. This old building had spawned thousands of stories from hundreds of writers.

Some of the writers were ghosts now. But that's the glorious thing about putting something on paper. Even when you're gone it's still there. Your words and thoughts. What you liked and didn't like. The characters you create never die. They live and speak and love and hate forever. The written word is eternal.

This building and the people in it, with its curious cross section of the writing world had contributed memorably to the fine art of writing—everybody but me.

Still, I felt that I was a part of it, just a small part now, but someday . . . the damn phone rang and without thinking, I picked it up instead of listening to the message machine.

It was Frances Vale.

"Hello, Alex."

"Hello, yourself. Are you back in town?"

"Nope. Chicago . . . I think."

"You think? Franny, are you okay?"

"Sure I am. Just kidding. Everything's great. Alex, Mike called and told me that you rescued Goldie. How's she doing?"

That Meadows did have spies everywhere and knew every damn thing. I hadn't told him about Goldie and Big Bear and all the rest, but obviously he knew, and had told Frances Vale. I wondered what else he knew.

"She's doing all right, Franny."

"Mike said she was in the hospital."

"Yeah."

"Give her my best."

"Sure."

"And, Alex, Mike told me about the Marion Davies picture. I think it's a great idea."

"You do, huh?"

"A hell of a part. It's got everything. Love. Humor. Tragedy . . ."

I could just hear Meadows making the pitch, selling it to her.

". . . of course, I don't want to play her too old, at least not in the first half. We've got to see her in her prime—young, vivacious, full of life, conquering Broadway and William Randolph Hearst and then Hollywood—the silents and talkies—with all those great characters that were involved in her life—Valentino, Gable, Cary Grant. Alex, who do you see as Hearst? Well, Mike'll find somebody, maybe an unknown. Do you think I'm too tall? I mean to play Davies. She was pretty short. Well, we'll just have to get taller people for the other parts, but not too tall. I don't want to look like a midget. The important thing is the love story—a love that could never be . . . be . . ."

"Sanctified."

"Yeah, that's it. Sanctified. And Mike told me about that part where she sells her jewels to save Hearst's empire, but not that Fabergé jewel she treasures most because it meant so much to both of them . . . and when he dies and she's alone with just . . ."

"Franny . . ."

"Yes, Alex."

"I know the story. You don't have to tell it to me long distance over the phone."

"But you are going to sell him the rights, aren't you, Alex? You'd be doing it for me, too, you know."

"Yes, I know, Franny. I don't own the rights, but . . ."

"Mike said you did."

"Not exactly. A newspaperman and I are working on it—but whatever we come up with, Mike'll get first crack at it—and so will you."

"Great, Alex. I know it's going to happen. I can feel it. I'm already preparing for the part . . ."

I remembered when Frances Vale's idea of preparing for a part was to spend two hours in front of a make-up mirror and now she was going to out-Stanislav Stanislavski while thinking up an Academy Award acceptance speech.

A year ago she couldn't get a walk-on in a television series—and tonight, as Sid Skolsky used to sign off in his syndicated column—"but don't get me wrong, I love Hollywood."

And Hollywood loved Frances Vale—at least for now.

"Franny, it's getting pretty late back there in Chicago—past midnight."

"So? I don't have an early call in the morning . . ."

"But *I* do."

"What're you talking about?"

"I'll explain it all when I see you. Get some beauty sleep, Beauty."

"Okay, Alex, but say it once more. I love to hear you say it."

"Fairest of the Rare. Rarest of the Fair, good night." I hung up.

I didn't tell her that the location of my early call was the Hollywood Forever Cemetery and that the leading lady was Marion Davies.

Chapter XXXVII

There's something about a cemetery at night that's eerie—and around midnight it's downright spooky. The newer cemeteries that only have markers flat against the ground aren't so bad. They look almost like a golf course at night; open and innocent.

But the old-timers like Hollywood Forever are planted with tombstones, statues, crypts and mausoleums with all sorts of places to hide. Where anybody or anything can jump out at you and say "boo"—or worse.

So it was that night when Elliot and I found ourselves within the domain of the dead.

I had picked him up from his Beverly Hills bungalow about a half an hour earlier and listened to him complain all the way into Hollywood about the discomfort of my sparkling blue Sebring. Everything was too low, the seats, the ceiling, the hood—everything—"a veritable sardine can."

I believe that this was the first time I ever saw him wearing anything but a suit or tuxedo. He was garbed in dark trousers and black turtleneck sweater like "Cary Grant in *To Catch a Thief*" so he said. But Elliot looked nothing like Cary Grant. He had a chest like an ironing board. But then neither of us looked like Cary Grant. Nobody did.

I had driven east along Melrose and turned north on Gower along what used to be RKO Studios and was now a part of Paramount.

A. Night In Hollywood Forever

About halfway up the block Paramount ended and Hollywood Forever began. The ten-foot-high wall at the cemetery was topped with barbed wire.

"Is that to keep people out, or to keep spirits in?" Elliot remarked.

I just shrugged.

"Or don't you believe in the spirit realm?" He didn't give me a chance to answer. "Well, I certainly do and I intend to return, barbed wire or no, and haunt certain sites, the Writers and Artists Building for one. And when I do, be respectful of my shade, or else."

"Or else what?"

"You'll find out, my fustian fellow—what the devil are you doing?"

"I'm making a right turn."

"This infernal machine feels like it's going to tip over, not at all like . . ."

"That battle cruiser Carstairs drives."

"Correct."

"We're almost there, Elliot, hang on."

"I'm hanging."

We drove east a few hundred yards along a seedy mall containing a dozen small auto repair, muffler, and transmission shops, all dark, all closed, past a large lawn with a wall sans barbed wire, to the gated entrance.

I made another right turn and drove to the gate that had been opened and where a security guard stood as sentinel. He was obviously expecting us because he waved us in.

I parked the Sebring in the nearby handicap zone while the guard closed the gate and locked it.

"Mister Elliot and Mister Night, right?"

"Right," I responded.

"I'm Ricardo. Mister Cassity's expecting you."

"Where is Tyler?" Elliot inquired.

"At the crypt. Corridor B."

"Alone?"

"Well, yes, I guess you could say that."

Flashlight in hand, Ricardo led us past the flower shop and then the chapel.

" '*Even he who is pure of heart,*' " Elliot whispered, " '*and says his prayers by night, may turn into a wolf when the wolfbane blooms . . .*' "

" '. . . *and the autumn moon is bright,*' " I finished the quotation from *The Wolfman.* "But there isn't much of a moon," I added, "and it isn't autumn."

"Then we have nothing to fear."

I think Elliot was smiling—and whistling in the dark.

Inwardly, I was doing a little whistling myself. It was one thing to quote Curt Siodmak's movie quatrain about the curse of the werewolf, it was quite another to be actually walking along this path with countless graves, monuments and mausoleums on all sides. Life's inevitability is death, and the paths of glory lead but to the grave. But I was hoping that this path would lead to something else—a key that would unlock one of the great, unsolved mysteries of the twentieth century—the fate of The Tear of Russia.

We had been walking in somber silence for too long. I felt the need to say something to break through the gloom.

"Ricardo . . ."

"Yes, Mister Night."

"Say, what's your last name?"

"Riley."

"Riley? Ricardo Riley?"

"That's it."

"Ricardo, are you armed?"

"No. We're not permitted to carry."

"What happens if something goes wrong?"

"We call the police." He pulled out a cell phone from a pocket.

"Well, just so you know, I am."

"You are what?"

"Armed." I pulled out the .38 from its holster.

"Hey, you're the one who had that run-in at the Douras Mausoleum, aren't you?"

"I am."

I put the .38 back into its holster and he replaced his cell phone.

"Congratulations," he said.

"On what?"

"Surviving."

We came to a solid iron gate which had been opened.

"This is Corridor A," Ricardo said. "We go through here."

We did.

It was a long marble structure, with a long marble pathway bordered on both sides by hundreds of marble crypts, most all of them with brass plates and names and dates, all too dark to read.

After about fifty yards we came to a colonnade beneath a skylight which didn't provide much light from the crescent moon somewhere above.

And there on a marble bench sat Tyler Cassity like Rodin's "The Thinker" waiting patiently and thinking about I don't know what.

There was a work light on a stand in the center of the colonnade which didn't provide much light to work by—but enough.

"Hello, Elliott." Cassity stood. "And Mister Night. Good to see you again."

"Thanks, Tyler," Elliot said. "We appreciate this."

"Right. Well, let's get to it."

There were seven alcoves in the Corridor B colonnade—family crypts.

Tyler picked up a strange looking gizmo from the bench. It was metallic, triangular, with three suction cups about four inches in diameter, each cup with a clamp on top, all attached to a handle.

He walked to the center alcove and we followed. He stopped in front of two marble crypts lined against the wall, unmarked, no nameplate, no designation of any kind—at least, that I could see. But he saw something even in the dark and checked with a small card out of his shirt pocket.

"3030—W.H.R.," Tyler said. "3031—M.D. The lower one was for Davies. At least we think it was. Shall we find out if anything's in it?"

"By all means," Elliot said.

"No." Cassity held up the gizmo. "By this means."

He pushed the gizmo with the suction cups flat against the front of the marble and pressed down each of the clamps. With his hand on the handle he moved the gismo slightly to the right, then to the left and—*violà!* The whole marble cover was dislodged.

"Ricardo, give me a hand here."

Ricardo took hold of one end, Tyler took hold of the other. Together they lowered the marble slab to the floor.

The open crypt was maybe seven feet across and four feet high. Couldn't tell how deep. It was dark, very dark.

"Give me your flashlight, Ricardo."

Tyler took the flashlight and pointed the beam inside the crypt.

"See anything?" Elliot asked.

"Nope. Not yet. Not a damn . . . hold on! Hold on! There is something. Deep in the corner . . ."

"What is it, Tyler?! For heaven's sake! What the hell is it?!"

"I don't know. Just a minute and we'll all find out."

Cassity reached in with his other hand.

"I can't quite get to . . ." He pushed his shoulder farther into the crypt. ". . . I got it! I got it!"

"Got what!?" Elliot nearly screeched.

"A pouch . . . pretty heavy. Here, somebody take the flashlight."

I took it . . . and Tyler took the pouch out of the crypt.

I beamed the light onto the pouch. It was leather and had drawstrings on the top.

"Loosen the damn thing!" Elliot commanded.

"I am. I am."

He did . . . and lifted out the presentation box just as Charles Oliver Dash had described it in his folder.

The box was just over five inches high and just under four inches deep—made of gold translucent enameling over a sunburst quilloché design set with diamonds and centered with the Romanov double-headed eagle, crowned with a diamond monogram of Nicholas II. The sides of the box were basket weave.

"Open it, Tyler!" Elliot gulped. "Open it before I faint dead away!"

"Here goes." He unlatched the box and opened it.

There it was against the blue velvet lining.

The Tear of Russia, glimmering in the beam of the flashlight. The last and most precious of Peter Carl Fabergé's Imperial Eggs.

Cassity put the pouch and presentation box back into the crypt, held The Tear of Russia closer to the light and turned it slowly while we all savored the moment.

"Well, there it is," I finally said, "all in one handful.

Nothing else quite like it in the whole wide world. Worth over ten million dollars."

"Thank you very much," the voice came out of the darkness. "I'll take that off your hands, gentlemen."

It was a nice voice, if you like gravel.

Chapter XXXVIII

"Freeze" is the oft-used exclamation by cops in movies, television—and in real life.

Gravel Voice didn't say freeze, but we were all frozen. Elliot, Cassity, Ricardo, and me.

Even if I were able to pull out my gun I wouldn't have known what the hell to shoot at, because at first it was just a voice in the darkness.

But then they stepped out of the darkness. Three of them. All dressed in black, including the stocking masks, gloves, and their guns. Big men. Gravel Voice was the biggest. High-shouldered and deep-chested.

One of them had a knapsack on his back.

"Hand it over," Gravel Voice said.

Cassity handed it over.

The one without the knapsack patted us down and took away my .38. He cracked open the cylinder and let the slugs spatter on the marble floor, then placed the gun on the bench. He then confiscated Cassity's cell phone and Ricardo's, and dropped them on the bench.

"All right, all of you, back to back," Gravel Voice ordered.

Elliot and I, then Cassity and Ricardo obeyed.

The one with the knapsack slung it off his back, removed a web-like something from out of it and flung it over all four of us.

"On the floor," Gravel Voice pointed his gun.

Again we obeyed while Knapsack pulled the web around us tight –and there we were—fish in a net on the cold deck of the crypt. He tied the cord into a square knot and let us squirm like floundering mackerel.

"It shouldn't take you too long to get out, gentlemen," Gravel Voice said. "But long enough. *Bonsoir.*"

In less than five minutes we had discovered a treasure worth more than ten million dollars, lost it, and wound up tangled together in a chunk that had broken loose from hell, while Gravel Voice and his two Dark Angels made off into the nether world.

Either they had come in too late to know about the presentation box—or didn't care. They got what they came for, but how did they know what we were up to?

At that time, lying facedown on the floor with Elliot on my back, I didn't know—or didn't care. The four of us were close enough to eat grapes off the same stem.

All I wanted to do was get Elliot off my back, get out of the damn net, and get after Gravel Voice and his sidekicks.

It would do no good to holler for help. Help was too far away unless we could wake the dead.

The net was a close weave so we couldn't get our hands through to try to untie the knot, but we could get our fingers through.

I had a plan. I didn't think much of it, but it was worth a try.

"Fellas," I said, "let's see if we can roll over to the bench."

"What the devil for?" Elliot asked.

"For one of those cell phones."

It was a scene out of *The Three Stooges*—only we were four stooges—and it wasn't funny. We rolled and twisted and tumbled, but finally got to the bench while punishing the hell out of each other, until Cassity managed to poke his fingers through the net, take hold of the tiny instrument, flip it open and bring it up to his face while practically strangling the rest of us. Evidently he was able to punch in three numbers because we heard him say—

"Hello, 9-1-1."

Lieutenant Frank Rodriquez of the LAPD, Hollywood Division, was not amused when sometime later in Cassity's office I said to him—

"Lieutenant, you know, the more I look at you, the more you remind me of that actor who played the detective in *Chinatown*, what was his name . . . Perry . . . Perry . . ."

"Lopez."

"Yeah, that's right, Perry Lopez."

"Perry Lopez happens to be my uncle."

"No kidding? How is he?"

"He's fine, but never mind that, let's get back to what happened."

"Sure, Lieutenant, but how come you're here? You're with Homicide, aren't you?"

"That's right and there's been a homicide . . . two homicides."

I looked around at Elliot, Cassity and Ricardo. As far as I knew none of us remembered killing anybody or being killed.

"Two homicides?" I said. "Who? Where?"

"A couple of dead men on the Hollywood Forever lawn by the Santa Monica wall."

"Dressed in black? With stocking masks?" I speculated.

"And blood leaking out of their brains."

"God almighty!" Elliot exclaimed.

"Yeah." Rodriquez looked at me. "And like I said the last time, every time you show up around here the bodies pile up like cordwood . . . freshly dead bodies."

"Don't look at me, Lieutenant, I was tied up at the time with three witnesses who are right here in this room."

"I know that. I didn't say you killed them . . . this time."

But Elliot, Cassity, Ricardo and I knew who did. Gravel Voice had no intention of sharing the spoils with the two Dark Angels.

"Evidently," Rodriquez went on, "they used hooks and rope ladders to get over the wall, wrapped the four of you up, took whatever they took . . . back over the wall, then one of them ventilated the other two and went on his way."

"A brilliant deduction," Elliot said. "Worthy of Poirot."

"Never mind that. Tell me again what they took and . . ." Rodriquez pointed at the presentation box and pouch on Cassity's desk. ". . . and what they left behind."

We told him again, as cogently as we could.

He was just as incredulous as the first time around.

"Ten million dollars!" Rodriquez repeated.

"Maybe more," I said.

"And how much you figure that thing is worth?" He pointed again at the presentation box.

"Maybe a half million," I said. "Maybe more, maybe less. But the Egg is what they were after. At least the leader was. The other two might not even've known what he was after. Just hired help."

"Yeah," Rodriquez nodded. "And they got paid off in lead."

"Lieutenant," Elliot took a step toward the presentation box. "What are you going to do with this?"

"I don't know yet. It's evidence. I'm going to hold it as such until it can be verified, then talk to my superiors."

"Sir," I said as respectfully as I could. "Is there any reason why the part about this box has to be released to the media?"

"No, there isn't, and I don't intend to release anything except the fact that two dead bodies were found in the vicinity of Santa Monica and Gower shortly after midnight, that's all, until we can identify them and sort things out."

"Excellent!" Elliot proclaimed.

"Glad you approve, Mister . . ."

"Elliot. E. Elliott Elliot."

"Right. Now, Mister Cassity, you are a respected citizen of this community. If you care to stay that way, I suggest that you inform my department of any investigative activity on your part before you proceed with such, and we'll be glad to cooperate, before you . . ."

"I understand, Lieutenant, and I promise that you'll be the first to know."

"Swell."

"Lieutenant."

"Yes, Mister Night."

"Are we free to go now?"

"Yes, Mister Night . . . and I wish you'd go far, far away from my territory."

"Come on, Elliot. I'll drive you home."

"The hell you will."

"What?"

"I'll be damned if I'll ride in that peripatetic sardine can of yours. I intend to call Carstairs. Tyler, may I use your phone?"

I drove home alone . . . in my peripatetic sardine can.

Chapter XXXIX

The next morning while I was eating breakfast I answered the knock on the door.

Linda Bundy stood there dressed in a tailored suit and oversized dark glasses.

"You'll want to listen to what I have to say," she said.

"Come in and say it."

She came in and I closed the door.

"Want some coffee?"

"No."

"You want to take off the glasses? The sun's not too bright in here."

"Just sit down and listen."

I sat and she sat across the table. It seemed to me that it took some effort on her part.

At first I thought she might be drunk, or suffering from a monumental hangover—or maybe she had shot herself up with some kind of dope. Whatever it was, she wasn't the same Linda Bundy that came up to see me that first night when Shenko had sent her with an envelope stuffed with $12,500—when she looked like a dream walking and had offered to stay the night and make that dream come true.

No, this was a different Linda Bundy, not some high-priced "Executive Assistant," or taunting temptress who knew her way around. There was something about her that morning that made me feel sorry for her.

"You in trouble?" I asked.

"Not anymore."

"Good. Then what can I do for you?"

"It's what I'm going to do for you, though I'm not exactly sure it's a favor, but I'm going to do it anyhow, before I leave . . . if you want to hear it."

"Whatever it is, I want to hear it."

"I know what happened last night and who's involved. He goes by the name of Sebastian . . . some of the time."

"Who does?"

"The one who took the Fabergé from you at the cemetery."

"You mean Gravel Voice?"

"There isn't always gravel in his voice, sometimes it's caramel—and sometimes with an accent—German, French, or . . ."

"Russian?"

"That's his native language, but he has several passports and speaks a half dozen other languages, and he's very good at disguises, and . . . other things."

"About the cemetery, how did he know . . . ?"

"He knows everything. Your office is bugged. So is Elliott's. Those men from the Planning Commission, they're *not* from the Planning Commission. They work for Sebastian."

"And who does Sebastian work for?"

"For himself, but he was hired by . . ."

"Your boss?"

"That's right, Andre Shenko, my *ex-boss*, but he doesn't know that yet."

"And who the hell is this Sebastian?"

"A serpent. Years ago he was one of Shenko's operatives in the organization."

"The KGB?"

She nodded.

"But since then he's operated out of Switzerland . . . smuggling . . . assassination . . . gunrunning . . . narcotics . . ."

"I get the picture."

"After you killed Shenko's hoods at the cemetery he got in touch with Sebastian. Two hundred thousand dollars just to come here. Another million when he delivered the Fabergé to Shenko."

"Cheap."

"He was going to get more later and besides Sebastian thought it would be easy."

"It was. He just came in and took it . . . then killed his two pals."

"That's Sebastian. He's . . ."

"Yeah, a serpent."

"With no compunctions or conscience."

"You seem to know him pretty well."

"I do."

"Go back a long way, do you?"

"I only met him recently, once. Once was enough."

"He made quite an impression. What happened?"

"I'm the one who delivered the two hundred thousand to him."

"For Shenko—like you did to me."

"No. Not like I did to you."

"Look, Linda, I don't want to appear skeptical or anything, but why did you come here this time? And why are you telling me this?"

She removed the dark glasses and set them on the table.

Her left eye was swollen and discolored. Her right eye was shut, black and blue and puffed. From that eye she had to be blind as a bean.

I swallowed hard. I couldn't help it.

She put the glasses back on.

"Not just that. You don't want to see me naked."

I thought I was going to vomit.

"You can't imag—"

I could, but I didn't want to.

"He has all sorts of . . . tricks."

"Okay. But didn't he know you'd tell Shenko?"

"He didn't care. He wanted me to."

"He *wanted* you to?"

"Why not? Just to prove that he could do it—to me and to him. He and Shenko are the same perverse breed . . ."

"Did you tell him?"

"I showed him . . . 'My dear Linda,' he said. 'If I have to choose between you and the Fabergé, it's an easy choice, no contest—your wounds, your pride, will heal—I'll just send you away for a time—and you're welcome to come back.' Well, I am going away. But I'll never come back. Not to him. I've managed to save enough to get by . . . to more than get by."

I bet she had. She was some piece of work.

"You still haven't told me why you came to see me."

"You want the Fabergé, don't you?"

I nodded.

"Well, I don't want them to have it. Either one of them. If you hurry, maybe you can get it . . . and them, but as I said, I don't know if I'm doing you a favor by telling you."

"Let me worry about that. Go ahead and tell me."

She did.

She walked to the door and turned back.

"Remember you said, 'there's a price no man will pay—or woman.' You were right. You're a good man, Mister Night."

"And you're a good girl, Linda—in spots. Trouble is, you wound up with people who were a little too much like you."

"I'll be back."

"Sure you will."

Chapter XL

Neither one trusted the other. Not Shenko and not Sebastian.

They had to meet at a place that was public, but not too public. A place where they could hide in plain sight. Not exactly hide, but do business without either one of them pulling a fast one. One million dollars in cash for The Tear of Russia Imperial Egg—and an additional sum to be deposited later in a Swiss bank account.

That's part of what Linda Bundy had told me.

I was heading toward the other parts. But first I had called Lieutenant Myron Garter. It was Sunday so I knew he wouldn't be at the office. I called him at home. Rhoda answered.

"I'm sorry, Alex, but Myron went to Home Depot. He ought to be back in about a half hour. Can I give him a message?"

"Yeah, tell him I'm on my way to the Empyrean Waste Disposal Plant in LaMadrina and I need help as soon as he can get there."

"Alex, are you . . ."

"Rhoda, I can't explain over the phone. Tell him it's about the Fabergé. He'll understand . . ."

" 'Waste Disposal Plant . . . LaMadrina . . . Fabergé. I'll tell him . . ."

I drove west on the I-10, then merged onto the I-405.

Yeah—I knew I shouldn't be pulling a Charlie Bronson and going after them alone. I should wait for Garter and the proper authorities—like I should have done at Big Bear. But up there Goldie's life was at stake and time was of the essence. This time nobody's life was at stake, except maybe mine—but still time was of the essence. I had to catch both of them, Sebastian and Shenko, in the act—with the money and the Fabergé on them. Otherwise Sebastian would disappear and I'd have no proof that Shenko had possession of the Egg—he sure as hell wasn't going to put it on display—and even if he did later on, I couldn't prove how he got it—I couldn't count on Linda Bundy coming back to tell her story—and even if she did, it was her word against Shenko's—and—and—and—the truth was that I was mad and was making bullshit excuses—even though most of them were true—I was mad and sick and tired of being pushed around, tied up and made to look ridiculous by a couple of no-good sons of bitches who lost the Cold War and were taking advantage of an innocent bystander. My Greek blood was boiling and I had no intention of standing by—or even of being innocent. Them and their dirty tricks—if I had to—I'd be trickier and dirtier.

It had started out with Charles Oliver Dash, Vladov and Sonja, Shenko and Linda Bundy, Serge Goncheroff, Ski Mask, the two hoods in the cemetery, then Sebastian and his two erstwhile accomplices—and it had all filtered down to Shenko and Sebastian—and me—if I could get there in time.

It looked like I did—maybe. I had made a right turn off Vista Del Rey, traveled about a hundred yards past parking areas on both sides and spotted the two of them, both on foot, just outside the security gate of the Empyrean Plant. Shenko was wearing a blue blazer and carrying a large briefcase. He was talking to a man whom I presumed to be Sebastian, even though he was wearing a hard hat and an orange jacket with the word SECURITY printed on the back—a man who was high-shouldered and deep-chested holding a clipboard in one hand and a black lunch pail in the other.

My first inclination was to crash the Sebring into them—and kill the two of them—but that might not be considered justifiable homicide by the authorities. I followed, instead, my second notion—park the Sebring and get to them before they recognized me . . . and my .38.

It almost worked.

Almost.

I parked the Sebring alright, patted the .38 on my hip so it would know that I was getting ready to use it, and started to walk alongside the other parked cars so they wouldn't see me.

But they did. Shenko did. He was facing in my direction and just as they were making the transfer—the briefcase to Sebastian and the Egg in a brown paper sack to Shenko, Shenko hollered—

"Night!"

It all happened fast—just like on MTV.

Sebastian spun, dropped the clipboard and lunch pail, pulled a gun and fired twice, producing two spider webs on the windshield of the car I was standing next to—a security guard from inside the gate opened it—gun drawn—to see what was going on—it was his last mistake—Sebastian shot him in the heart—Shenko stood mumchance—Sebastian shot Shenko directly between the eyes—grabbed the briefcase—tucked the bag with the Egg into his pocket—and had only one way to go, inside the gate because I fired, just missed Sebastian and had his path effectively blocked.

Workers on the inside of the gate scattered as Sebastian ran through with the briefcase, waving the gun.

I scrambled through the parked cars, jumped over Shenko's body and ran through the open gate after Sebastian.

Another security guard, gun drawn, was also running toward the gate from inside.

He saw I was holding a gun and pointed his at me.

"What the hell's going on?"

I pointed at Sebastian who was just making his way past a crowd of civilians and through a door to the inside of the plant.

"That one just killed a guard and another guy." Then I motioned toward the dozen or so people still standing near the plant entrance. "What are those people doing?"

"Just about to start a tour."

"Can you close off all the doors?"

"Yeah."

"Close 'em. Nobody in or out—after I get in."

"Who the hell are you?"

"Lieutenant Donovan. More cops on the way. Shut the place down and call for more backup."

"Right!"

He pulled out a cell phone and I ran toward the plant entrance. By then the dozen or so tour people were no longer standing, milling. They were making their way toward the gate.

The inside of the Empyrean Waste Disposal Plant looked like something out of H. G. Wells' *Things to Come*. All that was missing was Raymond Massey. But I wasn't looking for Raymond Massey, I was looking for somebody called Sebastian with a briefcase holding a million dollars, a brown paper bag containing a Fabergé Imperial Egg and a gun that had fired four shots.

I heard a voice.

It wasn't Sebastian's.

A. Night In Hollywood Forever

It came from a loudspeaker.

"Welcome to the Empyrean Treatment Plant. We would like to take this opportunity to acquaint you with a few highlights of our operation . . ."

As the voice droned on I caught a glimpse of the man with the briefcase running across a vast expanse of a room populated with generators, turbines and other gleaming mechanical monsters in the process of doing whatever they were doing.

"Six thousand five hundred miles of underground pipes are used to convey wastewater to Empyrean. There's enough pipe to build a tunnel between the coast of California and mainland China . . ."

Sebastian was about fifty yards away twisting the handle of a door—but the handle wouldn't twist—at least it wouldn't twist open.

He turned and spotted me. He started to take aim but thought better of it. I was too far away. Instead he started to climb up a shiny steel stairway that led to an upper landing.

"Empyrean is designed to treat four hundred fifty million gallons of wastewater every day . . ."

I was closing the gap to the stairway fast.

"Empyrean's twenty new modified egg-shaped digesters that stand seventy feet tall are the largest complex of egg-shaped digesters in the world . . ."

The only egg shape I was interested in was a Fabergé. I made it to the shiny steel stairway and started climbing.

"Empyrean was one of the first treatment plants in the world— 1950—to capitalize on the energy value of methane gas produced in our digesters . . ."

From the landing Sebastian fired once and the slug sent up sparks on the rail right next to my left elbow. That was shot number five from his gun. I let loose with one of my own just to discourage him—and kept climbing.

So did he, up another stairway to a higher landing.

"Our primary tanks are Oldies but Goodies. Built in the 1950s, they were considered radical for their time due to their huge size. More than a half century later they are still among the top-performing primary tanks in the world . . ."

I made it to the first landing and started up the second stairway. Sebastian had other ideas.

He flung the briefcase with all his might toward my head. I ducked. The briefcase struck the rung just above me and burst open.

It wasn't raining rain—or violets—it was raining hundred-dollar bills—fluttering and floating—over, around, and beneath me—gliding gently toward some surface below.

"The facility's six Sharples DS-906 centrifuges are the world's first centrifuges capable of providing 600 to 1000 gallons per minute of anaerobically digested wastewater sludge while producing a wet cake product in excess of 30 percent solids."

I made it to the second landing and several signs in large red letters proclaiming:

DANGER
DO NOT ENTER

NO ONE PERMITTED
BEYOND THIS POINT

NO ADMITTANCE

I went on. I had him cornered.

"Eighty-five percent of Empyrean's wastewater comes from households and the remaining fifteen percent comes from industry and business . . ."

Or did I? He fired again. Just missed. That was shot number six. That was it. His gun was empty.

As I started toward him I found out something. The son of a bitch had another gun and was aiming and firing.

I ducked and fired back.

"All bio-solids generated at the Empyrean service area are treated at this facility, including solids removed from the upstream reclamation plants . . ."

He missed twice but close. I missed once. The second one caught him near the left shoulder. He fell and rolled over.

The brown bag came out of his jacket pocket and the Imperial Egg with it.

He reached out, picked up the Egg, aimed and shot at me.

I went blind with shock and the pain at the side of my skull but only for a second. I emptied the .38.

Still clutching The Tear of Russia Imperial Fabergé, Sebastian crashed back then over the rail into the wastewater reclamation tank.

I remember hearing the voice from the speaker but can't remember the exact words, but the gist of it was that what would be left of Sebastian and the Imperial Egg—after the process—would be discharged along with its digested sludge, through a seven-mile ocean outfall, into Santa Monica Bay.

I sat down along the wall, wiping the blood away from the crease in my skull and waited.

For how long, I don't know.

Until I heard Lieutenant Myron Garter's voice.

"Alex, this is getting to be a habit."

"Not anymore," I said. "I just broke the habit."

"Yeah. Until next time."

Chapter XLI

My life in the last few days had been a chessboard of chases, clashes, checkmates, near misses and a slight tunnel on the left side of my head requiring a score of stitches.

The whole thing started when I was chasing a demented, bogus priest who was holding on to a gem worth a million dollars—he done a Brodie, but I managed to hold on to The Star of Good Hope. Along the way there was Ski Mask at the garage, stocking masks at the mausoleum, a wife-beater turned to toast at Big Bear, three comrades at the Davies crypt, and finally a running gunfight with somebody called Sebastian—I didn't know if that was his front name, back name, or no name—but I lived through it. He didn't.

Sayonara, Sebastian.

Farewell, my Fabergé.

Only it wasn't *my* Fabergé.

It was nobody's.

Not anymore.

It was chewed up and spit out to sea.

Still, it made a hell of a story. Since Charles Oliver Dash was still in the hospital and in no shape to—as Dr. Fay Lee said—"write a postcard!" I wrote the story myself, including most of the main characters—William Randolph Hearst, Marion Davies, Vladov, Shenko, Goncheroff and Sebastian, with all the attendant drama and mystery and suspense—ending up at Empyrean, but without most of my part in the caper. The story gave Lieutenant Garter and the security guards at the plant credit in the chase, confrontation and conclusion to what Arthur Conan Doyle might have called *The Case of the Imperial Egg.*

I bylined it Charles Oliver Dash and told Jim Addison at the *Chronicle* that C.O.D. had asked me to deliver it.

Addison read it, nodded, looked at me and smiled.

"Charlie Dash," he said, "drunk or sober, is still the best newspaperman in the business. Tell him I'll print it . . . and submit it for a Pulitzer."

Print it he did—and I had a hell of a time talking Dash out of writing another story giving me credit for what really happened—and how it really happened.

"Charlie," I reminded him, "you know the old John Ford line about 'print the legend'—well, the legend's already been printed. Don't screw around with it. It was your idea—your research—your story—I just did a little legwork for you. Let it go at that."

He did—finally.

Most of the million dollars from the briefcase was gathered up—but nobody claimed it. The authorities are still trying to determine what to do with it. Not my problem, I never had a million dollars.

Just as I got home my mother called.

"Alex, I've been thinking."

"About what, Mom?"

"Maybe you and I should get cell phones."

"What do we need cell phones for?"

"So we can keep in touch. We haven't talked much lately."

"We haven't?"

"No, we haven't. What have you been doing, besides working on the novel, I mean?"

"Just mostly that, Mom."

"How's Goldie?"

"I'm on my way to see her."

"Tell her I'll be by. Is she still in the hospital?"

"Yeah, a few more days. I'll tell her, and so long, Mom."

"Well, what do you think?"

"About what?"

"The cell phones. I see them advertised all the time . . ."

"Okay, let's think about it. Talk to you later . . ."

"Later. Always later . . . Alex, that cemetery? Is it *really* nice?"

"Really nice, Mom."

"Okay . . . we'll talk about it . . . sometime."

She hadn't read the story in the *Chronicle* yet, but Mike Meadows had when he called right after I said so long to my mother.

"Alex, that's a hell of a yarn about the Fabergé, but I don't know how much of it we can use in the movie—it's mostly going to be about Marion Davies and Hearst—and the Egg, of course. About the price . . ."

"Mike, whatever you think is fair, but the money goes to Charles Oliver Dash."

"Frances says she won't do it unless you get paid, too."

It was decent of Meadows to tell me that, but then again, he knew that Franny would tell me anyhow.

"Okay. Tell her I say hello."

"She'll be back tomorrow. I'm sure she'll call you."

"So long, Mike."

When I got to the hospital Elliot and Dash were in the room with Goldie. Goldie looked much better. So did Dash. Elliot looked his usual self with his usual faultless attire and walking stick.

Goldie had a copy of the *Chronicle* on the bed next to her.

"Alex," she smiled, "Mister Dash told me about this." She held up the paper and pointed to the article. "What you did . . . and that you wrote the story, and . . ."

"Mister Dash," I looked over at him, "sometimes talks too much."

"And drinks too much." Dash grinned his Charlie Grapewin grin. "Blame it on my youth . . . besides I said I wouldn't tell the world. I didn't say I wouldn't tell your sweetheart. It was bad enough I took credit for the story. Allow me not to be a complete heel."

"Charlie's right," Elliot said. "Besides, 'all's well that ends well.' "

"I'm not so sure it's ended." Dash pulled at his earlobe.

"What do you mean by that," I said. "The Presentation Box has been authenticated and The Tear of Russia ended up somewhere in the Santa Monica Bay."

"Did it?"

"Yes, Mister Dash," I replied. "It did. I was there. Remember?"

"Maybe . . . and maybe not."

"Go on!" Elliot prompted.

"Remember when I told you that the prop-master on that picture, *The Last Empress*, made a duplicate Egg . . . and that he disappeared shortly after the picture was canceled? Suppose that . . ."

"Suppose *what?*" I said.

"Suppose he gave them back the duplicate."

"But the Presentation Box was . . ."

"Authentic," Dash nodded. "Of course it was. He was smart enough to do that and he was smart enough to take the real Egg and vanish off the face of the earth. But what about the real Egg? It could still be out there, somewhere . . ."

"By gad!" Elliot exclaimed. "You're absolutely right, Charlie. What we must do is . . ."

"What you must do," I said, pointing to the door, "both of you, must get the hell out of here. I don't want to hear any-more—ever—about *eggs*, Fabergé Eggs, scrambled eggs, hard-boiled eggs—or any other kind of eggs—so put an egg in your shoe and beat it!"

When they left, still mumbling about eggs, Goldie held out her hand and I took it.

"You're a hell of a fella, Mister Night."

"Never mind that. You're still my sweetheart aren't you, Miss Rose?"

"Alex, before we go any further, do you want me to tell you what happened up there . . . with him? I think you have a right to know."

"Would it help if you told me about it? Help you?"

"No."

"Then I don't want to know. Forget the past. We've got to start talking about our future. You know what Doctor Luck said . . . it's not going to be easy . . . it'll take time, but . . ."

"Alex."

"Yeah."

"You're always talking about movies. Do you remember *An Affair to Remember*, Cary Grant, Deborah Kerr?"

"Sure. What about it?"

"They were going to meet at the Empire State Building but she was hit by a car and crippled. He had been trying to be an artist, a painter. Months later, after he succeeded, he came to see her not knowing about the accident. He found out in that last scene, the doctors had told her she might never walk, but she said to him, 'Nicky, if you can paint, I can walk.' Remember?"

"Sure."

A. Night In Hollywood Forever

"Well, Alex," Goldie held up the newspaper. "If you can write, I can walk."

Goldie Rose did walk.

She even made it up the stairs of the Writers and Artists Building a couple of times. But mostly she's been working at home. She's slowed down a little. Now instead of writing a novel in eleven days, it takes her two weeks.

Me? I haven't slowed down. I'm still writing at the same pace on my great mystery novel, *The Big Changeover*.

I realized that I hadn't been to the YMCA in a couple of weeks and that I never felt better in my life, but I started going back anyhow.

And I'm still bumping into the same characters—Jim and Marsha at Kramer's, still selling cigars, cigarettes, and pipe tobacco and warning their customers about the dangers of smoking—Henry Fenenbock and Judy Kirk, still running the Writers and Artists Building and relieved that the inspectors from the City Planning and Engineering Department weren't from the City Planning and Engineering Department and that the "bugs" have been removed—Morgan Noble, still reading Elliot's trade papers—the Bernstein brothers, whose cable reality series is still in development and now called *Payback Your Mother-In-Law*—Wes Weston, now working on a biography of the Duke called *Me and John Wayne*—E. Elliott Elliot, still the gracile Beverly Hills busybody and still theorizing with Charles Oliver Dash about the whereabouts of the real Tear of Russia—Chief Dave Snowden, still running the most elegant police department in the USA.—Lieutenant Myron Garter and Rhoda, currently cruising on the QM2—Tyler Cassity, Andy Martinez, Annette Lloyd and Homer Alba, still at Hollywood Forever, reaping a second glory for the cemetery—and, of course, my dear, dear mother, who decided against a cell phone, but who, I happen to know, jumped into her Jeep and toured the environs of Hollywood Forever, but still won't talk about it.

Would I change any of it? Not for all the oil in hell.

Goldie and I are still discussing a date for the wedding at Saint Sophia's . . . but in the meantime there are still those *"trips to the moon on gossamer wings."*

About the Author

A. J. Fenady, still smelling of college in the 1950s, went to work in Los Angeles for journalist-TV personality Paul Coates as a legman/ troubleshooter, and all 'round factotum in the creation and production of *Confidential File*, a local, then national exposé television series that was the precursor to *60 Minutes* and other investigative programs.

Fenady wrote and produced more than 150 episodes which won three Emmys. The documentaries directed by Irvin Kershner took the two of them from the kid gangs of Watts, the alleys of South Central to the sophistry of the Sunset Strip and the night-lights of Beverly Hills—and led to Fenady writing and producing his first feature, the acclaimed *Stakeout on Dope Street*.

Then for a couple of decades Fenady went Western, creating, writing and producing several TV series, among them *The Rebel, Branded, Hondo*, as well as Western features including *Chisum* for John Wayne.

Fenady returned to the mean streets with his novel and feature film *The Man with Bogart's Face*, Edgar Allan Poe Mystery Writers of America Award winner.

Now, after a dozen highly successful Western novels, Fenady mixes the movie stars he's known and worked with *roman a clef* characters in another knuckle-busting novel ranging from the Academy Awards ceremony to the plush mansions in Beverly Hills, and everywhere in between.